# Lost Luggage

## Books by Wendall Thomas

*Lost Luggage*

# Lost Luggage

## Wendall Thomas

Poisoned Pen Press

Poisoned Pen Press
4014 N. Goldwater Boulevard, #201
Scottsdale, Arizona 85251
www.poisonedpenpress.com
info@poisonedpenpress.com

Printed in the United States of America

*For my husband, James Bartlett,*
*who makes every good thing in my life possible,*
*and who is living proof that travel leads*
*to laughter, adventure, and—*
*if you're lucky—true love.*

# Acknowledgments

My first thanks goes to New Scotland Yard's Metropolitan Police Wildlife Crime Unit. Former Head Andy Fisher and Retired Sergeant Ian Knox gave me invaluable insight into the tragedy and mechanics of endangered animal smuggling and were extraordinarily generous with their time. Former Special Agent John Gavitt of the U.S. Fish and Wildlife Service—the first enforcement agent for the CITES Secretariat—offered a crucial perspective on U.S and multi-agency operations. In their tireless pursuit of wildlife criminals, these officers and their colleagues are the real heroes of this book.

Special thanks to Ellen Thomas, Chadwick's Gerry Morris, and BookMark Shoppe's Christine Freglette and Bina Valenzano in Bay Ridge, who were all beyond kind to me. I hope they will forgive my fictionalizing parts of their wonderful neighborhood. Fellow travelers Brett Smith and Richard McGarry offered priceless observations on safari travel, Swahili, and Tanzanian customs and etiquette. Everyone's information was impeccable; any errors in the book are entirely my own.

Eternal gratitude is due to Sisters in Crime Los Angeles for their help and support, particularly to Rochelle Staab, Tammy Kaehler, Holly West, Naomi Hirahara, Matt Coyle, and Ellen Byron.

Thanks to Keith Sears for advice and enduring friendship, and to all the generous people who read and supported the story, and me, over the years: Michele Mulroney, Karin Altmann, Linda Lael Miller, Smith Richardson, Kim Thomas Stout, Claire Dobbin, Ray Stout, Catriona Mitchell, Billy Mernit, Stephanie Moore, Ranjiv Perera, Marta Suarez, Carol Bartlett, Karin Williams, Effie Hortis, Carolyn Thomas, Bill Thomas, Ashley Gardner, Happy Kang, James Utt, Carter McGarry, and Simón de Santiago Areizaga—the first one who laughed at the idea of Cyd taking out bad guys with an armful of street market bracelets.

Thanks to Annette Rogers and Barbara Peters, the best editors a writer could hope for, and to Robert Rosenwald, Diane DiBiase, Beth Deveny, Holli Roach, Raj Dayal, and everyone at Poisoned Pen Press for stellar support.

Ninety-five percent of this novel was written in restaurants, so a huge thanks to the folks at Twist

Eatery, Xiomara on Melrose, El Coyote, and Maggiano's at the Grove, who let me sit. And sit.

Finally, thanks and love to Jim and Dianne Frazier, who inspired my love of mysteries, and to my father, Grady Thomas, who gave me my own steering wheel when I was three and has supported every trip I've ever taken, however harebrained.

# Chapter One

October 2006

Travel is my business. Or at least it was. After the last two weeks, no one may trust me with a drink order, much less their seat assignments, cabin preferences, or credit card numbers. Let's face it, travel is about trust: the instant you zip up that rolling bag, you're taking a leap of faith. You're putting your life in the hands of strangers. Total complete lying son of a bitch strangers, in my case.

If you're like most people, you just assume that every taxi driver, airline pilot, and bellboy has your best interests at heart. Of course they aren't criminals or terrorists. Of course they always check the brake fluid on that rental car. And, because 91.6 percent of travelers survive their vacations, most of the time you're right. It's the other 8.4 percent of the time you have to worry about.

That's where I come in. I'm Cyd Redondo and

for the residents of Bay Ridge, Brooklyn, I'm the first line of defense. It's my job to anticipate and prevent any and all travel disasters for my clients, especially since lots of them have pacemakers or might not survive a bad fall. But this time the disaster was mostly my fault. And it happened because I really needed a vacation.

It was October, the month when the sun hung straight over the Verrazano-Narrows Bridge and shot through the row houses and churches all the way to Third Avenue. You'd catch it in the glint of a shop window or in a halo around someone's new bleach job and bouncing off the spider webs and skeletons draped across every yard; no one in Bay Ridge did Halloween halfway.

I'd been getting into the office before eight lately, as we had a big promotion on. I liked being up early, when I was only interrogated by three or four relatives before I could get out the door. I walked the six blocks to work, up 77th to Third Avenue and down to 83rd. I usually went in the back way, as otherwise, Mrs. Barsky from Pet World would be straight over. She had a lot of ailments and conspiracy theories she loved to discuss—in detail. I needed coffee before I was ready for an alphabetized list of stroke medications. I came around the corner and saw the agency back door was open.

There might have been a logical explanation,

but logic wasn't my strong suit. I pulled the black market Mace from my purse and moved just inside the door, squeezing past the extra water jugs and jabbing myself in the neck with the coat rack. I stood still for a minute, not sure if I should turn on the lights or surprise the hell out of whoever it was. I decided on lights; I wanted to see the bastard. Just in case, I unhooked the fire ax in the hallway. With the ax, the Mace, my red vintage Balenciaga bag (which weighed in at about forty pounds), and three years of kick-boxing classes, I could hold my own. I hit the central switch and heard the knock of the fluorescent lighting, but nothing else. There was a slight odor, like someone had left milk out overnight.

First, I checked the front office. My desk was right by the door so I could greet customers immediately and, if they had walkers, help them in. There was a desk for my usually absent, terminally lazy cousin, Jimmy, and bookshelves filled with my collection of every Fodor's Guide since 1970. The petty cash drawer still had $365.47 from yesterday.

I inched down the hall to our kitchenette and found nothing but a dripping faucet—until I saw Uncle Ray's office door was open. I stopped short. My Uncle Ray, a cautious man, always left his office locked. I braced myself on my four-inch heels and lunged in. Something lay on the desk, oozing bright, sticky red.

A massive royal blue parrot with bright yellow eyes, wrapped in our "Tanzania: The trip for the life you have left" brochure, was speared to my uncle's mahogany desk with a steak knife like some gruesome Tiki Room shish kabob. At first I thought it might be one of Jimmy's practical jokes. He was the kind of idiot who went in for whoopie cushions and rubber vomit, so I wouldn't put a faux pet corpse past him.

I touched the feathers. It was no joke; the bird was real. And it wasn't breathing. Could you do CPR on a parrot? After a minute or two I had to admit it was completely dead. I felt horrible for the tortured bird, and pretty freaked out myself. I had to believe bird homicide was out of even Jimmy's comfort zone. What kind of psychopath had been in our office?

I was shaking. It seemed smart to put down the ax. Where was Uncle Ray? Redondo Travel was his baby. I'd worked there since I was ten and handled the day-to-day business, but I wasn't in charge. I needed to calm myself down before I called him. He knew my voice too well and freaking out wasn't good for his blood pressure. I made coffee: a double espresso for me and a large, watery decaf for Mrs.

Barsky, who'd be over any minute. Then I called my uncle's import/export office and left a message.

Ten seconds later, the phone rang.

"Cyd Redondo, Redondo Travel."

"Who died?" It was Uncle Ray. I sighed. He always knew.

"No one. Well, actually, some wildlife."

"What?"

"We had a break-in. Nothing's missing, but there's a massacred parrot on your desk."

"A what?"

"A parrot. A big blue one. There's a serrated knife through the poor thing's chest. Should I call the Precinct?" We did all the travel for the 68th Precinct and they owed us big-time. Hence, the Mace.

"Don't overreact," he said in that loving, patriarchal way that meant *because you're a woman and weak*. "I'm sure it's just a prank, maybe one of Jimmy's friends. We can both agree he has some sleazy ones." He did. Still.

"Prank or not, the precinct should know. We can't leave parrot stabbers on the loose. Do you think the bird's Mrs. Barsky's? Should I tell her?"

"And wind up on WikiLeaks? Life is too short. I'm just glad you're safe. I'll make a quick call to the 68th, then call Gonzo for some new locks." Gonzo Gonzales, a long-time client, owned the locksmith shop four doors down. He summered on Lake Michigan, wanted his firewood pre-cut, and preferred an aisle seat.

"What should I do about the parrot? It deserves a decent burial at least."

"I don't want you touching that bird—it could be diseased."

I decided not to mention the CPR.

"Just lock my office, kiddo. I'll deal with it. By the way, how are the Tanzania packages going?" If I booked fifteen package tours, our partner company was offering a free safari for me and a plus one.

"I need six more to fill the quota. I've got seven 'possiblys' from the Gray Panthers, three 'I've always wanted to go to Africas' from Bingo, and four 'I'll ask my husbands' from Our Lady of Angels."

"In other words, time for a few cold calls."

"Exactly my plan."

"Great. Let's do a real push this week. I want you to win that trip."

"You do?"

"Of course I do."

I reminded him that I was headed to the cruise terminal in the afternoon.

"Drive carefully," he said. "Seat belt. Love you." He hung up.

It felt weird doing nothing about the whole parrot situation, but I trusted my Uncle Ray more than anyone. He had erred on the side of caution with me since I was four—when my dad died on the JFK Expressway, broadsided by a chicken truck on his way to a Mets game. Dad didn't believe in insurance so there wasn't any. In the end, Uncle Ray took me and my mom into his huge house on 77th Street to live with him and his wife, Noni, their four boys, and most of the extended Redondo family. My mother and I were outnumbered and overprotected from then on. As the only girl cousin, and the youngest, I was subjected to daily torture at home, but the first time anybody outside the family came near me, my three uncles and my ten "brousins" made sure it was the last. So, from the moment I moved into the attic room with the gummy wallpaper, someone monitored my every move. If I called the Precinct myself, Uncle Ray and everyone else in the family would know.

I made the sign of the cross, draped a yellow St. Pauli Girl bar towel over the murdered bird, locked the door, headed back to the front office, pulled up our Venetian blinds, and sat down. I looked longingly at a brochure for the travel agents' convention coming up in Atlantic City, but Uncle Ray would never say yes. I slipped it in the drawer. The phone rang at 8:01.

"Cyd Redondo, Redondo Travel."

It was one of my regulars from the Bingo hall,

wanting price quotes on a summer rental in Maine. I suggested our Tanzania package as an anniversary present for her son and daughter-in-law, but she said she hoped the marriage didn't last that long and had I heard about Donna La Sorda and the UPS guy? I listened for another ten minutes, out of respect for her years and because I couldn't get a word in edgewise, not even "gotta go."

In our business, patience was key. The Internet made travel agents obsolete enough, but when you added suicidal pilots, cruise ship fires, and shocking fares, fewer people were traveling and fewer of those needed help to do it. Like any endangered species, we'd had to adapt.

Still, we had our pride and a paid-off building, so instead of selling out to a big firm, we now specialized in clients who were more comfortable with people than computers. In other words, seniors. And occasionally the blind. Granted, the majority of our target market would die in the next five to fifteen years, but it bought us time for Plan B, whatever the hell that was.

It was easy to choose this particular market because, as luck would have it, we were based in one of the few NORCs in the United States. In travel consultant vernacular, a NORC is a "naturally occurring retirement community." In short, people were born in Bay Ridge and never left. Our parents' high school classmates weren't golfing in Palm Beach; they were using walkers in Foodtown on Fourth Avenue.

That's why our new Tanzania safari package was a tricky sell—by the time most people are seventy-five, they don't really feel up to bouncing in the back of a jeep or running from a lion while covered in bug spray. Still, I was only six short of my free trip, so I wasn't giving up. My sell was heavy on pith helmets and khaki, insect repellent torches, egg yolk sunsets, free-standing bathtubs—with safety handles—rum drinks, and all things "Colonial." I used *Out of Africa* a lot.

I was just firing up the computer to e-mail the Quilting Club when my FedEx guy, cute as ever in his purple shorts, came through the door.

"Cyd? Would you sign for this Pet World delivery? I'm in a rush on the ten-thirties and she's not answering."

"Sure." I smiled, happy I'd remembered my Conga red lipgloss.

I put the box down on my desk and noticed Mrs. Barsky's cold coffee. She was usually in my office the moment she sensed movement. Every day I counted her pills as she sucked them down with my decaf, to make sure she didn't miss any before she opened for business at eight-thirty sharp. She'd only varied that routine four times in my memory, once for each stroke.

I'd been so thrown by the parrot, I hadn't even checked to see if she'd had a break-in too. I was scum. I grabbed the phone and dialed. After her husband died, she'd sold her house and moved into a cute, if pungent, walk-up over the pet store. I could hear her faded pink rotary phone ringing over my head.

I admit, I've been known to complain about Mrs. Barsky. She moved slowly, talked fast, had eight thousand conspiracy theories, and made frequent madcap requests—like would I get her fifteen lime green shower caps at the 99 Cent Store?

Still, she had sold me my one and only gold-fish, Vince. And she had been my style icon in the day, with her miniskirts, flared pantsuits, and DayGlo fishnets to die for. She remained the octogenarian version of Angie Dickinson, and though her blond flip now came from Wig Explosion, she still tossed it back whenever she lit a cigarette. Hence the strokes.

Her smoker's voicemail kicked in: "I'm in the store."

I reached into the drawer for her keys. Dammit. Jimmy hadn't put them back. I headed next door.

The light was on, but the door was locked. I

couldn't see past the eight thousand birdcages, so I ducked next door into One Hour Martinizing.

"Have you seen Mrs. Barsky this morning?"

"She probably had another stroke." Mr. Tacchini crossed himself.

I grabbed one of his wire hangers. "If you hear a window break, it's just me."

"Knock yourself out." He went back to rotating suits.

I should have checked on her earlier. If something was wrong, it was on me. I straightened the hanger and maneuvered it through the letter slot and contorted my arm just enough to turn the inside lock, praying she was okay.

# Chapter Two

The slap of the pet store smell—part puppy, part gerbil droppings, part Clorox—was nothing compared to the racket the birds were making. Mrs. Barsky loved birds. Her mynah, Myron, had died last year and had gotten a bigger farewell than her husband.

Kittens were mewing in their metal cages and even the fish seemed agitated. I saw something hop on the floor to my left, but when I turned, it was gone. Nerves, I thought. I moved toward the counter and saw a stack of packing boxes and paperwork beside the "ferret hammock" display.

"Mrs. Barsky?"

"Mrs. Barsky's a fox! Mrs. Barsky's a fox!" a cockatiel squawked, giving me half a coronary. I tripped, flying toward the floor and catching myself on one elbow, while my other hand slid on something acrylic. And blond.

Mrs. Barsky's platinum wig was splayed and horribly empty under my palm.

I turned to my right and saw her tiny head. Her real hair, or what was left of it, was pressed into tiny whitecaps under what looked like control-top panty hose. I reached for her neck, hoping for a pulse, and got nothing but wattle. I knelt into CPR position as I grabbed my phone, calling 911 between breaths. After seven minutes of trying, all I could do was hold her hand.

One of my old school friends, Hank, was the first uniform through the door, followed by three other guys from the neighborhood. They all nodded as Hank pulled me up. He and I had played doctor in second grade. I guess, with him, it stuck. Hank worked on Mrs. Barsky for another five minutes, then closed her eyes. He called the coroner, then patted my arm.

"Cyd. There was nothing you could have done."

In my experience people only said that when there had been. "We had a break-in last night, maybe she heard it and it pushed her heart over the edge."

"The woman was eighty-three, she'd had four strokes, she was still smoking—a flea bite could have pushed her over the edge." He pointed to her freshly scarred and bitten hands and forearms, the price of pet-shop ownership. "Okay?"

"Okay." I wasn't okay.

"Do you want me to call Joni?" Hank patted my other arm.

I shook my head. "No, I'll do it." Joni, Mrs. Barsky's daughter and my former babysitter, lived in Syracuse. I moved away from the body and called her at work.

"Those damn cigarettes," Joni kept saying over and over. She wouldn't be able to get down until the next day and would I please put up a sign and lock up the store? I had been the flower girl at her first wedding. I said of course.

Joni hesitated. "And could you take care of the autopsy?"

"The what?"

"The autopsy. Remember? It's in her will."

I did remember. She wanted proof the government had it in for her. After her son, Bobby, was wounded in Vietnam, she had chained herself in protest to the bike rack outside the local Army recruiting station and wound up in jail. She was convinced she'd been under government surveillance ever since.

"Mom will feel better wherever she is if she knows she wasn't poisoned by the CIA. Of course she was crazy, but I promised her. You know Dr. Paglia, right? He won't talk to me after that whole prom night fiasco."

"Okay. Do you know where Bobby is?"

Joni sighed. Her older brother Bobby, a former Green Beret, had shipped out in the last days of the Vietnam war, decided he liked Southeast Asia, and stayed. Though he called his mom on holidays and sent the occasional postcard, he'd only been home twice in thirty years. His absence had broken Mrs. Barsky's heart. "Last address I had for him was someplace in Indonesia, but his birthday card came back."

"E-mail?" I asked.

"No way. He's as paranoid as Mom." Joni hung up.

There was a knock on the window. I had completely forgotten about Gonzo. He was waiting outside Redondo Travel in freshly pressed overalls, his thick black hair gelled off his forehead, stiff as marzipan. He had a shiny silver thermos, a tool box the size of Connecticut, and a burlap bag. The locks were already done.

"Mrs. Barsky?" He nodded toward the body. "The government always gets us in the end."

We went into my office, where he poured two cups of grappa from his thermos and we toasted our fallen friend. He gave me a new set of keys and warned me, as always, that life was a burglary waiting to happen. I gave him Circle Line Tour tickets for his grandkids, wrote him a corporate check for two hundred dollars, and went back to Pet World.

By then, our neighborhood medical examiner and travel client, Dr. Paglia, was leaning over Mrs. Barsky's body while he sucked down a triple espresso. He was a gambler who specialized in card-counting, so I alternated his trips to Las Vegas, Mississippi, and Atlantic City.

"Cyd. How's the most beautiful travel agent in Bay Ridge?"

"Sad."

"Yeah. She was a genuine broad. I'll give her that." He straightened his creaking knees, snapped off his gloves, and nodded to his assistants. "You can take her."

As they wheeled Mrs. Barsky out, I ran behind them, finger-combing her wig and putting it on the gurney. "She'd want it." I turned to Dr. Paglia. "Will you let me know what happens with the autopsy?"

He didn't have enough espresso left for a full spit-take—it was more of a dribble. "What are you, nuts? The woman's had five strokes, four would have been enough."

"I know, but she's requested an autopsy."

"What, from the grave?"

"It's in her will."

"People don't get to request their own

post-mortems. Besides, she sold my daughter one of those turtles that gave her salmonella."

"Doc, I promised Joni. She'll pay for it. Come on. I'm the one who found the body and I'll sleep better if I know it happened before I got into the office. I'd hate to think she was lying there dying while I was checking my horoscope. I feel bad enough already. Please? I have a new Atlantic City promotion coming in December. I could comp you a room."

"Alright, alright. Smoking, high floor. Should I call Joni with the results?"

"Call my client line. I have a better bedside manner than you."

"Hey, I don't hear anyone complaining."

"Just do it when you can."

"You got it, doll." He tossed his cup into the trash, and left me alone in the store.

I called my brousin Jimmy and let him know what had happened, asking him to come in and feed the animals. I didn't mind the kittens and hamsters, but I wasn't about to go into the reptile room. The neighborhood boys had begged Mrs. Barsky for years to add snakes, lizards, and frogs. She had finally agreed when Jimmy offered to help her out. She must have been paying him under the table. I'd ask him about the parrot later.

That reminded me of our break-in. I took a

look around to make sure Pet World hadn't had one too. The back door was still dead-bolted from the inside and everything else looked normal. I picked up a few empty FedEx boxes off the floor and put them in the trash, then grabbed the paperwork off the counter and took the cash from the till to save for Joni.

Before I left, I looked up at the picture above the cash register: a young, glamorous Mrs. Barsky was leaning against Bobby. He was in his Green Beret uniform. They had the same unfortunate ski-jump nose, but they looked happy. I hoped Joni could find him.

It wasn't like I hadn't lost clients or friends before, but I couldn't imagine a day without Mrs. Barsky's left-wing theories, hot-pink pill dispenser, and horrible Russian tea. I said a quick prayer that they had a smoking section in heaven and locked the door behind me. It was the end of an era.

Back in the office I saw the clock. I had to get my favorite clients, the Minettis, on the *Queen Mary 2* by noon. I couldn't let any more AARP members down today.

Herb and Maria Minetti were my favorite clients because they were still in love. They were always touching each other lightly, like you would a rabbit's foot, for good luck. By the time I was born, they had already been married for thirty years and lived one block down in a red brick house covered with thick, shiny ivy that climbed to the second floor. It had a white metal awning that popped and bounced when it rained. They had never had any kids, which was sad for them, but great for me, as they were always inviting me in. Sometimes Herb played checkers with me on a Sunday after he got home from grinding pork. I remember their house as an oasis of lovely flowery smells, unlike the mixture of garlic, dirty sweat socks, and Lysol that hit you the minute you entered ours.

Booking this trip for their sixty-fifth wedding anniversary was the pinnacle of my travel-agenting career. To my delight, they allowed me to fold my Tanzania package into the trip. I called in a couple of favors for a room on the *QM2*, British Airways London to Tanzania's Dar Es Salaam on frequent flier miles, two days on romantic Zanzibar, and four days at the Serena Lodge in the Ngorongoro Crater. I'd designed the trip for maximum vehicles and minimum bugs. After all, they were in their eighties, if spry.

I headed into my supply room/gym. Although I did most of my kickboxing at Alana Health and Fitness on 86th, I kept a hundred-pound punching bag and a pair of remaindered pink gel Everlast gloves at the office, in case I felt like punching

Jimmy but didn't feel like nursing him afterwards. He was a bleeder.

The supply room was also stocked with standard office items, fashion-emergency staples, and every possible size and shape of Tupperware. Its inventor, Earl Silas Tupper, understood life was messy and needed to be contained—in something that didn't leak. Each Redondo Travel customer got nesting containers as well as Redondo Travel visors, luggage tags, phrase books, and a special emergency kit.

I found a textured pink sheet cake container for the documents, grabbed my bag, and reached for a magnum of Dom Pérignon. I checked Uncle Ray's office as I was leaving. The parrot was gone. It must have been in Gonzo's burlap bag. I shuddered as I went out the back door. The instant I pushed it open, I heard the growl of a V-6 engine and watched a Lincoln Town Car reverse in a swirl of gravel and head down the alley. Could it be the parrot stabber? I ran across the lot as fast as I could, but the car disappeared before I got to the corner.

# Chapter Three

I rechecked the new locks, then headed over to pick up the Jade Palace. My emerald green 1965 Ford Galaxie 500 was the cruise ship of cars, wide as a walk-up and built when more was more, gas was plentiful, and children were well-behaved.

The car was on its third transmission, but it was still on the road, thanks to my standing arrangement with an old grammar school buddy who ran a garage off Fifth Avenue and loved fly-fishing. I got him a discount package to Idaho every year, meals and complimentary gutting included. In exchange, he maintained and hid my car. Despite my age, my uncle still liked to keep track of me. Literally. My mechanic pal had found tracking devices twice.

I entered the chained lot filled with smashed bumpers and sagging exhaust pipes and found my old pal in the second bay, deep under the oil pan of a silver Mercedes. He rolled out and grinned, his shiny Tic Tac teeth the only part of him not under two layers of motor oil. We had dated, briefly, but he had wanted to settle down right out of high school and I hadn't been ready. A local waitress had been, and now they had three tow-headed, rambunctious boys.

"Cyd!" He got up, wiped his hands on a rag, and moved toward his wall of keys. "Where you off to today, gorgeous?"

"Red Hook," I took the slippery keys. "I'm putting the Minettis on the *Queen Mary 2.*"

"Are they still alive?"

"And kicking. It's their anniversary. Sixty-five years."

"I'll be lucky to make fifteen, the way things are going," he said.

"You don't know anyone in the neighborhood with a new Town Car, do you?" I was thinking of the break-in.

"What, besides every airport car service and undercover cop in the borough? Nope. They're shit cars. My clients know better."

Ten minutes later, after I had downed his special double espresso—brewed with a blow torch—I patted his cleanest shoulder and told him we'd grab a beer next week.

"Be careful. The front end is shimmying a little. Kind of like you." He winked as I swung myself onto the bench seat. I gave him the finger as I put my bag on the floor, buckled my lap belt, and started the V-8.

I could open it up better on Shore Road, so I took 86th there, winding along the water just above the Verrazano-Narrows. The bridge to Staten Island was the jewel of the neighborhood. On a sunny day, the metal frame shot quick, sharp flashes, and at night it glowed like a felled Christmas tree. When I was six, Uncle Ray squatted down, his knees groaning, and told me if I always kept the bridge in my sights, I'd be safe. He had kissed me on the forehead and sighed as I headed off for first grade.

Today, I was venturing out of the bridge's safety zone, heading up Fourth Avenue to the Fort Hamilton Expressway. I was grateful for the time to think. When you lived in a house with eight people, thinking was at a premium. So was anonymity. As I passed Owl's Head and headed into Sunset Park, I thought about the few times in my life I'd been allowed to go unrecognized. It was kind of sad that I remembered all of them. The first was when Ma took me to see *The Nutcracker* when I was nine. I sat in the plush seats mesmerized, not by the stiff, bright tutus or the flying shoes, but by something much more exotic: strangers. It was a completely new experience. No one called me "Cyd the Squid." No one asked me if I was eating my vegetables or if I had seen my brousin Jimmy, or if my spelling was improving. It was bliss and I wanted more. I wanted the whole world. Thinking about sunsets in Tanzania, I almost missed my exit.

I made the hairpin turn onto Terminal Drive with about two inches to spare. When I swung around, the whole city lay behind the top deck of the cruise ship. The Terminal at Pier 12 was a tiny, one-story white building with bright blue trim. Beside the luxury liner, it looked like a discarded drink napkin.

I braked for five reverent seconds in honor of the *QM2*, which resembled the world's most ambitious Lego project, complete with a Mercedes engine and Gucci fireworks. Happily, I had a special deal with my client, Lou Fagamo, who ran the parking service. Lou had gotten me an employee sticker in exchange for setting him up with Betsy McGuire, whom he later married. As long as the marriage lasted, so did my parking privileges.

I turned into the lot, waved to Lou, and parked. I decided not to tell the Minettis about Mrs. Barsky. Why ruin their vacation? I checked their emergency kit: tiny flashlight (for bedbug check), Band-Aids a tourniquet a snakebite kit, water-purifying tablets, rain ponchos the size of a sandwich, a laminated form with all their medications, allergies, and conditions, and a tiny currency calculator. I always included ten dollars in the currency of their destination, as a good luck gesture. Maybe the snakebite kit was over the top, but snakes scared the bejesus out of me, and the tourniquet could save a limb.

I headed down the dock, trying not to catch my heels in the slats. I'd dressed professionally, with a knee-length metallic green snakeskin skirt, a white tie-front blouse, and of course my Stuart Weitzman patent pumps. The heels were non-negotiable. I was five-foot two and couldn't leave the house in anything under three-inch heels if I wanted to stay alive in my family. Plus, stilettos doubled as a weapon. In flats, I just felt short and unarmed.

My skirt provoked a few wolf whistles, thank goodness. Really, if you can't provoke dock-workers, you may as well cash it in. I made my way inside where the Cunard greeter nodded and smiled.

A cruise terminal beat an airport every time: no luggage restrictions, no armed TSA guards, no need to buy soggy, expensive sandwiches to eat on the plane. Here, people laughed through security, gleefully flaunting huge bottles of shampoo and dressed for a holiday rather than an accident. It was one of the last truly hopeful places in the world.

I spotted the Minettis. They were pretty easy to spot, with their matching orange Hawaiian shirts, Bermuda shorts, and varicose veins. They were headed up the gangplank in identical Sketchers'

Shape-ups, with a sole curved so high I worried it might break their brittle bones. I thought about the way Herb always asked, with a slight blush, to be sure they had one bed instead of two. God bless them. I hadn't been around a lot of long-term marriages, including my own, so the Minettis were my gold standard. I hurried up to meet them.

"Did I tell you? That couples-only outlet mall is magic. You both look gorgeous." I grinned, pulling their paperwork from the translucent pink box and burping it closed. "Okay, open jaw return tickets, Dar Es Salaam to London to JFK—I got you the exit row—don't tell them about your hip, okay? Here are vouchers for free massages, and a "Midnight Oasis" dessert buffet. You want to change anything, you just call me, okay?"

Maria leaned forward and kissed me, smelling of Rive Gauche. "We know everything is perfect, Cyd. It always is."

"How about on your end? Sunscreen? Travel insurance number? Non-aerosol pepper spray?" They nodded. "Anniversary present?" I pulled out the champagne.

"Cyd, you shouldn't have. Not on your salary." Herb had seen my books.

"Don't be silly, nothing's too good for my best customers. And, anyway, I got it at cost. I'm so excited for you. It's almost as good as going myself."

"Yeah, Cyd, when are you getting a vacation? It's high time you got out of here," Herb said.

He was right. The truth was, at thirty-two, I'd barely made it past New Jersey. Every time I planned a trip, something would conveniently "come up" with the business or the family, or my mother would lay on the guilt about leaving her "drowning in Redondos" and I'd be forced to cancel. Not only was my lack of travel experience embarrassing, it occasionally resulted in professional errors, like putting the Collearys by the trash hold on the *QE2* or Mrs. Bialik and her daughter next to a crack house on Capitol Hill. I mean, our Owl's Head Park is one of the prettiest in Brooklyn, but if you haven't actually been there, you'd have no idea it sits above a sewage treatment plant and the smell practically knocks you unconscious. There were some things you could only know by being there.

The boat whistle blew. "Happy Anniversary!" I called out as they reached the deck, waving until they headed inside. Maybe it was the memory of Mrs. Barsky's frail, dead hand, but I wished I were going with them. What was I doing, sending all these seniors into the jungle alone, with nothing but bug spray? I had to win that trip, not just for me, but for my clients.

I needed a new pool of seniors and I knew the

best place to find them: the Travel Agents' Convention in Atlantic City. But could I make my escape without my family finding out?

# Chapter Four

By Sunday, I had my Atlantic City escape plan in place, but it didn't make saying good-bye to Mrs. Barsky any easier. I had offered Flowers!!! Flowers!!! a weekend on the Cape to make sure Redondo Travel sent the largest arrangement for her funeral. Most of Bay Ridge attended the service, and Joni and Uncle Ray gave eulogies. No one had been able to find her son, Bobby.

Joni had borrowed my waterproof mascara, but it hadn't done much good. "Thanks a lot," she said with a tone, then shook her head. "Sorry. My fricking mother." I handed her a catering napkin and my compact mirror. "After the five thousand times I've come down to take care of her, she makes Bobby the executor. She left you her apartment, by the way."

"Me? You've got to be kidding? Why would she do that?"

"She said you needed your own place or you

were gonna be an old maid. Really, I don't begrudge you that, Cyd, you kept her company, and Bobby can have the damn store. I hate that smell anyway. She left us all the cash. But if we don't find Bobby, none of us are getting anything." She slammed the compact shut. "I don't even know if he's alive. You know some P.I.'s. Can you help me find him?"

"Sure, of course."

"Thanks." She threw back her eighties perm and headed for the receiving line. Mrs. Barsky had left me her apartment with the pink rotary phone. I felt a real stab of grief. And guilt that I hadn't been there for her at the end.

Uncle Ray invited everyone back to our house after the service. He was being nice, but also strategic, as it kept our competition from working the funeral. There was nothing like a funeral for a "seize the day" pitch and we weren't about to give our nemesis, Peggy Newsome of Patriot Travel, access to our client base.

Ever since Patriot Travel opened a branch in Bay Ridge, Peggy had been trying to poach our customers, especially the Gray Panthers—Redondo Travel had been the official travel agent for the Brooklyn Chapter since its inception. Three days after Peggy arrived, I stopped by their headquarters with my weekly cupcake run to find a fifty-two-inch flat screen TV, with a plaque at the bottom that read, "Patriot Travel Cares." From that moment, it was war. The Panthers had a whirlpool the next week, courtesy of my Christmas fund. I was sure Peggy had come up with her new "Bahamas Bingo" package just to siphon off my potential Tanzania clients. Lucky for her and for me, she stayed away. I needed all my energy to pull off my Atlantic City trip. As the mourners worked their way through three trays of tiramisu, I tried to keep the excitement out of my face.

It was pretty impossible to keep a secret from my family. They knew everything I did and had vocal opinions on all of it, especially on Atlantic City. Uncle Ray headed my way. He was six feet tall and getting wider by the year. His strong, straight nose, black eyes, and salesman's smile meant he was still someone to be reckoned with. Had he sussed me out?

"I was going to drag you to the Firemen's Pancake Breakfast this Saturday, but rumor has it you're off to Debbie's for the weekend."

I had planted that rumor myself at the Third Avenue Merchants Association on Friday night. After a two-hour meeting on worker's comp, everyone was thrilled to hear about my friend Debbie's breakup and how I needed to help her pick up the pieces. I was pretty sure the news would get back to the family, but it was good to know for sure.

"Uncle Ray? You went to high school with Bobby Barsky, didn't you? Joni can't find him. Do you have any idea where he is?"

"Bobby? Jakarta, last thing I heard. He may not want to be found, you know. Your cousin Eddie thinks he's a mercenary."

"He's just jealous."

Uncle Ray laughed. "Well, that may be true. Sorry I can't help you, kiddo." He moved toward the buffet table, then turned back. "By the way, Frank caught the little monsters that left that parrot. They won't be doing that again." My brousin Frank was a detective for the Precinct and if I were a kid, I wouldn't want to mess with him either.

"Great." I was just glad it hadn't been Jimmy.

●  ●  ●  ●  ●

By Friday, the day of my escape, I had confirmed my last-minute room at the Taj Mahal. Debbie was on board for my alibi, and my ex-boyfriend mechanic had swept my Ford for bugs. I had e-mailed We Find Anyone—we used them for the few clients who were mobile enough to skip out on their bills—about getting an address for Bobby Barsky. It was a long shot, but at least I'd done everything I could for Joni. Now all I had to do was get through the rest of the workday. I had calls in to six clients and had booked a couple of fortieth anniversary cruises, but so far no more safaris.

I was so excited about Atlantic City, I couldn't sit still. I decided to head to the supply closet for a quick stiletto kickboxing session. It wasn't encouraged at the gym, but I was a realist—I figured there was a ninety-nine percent chance that if I actually had to use self-defense I would be in my Stuart Weitzmans—so I liked to get at least one session in a week in four-inch heels. I'll admit, they were hard on the bag, but balance was key in my favorite roundhouse kick combination and I didn't want to be wobbly on the R train or anywhere else. As usual, taping Peggy Newman's newest airbrushed flier on the top of the bag upped my game. Her haircut inspired me to throw in a few extra sidekicks and some elbow strikes, but I stopped myself before I broke a real sweat. I dabbed some loose powder on my face and headed back to my desk.

As I was straightening the office, I found Mrs. Barsky's FedEx package under a box of new Tanzania brochures. I had completely forgotten leaving it there the day she died. I was about to put it in the stack of stuff for Joni when I noticed the return address—a post office box in Dar Es Salaam. Why had Mrs. Barsky never mentioned she'd been getting packages from Tanzania? I'd only brought the country up about five thousand times. I told myself Joni didn't need anything else to deal with, but who was I kidding? I was too curious: I ripped the tab.

Inside I found a stack of documents with official stamps from the United Arab Emirates. Weird. I had just noticed a bunch of Latin words when the door chimes sang and a tall woman with a sleek black haircut and an Eileen Fisher heavy-linen tunic poked her head in.

"I hear you have a special to Tanzania?"

"Yes, absolutely. Please come in."

She sat down. Though the nubby charcoal fabric matched her hair and the flats were right for the outfit, something was off—she didn't usually wear those clothes. She had no idea how to manage fabric billowing in a flattering way around her hips. Hiding flaws around the middle was the cornerstone of the Eileen Fisher line. Happily, I hadn't had to resort to camouflage yet. Tight was still working better on me.

The woman wanted to know everything: times of flights, outbound and return, hotel details, in-country transportation, which safaris were available, etc. She wasn't big on politeness: when she wasn't typing into her phone, she surveyed everything on my desk, even staring at Mrs. Barsky's FedEx package until I moved it out of range. After half an hour, I asked if she'd like to book. She hesitated. It wasn't the hesitation that meant she'd have to check with her husband/partner/accountant. It was the hesitation of no. She stood up, saying she usually booked her own travel and had just wanted to compare prices.

"You're not going to get better prices anywhere, because no one else is partnered with someone on the ground there."

"That's what you think," she replied, her tunic barely moving as she jerked the door open and let it slam. I was disappointed but not surprised. The rich transplants in the neighborhood used us a lot that way, but I figured if they came in the door, I had to try. Had Peggy Newsome sent her? Maybe that's why she'd been so interested in my desk. I cursed them both.

By three o'clock, I had checked on all the Tanzania clients that were already traveling. Jack and Barb Anderson, who embraced skydiving and mountain climbing, had tons of frequent flier miles, and paid in advance, had arrived safely in Tanzania and checked into their hotel. My godparents, the Giannis, were en route to their safari; and Herb and Maria Minetti, my favorites, were mid-Atlantic on their *QE2* cruise and had eaten dinner with Elton John's husband, who apparently was lovely. Thinking of them, I vowed again to make the Travel Agents Convention in Atlantic City count.

I was just shutting down the computer when Jimmy slouched in. My youngest brousin was one of those guys who led with his feet, like the Keep on Truckin' guy. He was already losing his hair and was dressed in a grayish green Hugo Boss suit that didn't quite fit through the shoulders. He was on salary, but only made an appearance about twice a month, usually to borrow petty cash.

I hadn't wanted to yell at him at Mrs. Barsky's funeral, so I had days of irritation stored up. "Where the hell have you been? You left me with all the Wisconsin Cheese Tour paperwork."

"Cheese is your department. Any customers for me this week?"

"They're only your customers if you're here."

"I've been busy. What the hell are you wearing?"

"I suppose the guys who speared the parrot were friends of yours?"

"I don't know what you're talking about, Squid. What's with the outfit?"

Since Atlantic City was a work trip, I had paired my new crocodile pencil skirt with a black silk ballet-neck blouse, sheer black stockings, and my four-inch brown crocodile heels. I had pulled my hair off my forehead with a black suede headband, and added gold hoop earrings and Jackie O sunglasses—classic simplicity.

"I'm spending the weekend with Debbie. You know, girls' night." I spun professionally, hoping it would distract him. "Loehmann's Columbus Day sale. What do you think?"

"Too slutty. What are you up to?"

"Nothing. I'm trying to get Debbie out of the house."

"You know I'll get Eddie to find out, if you don't tell me."

I sighed. Eddie was my oldest brousin and my favorite. I really didn't want him involved. "If you must know, the National Association of Career Travel Agents is meeting this weekend. As the face of this agency it's a very important part of my job to keep up with travel trends."

"Dad's sending you? I find that pretty hard to believe, considering last time," Jimmy said, sitting on the edge of my desk and lighting a cigarette. "Well?"

"He's been so busy, I didn't want to bother him with it."

"Right. It's in Atlantic City, isn't it? He'll have a cow."

I was dead. All my planning was for nothing.

"Come on, Jimmy. Does he have to know? It's only three days and two nights with breakfast and Wi-Fi included. It's just New Jersey, for Christ's sake."

He leaned in, his gold chain swinging toward me, and it was all I could do not to knee him in the balls. It wouldn't be the first time.

"It's my only chance of filling the Tanzania packages. I've pitched the whole borough and their extended families already."

He took a long, cough-inducing drag on his cancer stick, and held out his hand, which seemed to sport a couple of new gold rings. I gave him a look and reached into the drawer for the $365.47 that I was going to have to replace out of my next paycheck.

"No ratting," I said.

"No getting lucky." He pocketed the cash and headed for the door.

"What are the odds?" I yelled after him.

To be honest, I hoped they were good. I'd been single for a year and even worse, celibate for about six months. I'd had a brief fling with one of my old high school boyfriends after he and his wife split up, but that was mostly sad, as he kept talking about her before, during, and after sex. Apparently she had psoriasis, but that just made her more attractive to him. Short of my contracting a disfiguring skin disease, the relationship had no future.

So I was ready for a fling. That's what conventions were for, right? I just wanted to meet someone who wasn't from Brooklyn. Romance would be preferable, but I'd settle for someone cute to talk to about finding bulletproof rental cars in Mexico.

Daydreaming was a mistake. I didn't trust Jimmy not to snitch. I had to leave right away. I jammed Mrs. Barsky's FedEx envelope into my purse and headed out.

# Chapter Five

I headed down 92nd Street and onto the ramp for the Verrazano Bridge and before I knew it, I was on Highway 9, headed for Atlantic City. Most people don't consider New Jersey a destination location, but as far as I was concerned, Trenton was practically Tahiti.

I put my "Basic Swahili" Berlitz tape into the ancient cassette player and practiced saying *jambo*, which meant "hello" and *hujambo*, with the emphasis on the second syllable, which meant "How are you?" There was something great about driving past a toxic chemical plant while saying *Ni siku nzuri sana*: "What a beautiful day." I was so caught up in perfecting my pronunciation that I almost missed the Garden State Parkway. An hour later, I merged onto the Atlantic City Expressway East and minutes later, I could see the ocean, the Boardwalk, and my destination, the Trump Taj Mahal, where the marquee read "Travel Agents Do It With Reservations."

I self-parked and headed to the lobby. The Taj had the blinding, combed-over arrogance of its owner, who seemed to move through life without apology or consequence. To live without apology. Or jail. What a concept. The lobby was a gold-plated tack-fest through the history of architecture: marble Arabian-patterned floors, classical white marble check-in desk, a Rococo ceiling with massive gold leaf clam shells, and a truly monstrous modern chandelier the size of my car.

I got into the check-in line. Normally, when I managed to sneak out of the borough, I booked myself under one of my assumed names—I had a friend in the credit card/passport business. I hated splitting up the rewards points, but it was the only way to throw Uncle Ray off the scent. This time I'd registered so late I'd had to use my real name. Chances were someone I was related to was going to drag me out screaming anyway, so I might as well get all the perks I deserved.

"Next?" called Rhonda from Fort Collins.

"Cyd Redondo, Redondo Travel."

She took my credit card details and handed me off to a bellboy. I always felt weird having a bellboy pull my carry-on luggage, but it seemed rude, and cheap, to refuse. I love a bargain, but the one place you never, ever, scrimp is tipping; it always pays off. I encouraged my clients to factor in at least twenty percent for tips in their travel budget. The bellboy opened the door and brought my luggage in. I gave him a ten.

"Nice legs." He ran for the opening elevator. See?

My room looked out over the ocean. It didn't matter that the water was rodent gray with waves the color of a yellowed t-shirt. It was the Atlantic and on the other side of it was France. Technically, I had a view of France.

I headed to the bathroom and put all the Aveda samples in my suitcase, so the housekeeping staff would replace them. I told my clients they should do the same; they were paying for it. I checked out the mirror. I still looked twenty-eight on a good day, largely because I hadn't had children and took kick-boxing. My mom always said it was unseemly for a woman to kick someone in the head, but growing up with so many boys, I saw the appeal. I redid my makeup for convention hall lighting, checked my bag for my box of one thousand business cards and Tanzania pamphlets, and put the Do Not Disturb sign on the door, with the TV on as a burglar deterrent. It wasn't foolproof, but it lowered your odds.

Then, for luck, I headed down to the biggest wishing well in New Jersey—the Atlantic Ocean. I put my shoes and stockings in my bag, and dug my bare feet in the damp sand. There's usually a mildewy, fishy smell about the Jersey shore, but that night it was fresh as a margarita. I wished for my clients to be safe, and for me to win the trip to Africa with my own "plus one." I threw in a whole roll of quarters, watched them sink, then dried off my feet with the mini roll of paper towels in my bag and headed back.

I had registered too late to snag a convention booth, so I was going to have to approach potential clients on their own turf. I figured I had about ninety minutes before they all disappeared for the Early Bird Specials. Safaris weren't cheap, so I needed optimistic, well-heeled seniors. I headed to the five-dollar slots and looked for smokers with Rewards cards. I spoke to seven different women, all with three-day-old hair-dos that had begun to collapse like angel food cakes taken out too early. I heard a lot about their children and Medicaid, but only one of them took my card. She said I should try the Bingo Lounge the next morning. I bought her a drink, then headed to the Convention Hall, hoping for some referrals.

As I neared the registration desk, I could have sworn I saw the Eileen Fisher woman who'd come into the office earlier today. This time she was wearing a severe navy suit and looked like she'd been born in it. I followed her to the elevator, but what was I going to say to her anyway?

Nancy from Go! Chicago! was working the registration outside the Apollo Ballroom. We had traded hotel coupons and services for years. She helped me find the best river tours and handicap access hotels and I got her Yankees tickets and suites at the Plaza. We independents had to stick together.

"Is she here?"

Nancy hated Peggy Newsome too. "Anne Klein pencil skirt, blouse unbuttoned three down, new Diane Sawyer haircut. She's already hosting at the bar."

"Why do the evil people never get cancer?"

"The poison in their blood kills it." Nancy handed me five drink vouchers. "She's in Eastern Europe, so I'd hit Asia or the Caribbean, to be safe."

"Thanks, Nance. Drink later?"

"Tomorrow. I'm on the desk all night. Have fun. See the world."

And that's what I did, by proxy. The convention hall was divided into destination locations, with individual travel service booths scattered throughout. I gave each of them a professional assessment. Sometimes the posters and pamphlets alone could tell a good travel agent whether the place was worthy of Mrs. Greenblatt and her chihuahuas. First, you looked at the paper quality of the brochure, font, number and quality of photos, etc. Anything under twenty weight or non-glossy meant the place was cheap and would probably skimp on shampoo, towels, bedding, etc. Obviously anything Xeroxed meant fly-by-night; any place that used italics was trying too hard. The photos were the most important. If they focused on tiny things—a chair in the lobby rather than a full view—it was a bad sign.

I checked out the travel agents too. The floor was full of optimistic clothing. It was always interesting to see people trying to look their best. Sometimes you had to say, "Really, this is your best?" Still, there was something sweet about it; I felt a wave of love for my profession, for the agents who were taking out second mortgages and managing commission cuts and still came here, full of hope. For me, it was the hope of giveaways. Those thousand business cards were not for nothing.

I entered every drawing and raffle, as many times as I could, sometimes flinging my card in from the side or over a cut-out, for trips to Venice (six days, seven nights with scooter included), Auckland, Hong Kong, Napa, and a barge down the Amazon, among others. I talked to the team from Singapore Airlines, who gave me some insider tips for seat requests, said hi to the folks at Europe On A Dime, and of course, I stood in line for Rick

Steves. The guy is a genius. I just wish he would stand up straight.

By the time I was halfway through the hall and had registered for tomorrow's lecture, "Making Terrorism Work For You," I had so many pamphlets, books, and business cards that I put them in the luggage room so I could start over.

For my second round, I chose a tote from the *New York Times* so I'd look smarter and headed for the Asian section. There was a tall, dark-haired man there with dimples who'd seemed to look at me in Prague and Key West, so I thought it would be easier on both of us if we were on the same continent. He was wearing a loose linen shirt, khakis, and sadly, sandals. Men in sandals are usually high maintenance to make up for their lack of sex appeal, but that was not the problem with this guy. At least they weren't flip-flops, but even if they were custom, it was a strike against him. I watched him listen to a pitch on Indonesian dive trips. He had a shy smile and eyes like jumbo Raisinets and I decided to ignore his feet for the moment. When he turned and stared right at me, I actually blushed. When you have ten brousins, you don't blush. He was coming my way.

I smoothed my skirt, then saw Peggy Newsome stomping toward me with what could only be described as a "look" on her face. The woman was evil and no amount of Cool Water could cover up the sulphurous, dragon lady smell that permeated the air around her. I really wasn't in the mood, especially as I might have spread a couple of small rumors about her at the Panthers' annual dinner dance last week. The words "bedbugs" and "identity theft" might have crossed my lips.

I ducked down behind an empty Thai Parasailing booth to gather my wits and accidently stepped into the trash can behind it, losing my balance and falling ass over elbow, flashing most of the South Pacific. Horrified, I got up too fast, knocking over a fifteen-foot Great Wall of China display. When the rolling fishbowls and flapping sails finally settled, the whole convention was staring at me. I closed my eyes, hoping this was one of my recurring convention nightmares. It wasn't. I was still on the floor when I heard a familiar, debate club voice.

"Cyd Redondo. What are you doing here? This is a travel agents convention." Damn you, Peggy Newsome. Now everyone in the convention knew who'd taken out Asian Adventures while showing her thong. "Ah, let me guess," Peggy said. "Ruining vacations wherever you go. That is, if you ever actually go anywhere."

Before I could spit out a retort, I felt a strong hand on my elbow.

"I'm so sorry," the guy with the Raisinet

eyes said, pulling me up and handing me my purse. "Sorry, folks. This was entirely my fault," he shouted to the gathering spectators. "It's just like me to turn all clumsy when I see a beautiful woman." His dimples turned almost inside out as he handed his card to the Great Wall of China reps. "Of course I'll pay for any damage."

He turned to Peggy. She shook her haircut and held out her hand.

"Peggy Newsome," she said. "If you're looking for a true professional, I would be happy to handle all your travel needs." I bet you would, you hag, I thought.

"That's very kind, but Ms. Redondo has yet to ruin any of my vacations."

"It's your funeral," Peggy said.

He made a half-turn, then looked back at her. "May I ask a personal question?"

"I'd love it."

"Have you had work?" he asked.

"No, all absolutely natural." She shook her hair again.

"Maybe you should consider it."

Peggy Newsome went as stiff and white as a half-baked meringue. "You're not going any-where," she snarled at me, then stomped off into Micronesia.

My hero winked and headed for the exit. If

I hadn't been in lust with him already, this pretty much did it. I went to follow him, but the parasailing guys surrounded me and by the time I had calmed them down, he was gone.

# Chapter Six

I ran to the lobby and spent a half an hour of pointless searching for the man who had taken down Peggy Newsome. At eleven, having reached the limit of my shoe pain, I gave up and headed upstairs. As I was taking off my eyelashes, the phone rang. Maybe it was him.

"Cyd Redondo, Redondo Travel." Nothing but breathing. I checked the locks and got into bed. I kept telling myself I needed my beauty sleep in case I ran into him again, but all that did was keep me awake.

Still awake at five, I decided to check out Mrs. Barsky's FedEx package. Maybe that would put me to sleep. The documents inside were full of Latin words, references to the United Arab Emirates, stamped "Captive Bred," and approved by something called CITES. It might as well have all been in Latin. I figured the sender probably didn't know about her death; I should give them a call.

They were seven hours ahead, it would be midday there and international calls were free on my weekend minutes. But when I tried the number on the waybill, it was disconnected. I added the P.O. Box address to my phone anyway and got up.

I ordered English muffins, bacon, and a pot of coffee. I was missing the complimentary buffet, but I didn't want to risk running into the sandal guy before I'd had caffeine and a mini facial. I took a cold shower to close my pores, then dressed professionally sexy, just in case: a pink Chantelle bra, a leopard skin knee-length sheath with a tiny crocodile patent belt, nude platform heels, and the real Tiffany studs I'd gotten in an estate sale in Fort Hamilton.

I went to two morning lectures, keeping my eyes peeled for my tall stranger, then headed to the Bingo Lounge, which turned out to be a bust. Or it was after I was escorted out by Security. Apparently, I distracted a hardcore regular with my pamphlet and cost him five hundred dollars. The guard was very nice, considering, but said there was no "solicitation" in the casino and if he caught me approaching guests again, I would be banned from all Trump resorts. No problem, there were other casinos.

To keep my spirits up, I headed to a reception for the Independent Travel Agents Association. This was one place I knew I wouldn't run into Peggy Newsome, as corporate bitches were not allowed. Nancy and I cashed in her drink vouchers.

"My only clue is his sandals," I told her.

"He's your Cinderfella. Security tapes?"

"If we were in Bay Ridge, no problem. Do you know the guy here?"

"Just the ones in Vegas." Nancy downed her pear martini. I was sticking to my usual Jack Daniels straight up. Things were complicated enough in life without having to make a decision about drinks: JD, red wine, coffee, water. Simple. This regime required whitening strips, but that was a small price to pay, especially if you got them online.

"Well, here's to finding your mysterious stranger." Nancy shot her drink. She was late for her date with a cruise director from Greece, so I hugged her good-bye and did another round through the slots until the security guard spotted me and I ducked into the closest ballroom I could find—the Herb World Expo. I figured I could hide for a few minutes in there—my mother would probably love a basil plant.

The ballroom entrance smelled more like gerbil litter than fresh rosemary, and featured a huge wall of what looked like mulch and cans of fertilizer. Personally, I would have gone for suede gardening gloves as a teaser, but maybe mulch was sexy to gardeners. When I got inside, instead of the colored clogs and capri pants I expected, the hall was crawling with faded black-light t-shirts, piercings, and male ponytails that looked like they were trying to wriggle off their owners' heads. Past the terrariums, I saw something familiar: a goodies table. Great—I was starving. The table was piled high with cake displays and white plastic carryout containers. It was like the high school bake sale of all time.

I headed toward what I thought was a carrot cake. As I reached for it, it moved. And it wasn't the only pastry in motion. Every cake plate, every coleslaw container and zip-lock was filled with reptiles: tiny colored ones curled up like licorice and huge brown boa constrictors masquerading as maple Bundt cakes. I felt weak.

I sprinted for the exit, running into the kind of thing that should be behind unbreakable glass, or safely dead and reincarnated as a handbag: a writhing, yellow and white python the length of a hallway, flicking its red tongue. The man it was wrapped around came straight toward me, smiling.

"Welcome to the Herp Expo." He held out a hand with about a fifth of the reptile in it. "Would you like a photo with Bubbles?"

# Chapter Seven

I came-to five minutes later in a plastic folding chair at the back of the convention hall and immediately screamed, as I had missed my opportunity before by being unconscious. A thick woman in a black leather vest and fifteen silver snake necklaces handed me a coffee.

"Wrong convention?" she asked.

"Slightly. Cyd Redondo, Redondo Travel. Thanks," I said, downing it as I looked right, left, and behind me. Reptiles everywhere. "How did I get here?"

She pointed to a familiar set of sandals. I looked up into those eyes and blushed. Again. This was the second time I'd keeled over in front of this man. What must he think of me? Well, if I let him get away again, I'd never know.

"Cyd Redondo, Redondo Travel." I held out my hand. He took it. It was like someone had thrown a toaster into my bathtub. And that was just my hand.

"Redondo Travel?"

I nodded.

"Sounds familiar," he said.

"We service the Greater Brooklyn area."

"Really?" He raised his eyebrows. "Roger Claymore. I didn't take you for the herpetology type."

"What was your first clue?" I said. "Did I land on the snake?"

"Luckily not. That snake is worth twenty grand."

My heart sank. "You're not one of the snake guys are you?"

"Chiropractor," he said. "Convention-hopping."

"Me too." I looked around. The more awake I became, the more I felt like slimy things were crawling inside my clothes.

"And you came in here?" he said.

I shook my head. "Misunderstanding." I looked up at him. Seize the day. "You've saved my ass twice. I probably owe you a drink. I have vouchers."

"Well, if it's vouchers."

"Any chance you can carry me back out?"

"Why. Do you faint a lot?"

"Only once before, when my brousin's bone was sticking out of his elbow."

"Your what?"

"Never mind."

He smiled. He had a small mole just beside his mouth. His hands were long, like a pianist's or a surgeon's.

"Men don't faint, right?" I couldn't take my eyes off his dimples.

"I wouldn't necessarily say that. Quick look on the way out?" He offered his arm.

A look, quick or not, was not my idea of fun, but I didn't want him to let go of me. I nodded. We passed terrariums filled with poisonous tree frogs, monitor lizards, and tarantulas. Behind us, I thought I saw a booth that read CITES, like on Mrs. Barsky's documents, and almost pulled Roger that way, but there were a few loose lizards on shoulders coming our way and so we headed for the exit instead. I was stunned by the prices for things most people in Brooklyn would slice with a shovel. Twenty grand. Thirty grand. For snakes. I started to hyperventilate. Everywhere, dealers were opening their reptile "takeout containers."

"It's safe, don't worry," Roger said

"It is not safe. Think about it. How many times do you wind up with coleslaw juice all over your pastrami or balsamic on your garlic bread by the time you get home? Those things are not secure." I saw a booth full of what looked like golf clubs. "What the hell are those?"

A lovely, petite blonde in a white golf shirt handed out her card: Ron's Reptile Control. "You use this end here to hold the snake down behind its head. We also have collapsibles," she said, taking a one-foot club, then shaking it out into four with a fencing flourish.

Roger steered me past a huge tub of crickets on broken egg boxes and a freezer full of dead mice. I didn't realize how hard I'd been holding his hand until I let go and he shook it out.

"Sorry."

"No problem. I will accept that drink, though. It might restore the feeling."

"Smart ass." I pointed to a purple bar. Roger looked back at the hall.

"What is it?" I looked back too.

"Nothing," he said "but there's a quieter bar up on the left."

We went around the corner and arrived at a gold-plated lounge. He pulled out my barstool. The bartender took our orders for a microbrew and a Jack Daniels straight up. I checked the mirror behind the bar in case fainting had flattened my hair.

"Okay, that was, hands-down, the weirdest thing I've ever seen. It's like a snake flea market. Is there really a demand for these things? Honestly?"

"Bigger than dogs and cats. Billions of dollars. It's massive online too."

"Snakes through the mail?"

"Absolutely. That's what the holes in the tops are for. And this is the legal stuff. Most of the reptile trade is black market. Like I said, billions of dollars of endangered animals every year. It's second to arms dealing."

"Wow. Lizards are a girl's best friend. Who knew? How do you know all this stuff?"

"They had brochures by the door."

"How secure are those animals at night?"

"You really shouldn't worry."

"That's easy for you to say. You're a chiropractor, you trade in calm. I'm a travel agent, I trade in emergencies. It keeps you a little bit excitable."

"Really?"

"Well, in certain circumstances." I took a stiff mouthful of the Jack Daniels. We looked at each other and my temperature went up about ten degrees.

Roger raised his glass. "To meeting on the Great Wall of China. And I do mean on it."

Two hours and a bottle of wine later, I had done the soft sell for my Tanzania package and he'd explained pressure points. For some reason, I told him about finding my neighbor dead without her wig. Then I realized it wasn't the most romantic topic, so I suggested a stroll on the boardwalk, preferably toward Nathan's. But first, I needed lipstick. I said I'd meet him in the lobby.

When I came out, he was in deep discussion with a sandy-haired man dressed in what could only be called a Eurotrash suit, slightly shiny and a bit too tight, with a t-shirt underneath and sporting over-long, pointy shoes. As I approached, the suit guy turned and smiled.

"Cyd Redondo, Redondo Travel." I gave his freckled hand a good shake.

"Graham Gant." He had a slightly Nordic accent. "Pleasure." We stood awkwardly. "So you're a friend of Claymore's?" I looked at Roger, who gave me a cautionary look.

"We know each other professionally."

"Really? Well, that's terrific. I don't want to keep you. Claymore, I'll be in touch." He turned and walked to the bar.

"I'm sorry. I didn't mean to interrupt anything."

"Don't worry about it." He took my hand, but looked after Gant. "Didn't you say something about Nathan's? It's famous, right?"

I dragged him down to the boardwalk and got a perfect Nathan's chili cheese dog. Roger went for the crinkle fries. I was a little concerned that he was a man who knew a lot about reptiles and didn't seem to like hot dogs. Who doesn't like hot dogs? I know they have nitrates and toes and things in them, but he was on vacation. Still, he apparently loved the fries, as I only got two, so I decided to overlook the rest. We stood there looking out on the water, slick as motor oil. My phone rang.

"I'm sorry, but this is my client emergency line."

"No problem."

It was Debbie, my alibi. "Your uncle called. He said he had some news. Honestly, if you're having fun, I wouldn't risk his hearing your voice. You're clearly about to have sex. Right?" Debbie and I had been friends since first grade. I laughed and hung up.

Roger had rolled up his pants and had his bare feet in the water. I wrangled out of my stockings and joined him, shoes in one hand, his fingers in the other.

"Still worried about snakes?" he asked.

"Any chance you'd care to check my room just in case?"

He squeezed my hand. We headed back to the hotel. When we got inside, I thought I saw the Eileen Fisher woman again, this time in a skin-tight leather dress, leaving with a miniscule Chinese businessman. Roger asked me to wait for a minute.

It gave me time to ask myself what I was doing. Roger lived in San Francisco, I might never see him again. But when he came back, twirling the collapsible snake handler like an Englishman's umbrella, I was in, for better or worse. It was a long elevator ride and an even longer wait while Roger actually checked the room. Finally, he turned. "I don't see anything, but they've been known to hide."

I'm not much of one to kiss and tell, but the next three hours were pretty much in the spectacular range. I couldn't get enough of Roger's narrow shoulders or the way his flop of hair slapped me on the forehead every time he kissed me. Somehow, I didn't mind that his chest was smoother than mine. I even came to crave his "green" kelp aftershave, a first for me. It's amazing how much genuine, crazy, mutual attraction can make every gesture, every movement, even every mistake the most erotic thing that ever happened. It was my favorite kind of sex, the kind where you could only breathe enough to laugh. The kind where the contact, the connection, not the technique, was what mattered. And we had that. We'd had it from the first moment he'd touched my elbow.

Not that Roger the Chiropractor didn't have technique—he basically managed to turn my back into a third breast. But I'm not sure I would have liked him any less if he hadn't. By the time he finally drew himself around me and we fell asleep, I figured for once, I'd done something right.

At three-thirty, I woke up to find him gone.

# Chapter Eight

At first I thought he was just in the bathroom, but after five minutes, I finally stumbled up to look. It was dark and empty, as was the rest of the room. I tried not to panic. Men had left quickly before, but usually they at least offered some lame excuse. Had I been wrong about the whole thing? My uncle always said my instincts would ruin me in the end, but I so didn't want him to be right. I turned on the bedside light, setting off sunspots in my slightly hungover head, and looked around.

His clothes were gone, but he had left his wallet and keys. Maybe he was just an insomniac and didn't want to wake me. Maybe he was hungry. I decided for once in my life to be cool, so I turned the light back off. After about a half an hour, I heard the key in the door and resumed my position, eyes closed. It was hard to be perfectly still when you'd just had possibly the best sex of your life with someone who had disappeared.

Roger eased the door shut. I could feel him moving to the table, where he replaced my key. Then he sat down in one of the chairs by the window. I really wanted to see what he was doing. Finally, I couldn't stand it anymore and squinted. He looked out the window, then leaned forward and put his head in his hands. This was not a good sign.

Finally, he got undressed and crawled back into bed, folding himself around me again and kissing me just above my ear. Needless to say, I didn't get back to sleep.

I don't think he did either. Finally, we accidentally turned at the same time, facing each other, about an inch apart. I put my hands on his smooth chest, rippled with small flat muscles. He slid out from under me and started to stroke my back, kissing it at the very bottom.

"You have the loveliest coccygeal vertebrae I've ever seen," he said.

"I beg your pardon?"

"It's this little bit at the very bottom of your spine. It's perfect."

He kissed it gently, covered me up, and lay back. He took my hand and wound his fingers through it. We just lay there for a long time. Later, he turned to me.

"I just want you to know I don't do this at

every convention. I mean, I've never done anything like this before. Ever. Have you?"

"You mean with a snake-handler?" I said. He laughed and kissed me. "God, every time you kiss me I forget what time it is. What time is it?"

"Ten-fifteen," he said. "I guess I should get moving." He got up.

While he took a shower, I kept telling myself, "Flings are short, that's the point," but I had that tiny little pain just under my breastbone. I looked over at the room service leftovers we had ordered at one a.m. and reached for my purse. I pulled out a stack of lime green Tupperware "minis" and put the cheese, the rolls, and two shrimp away for later. Those shrimp were about five dollars apiece, and the room was freezing, so I was sure they'd be fine. Mrs. Barsky's papers weren't in my purse—I must have put them in my carry-on. Roger emerged from the bathroom, dressed, and drying his hair.

"What airline?" I asked.

"American."

"They'll hold your seat until fifteen minutes before—they don't tell you that, but they don't want to lose a business customer."

Roger put on his belt. "You seem to be a hell of a travel agent, I have to say."

"I try."

"I'd definitely use you," he said. "Oh God, that

sounds awful. Look, I'm not usually this spontaneous. I like to think I am, but I'm not."

"You look a little pale," I said. "Do you want an aspirin?"

He smiled. "No thanks. I actually try not to take any drugs if I can help it."

"Aspirin's not a drug, it's more of a condiment," I said, popping a couple myself. We'd had a lot of wine.

He turned me toward him. "Look, Cyd, what I've been trying to say all morning is that I'll never forget this. This night with you." God, that sounded final.

"Me neither," I said. "Do you want my card?"

"Of course," he said. We exchanged numbers then he grabbed me and kissed me.

"Well, if you ever fancy a trip to Africa, give me a call." I was shooting for levity, which was hard when I could barely breathe.

"I will," he said. "Good-bye."

And he left. I got on my tiptoes and watched him through the peephole. He hesitated at the elevator, but then it dinged and he disappeared.

I finished packing and looked for Mrs. Barsky's FedEx package. I finally found it under the bed. As I was grabbing my last free toiletries, my phone beeped. I hoped it was Roger.

It was the morgue.

# Chapter Nine

"Cyd? It's Paglia. The Barsky broad? Murdered."

I sank to the bed. I was not going to faint twice in one weekend, dammit.

My pal the medical examiner took my silence for the WTF it was. "It's her. Believe me, the Precinct thought I was drunk too. Definite homicide."

"What kind of homicide?"

"Poisoned. I'll know more when the lab work comes back."

"Poisoned? Holy crap. Does Joni know?"

"Your cousin Frank said he'd let her know. Anything else?"

"Just call me when you have more info. I owe you one. Which casino do you want this time? I'm at the Taj now. Don't tell anybody. Seriously."

"Gotcha. How is it?"

"Full of snakes. I'll book it now."

Who would murder Mrs. Barsky? Had she been right all along? Had the government actually considered her "a threat to our way of life"? Had the cops searched the store yet? Did it have anything to do with our break-in? I didn't think kids would kill her, but it was a pretty big coincidence that Mrs. Barsky and the parrot had died on the same day. Did the police realize the papers I'd lifted were missing? They might be evidence. And what did they mean, anyway? I remembered the CITES booth downstairs in the Herp Expo and threw my stuff together. But by the time I had steeled myself to reenter the reptile ballroom, there was nothing left but dollies, takeout containers, and the mouse freezer. Damn. I needed to get back to the office. I'd look it up then. I couldn't face opening my e-mails on a tiny screen right at that moment, so I headed for the car.

As I took Exit 38 for the Garden State, I put in my Swahili tape and tried to think about how cute Roger would look in cargo shorts, but the image of Mrs. Barsky, cold and wigless on the floor, was the only thing I saw.

Two hours later, the bridge was in my sights, and ten minutes after that, I was back at my desk. I had a half hour before I was due for our mandatory Redondo Sunday supper and there was no caution tape around Mrs. Barsky's store. Yet.

Jimmy still hadn't put back the pet store keys, so I had to break in again. As I reached through the mail slot, I went cold. It was too quiet. I opened the door. The animals were gone. Just empty cages and a few feathers, and bird seed pellets on the floor. I hoped the birds and puppies were safe somewhere.

The old-fashioned cash register was open and the filing cabinets were empty, but there was no sign of a break-in; Joni must have cleaned them out. I headed upstairs to Mrs. B's apartment. Her drawers and closets were empty, but her lime green chenille bedspread was still there. I sank down on her bed and tried to process the fact that the apartment was mine.

My phone rang again. Not Roger. It was We Find Anyone, asking if I'd gotten their e-mail about Bobby's Barsky's last known address? It was in Tanzania—in downtown Dar es Salaam. Had the weird FedEx been from Bobby? And was he still in Tanzania? Now I had an even better reason to win my trip. I could look after my clients, find Bobby Barsky, and have the first real vacation of my life. It was fate. Mrs. Barsky's cuckoo clock startled me out of my daze. I had five minutes to get to family dinner.

The house, as usual, was ablaze. It was three stories of red brick on a long narrow lot, surrounded by the topiary that had been my mother's hobby during menopause. I guess she had to slice something up. There was a glassed-in sunroom on the left side and a bay window on the right, separated by an oak door heavy enough to withstand continuous brousin slamming. My tiny attic window was like an exclamation point at the top of the A-line roof. Jimmy had most likely grassed me. I felt nauseous. It didn't matter. Avoiding Sunday night supper would just make it worse.

I opened the door and was immediately assaulted by two of my nephews. Louie and David were twin boys of six and usually showed their affection by some form of warfare. I had taught them they could only throw things that wouldn't stain. As long as they didn't leave bruises, I let them have their fun.

I was shaking the almonds off my coat when Uncle Leon grabbed me. He always tried to pick me up, but now that he was sixty-eight, it usually didn't work. I had learned to brace myself against furniture and push off. It made him feel better, though I usually pulled something.

Leon was the uncle who looked most like my dad, so I had a soft spot for him. He was a taxidermist—the artistic one in the family. He consulted for the Museum of Natural History and took me behind the scenes when I was a kid. There's a picture somewhere of me at six in a diorama, hugging Neanderthal Man.

Uncle Leon gestured toward the kitchen. "Everyone's in there. Big powwow."

"About what?"

"About you," he said, winking and headed down the hall. Oh God, they knew about Atlantic City.

"Uncle Leon, wait."

"I'm going to watch that Rachel Maddow. Smart is the new sexy." He disappeared into the den. Just as I turned, Uncle Ray stuck his head out.

"Hi," I said, as casually as possible.

"Everyone's in here. Come on, I need to talk to you."

I moved down the long hallway, past the dining room on the right. The red flocked wallpaper and massive sideboard seemed more ominous than usual and someone had done my job—the silverware. This was going to be bad. I moved to the swinging door outside the kitchen, breathed, and pushed.

There was a huge roar and I walked into a bright orange banner with "CONGRATULA-TIONS CYD !!!!" across it. The whole family was clapping like crazy.

"What?" I said. "What?"

Uncle Ray put his arm around me. "You did it. You sold sixteen Tanzania trips. You're the Queen of Redondo Travel. The tour company is thrilled. I'm proud of you."

"But I only had nine. What happened?"

"You got the rest of the Gray Panthers. I ran into Dorothy at Mass. I guess they read something dodgy on the Internet about Peggy Newsome, so they switched over from her Barbados package for their spring trip."

I owed my computer-hacking guy a bottle of single malt.

"I can't believe it. I'm finally going somewhere. Oh, my God." No one was smiling. "What?"

"We'll talk about it over dinner. Come on, everyone's hungry." My stomach fell to my knees. I didn't grow up in this house for nothing. I turned to my mother who was busying herself with the gnocchi. I watched as she moved around the kitchen, pale as nonfat milk, her long strawberry blond hair flecked with gray and swinging in a braid down her back. Everything about my mother was long: her hair, her feet, her suffering, her name: Mary Bridget Colleen Colleary Redondo. She wouldn't meet my eye as we moved to the dining room.

"To Cyd," Uncle Ray said, raising his glass. "Our favorite girl."

"To Cyd!" everyone said, and drank.

"To Cyd," my Uncle Ray continued, "who always puts the family and business first. To Cyd, who never lets us down." Everyone clapped. They'd now clapped twice. "Isn't she the best? When she cashes in her trip, we can afford to upgrade our computer system." More applause, then everyone started to pass the antipasto. Just like that. I looked at their faces. They'd all discussed this and agreed. I was never getting out of there. Before I could respond, the doorbell rang. Everyone froze. People knew better than to disturb us during Sunday dinner. My mother headed to the door.

"How's Debbie?" Jimmy asked.

"Pissed off," I said, biting into a breadstick. Then I heard a voice in the hall. A male voice. And before I could stop her, my mother arrived at the table with…Roger.

# Chapter Ten

He was holding a bunch of lilies. For just a second, I forgot about my family. I could feel the blood rushing to my cheeks and my womb. In the opposite order.

"You didn't fly home," I said.

My mother cleared her throat. "Everyone, this is Roger. He's here to see our Cyd." Except for the sound of my uncle putting down a serving spoon too hard, there was complete silence. Uncle Ray rose to his full height. I was so dead. Then he held out his hand instead of throwing a punch.

"Ray Redondo. I'm Cyd's uncle and guardian and this is her family. What can we do for you?"

"Roger Claymore. Very pleased to meet you. I'm so sorry to have disturbed your dinner. I just wanted to bring these to Cyd." He turned to me. "I didn't realize you lived with your family. I'll come back later? Or see you tomorrow?"

My brousin Eddie, six-foot two and two feet wide, jumped up.

"No way. Eddie Redondo. Cyd's cousin. Nice to meet you. Why don't you stay? Any friend of Cyd's is a friend of ours." He brought in one of the chairs from the hall and put it between him and Uncle Ray. Roger squeezed in, while my mother brought another place setting. Louie threw an olive at Roger, hitting him in the forehead.

"Nice shot." Roger grinned at my nephew and looked at the mountains of sausages, rigatoni, antipasto, and cheese. "Have I interrupted a special occasion?"

"Not really," I said. David pelted him with a parmesan ball.

"So, Roger, how long have you known our Cyd?" Eddie asked. "I don't think we've heard about you yet."

"Yeah, where did you guys meet?" Jimmy said. I would have kicked him, but he was too far away.

"This weekend," Roger said as everyone leaned in. "In Atlantic City."

I think I actually squeaked. The entire table swiveled in my direction. My Aunt Helen yelled "Not again," made the sign of the cross, and sucked down the rest of her Chianti.

"Atlantic City?" Uncle Ray said. "Well, Cyd, you haven't been there in a while."

The last time I'd gone to a convention in Atlantic City, I'd made a small mistake—I'd gotten

married. I was twenty-nine at the time. It happens.
The family tried to get it annulled, but I refused: I
was in love. When we moved into a duplex three
blocks over, my uncle gave me a list of everything
that would go wrong in the next six months. Every
single thing he'd said came true. After that, my
family was even more determined to keep me at
home and I'd been brokenhearted enough to stay.

"So," said Uncle Ray, "Sin City."

"NACTA Convention at the Taj. Didn't
Jimmy tell you? It's far and away the best place to
keep informed," I said.

"I bet," Jimmy said. "You look informed." He
and Eddie shared a look.

"So Roger," Uncle Ray said, "are you in the
business too?"

"Oh no, I'm a chiropractor."

"And where are you from?" my mother asked.
Everyone's forks stopped. She rarely made herself
heard in this family.

"San Francisco," he said. "I grew up just north
of the city."

"Earthquakes," she said in an aside to me.

Roger took a bite of eggplant, oblivious.
"This is absolutely delicious. It's very kind of you
to include me. It must be great to have big family
dinners like this."

"You don't have family dinners?" Aunt Helen asked.

"I'm an only child."

"Cyd is too," Jimmy said. "You're perfect for each other. Look, Eddie, look at Squid. She's all red."

I decided in that moment to tell Uncle Ray about the missing petty cash, if he ever spoke to me again.

For the first time in my life, I was having a hard time getting eggplant parmesan down. I needed to do three things. First, get Roger out of here. Second, give my uncle time to cool down. Third, move into Mrs. Barsky's apartment, possibly tomorrow. In the meantime: diffuse.

"Roger is interested in parasailing packages and seeing the Great Wall of China."

"Well you've come to the right place. We've been around for forty-two years, about ten years before Cyd was born," Uncle Ray said. Really? Did he have to give up my real age? "And Cyd's the life and soul of the business."

"It's almost like she's married to it," my cousin Joey chimed in.

"Yeah, no one else will take her," Jimmy said, laughing. The nephews laughed too.

"Oh now, boys, you know that's not true, is it Cyd? But enough about the business. We all want to hear about your trip," Uncle Ray said. "Do you have any announcements for us this time?" They all waited. I looked at Roger's dimples and the way his hair was falling over his eyebrows. Enough, I thought. Time for drastic measures.

"Yes, I do. Roger is my 'plus one.' For the Tanzania package."

"You won the trip?" Roger asked.

"I did. I just found out."

"Great. Uh. That's fantastic."

I took a breath. "Do you still want to go?"

"Of course. Of course I do." He looked worried. My family will do that to a person.

"I thought you just met," Uncle Ray said. "Isn't it a bit early for a safari? You know what they say—nothing ruins a new romance like traveling together."

"We've been dating on the Internet for awhile, haven't we Roger?" I kicked him under the table. At least I hoped it was him.

He looked at me. "She's even more wonderful in person, but I don't have to tell you that."

"Let's have our dessert in the den," my mother said, rising. "Ray, you and Eddie look after Roger while Cyd helps me in the kitchen."

I had to let them take him. I had no choice.

As soon as the kitchen door closed, both my mother and my Aunt Helen were all over me. Who is he? How could you meet someone on the interweb? But a doctor, how great. Unless he was a serial killer.

"He's a chiropractor, Mom. He's very, very nice. In fact, he even defended me against Peggy Newsome." That shut them up for awhile. I started scraping red sauce into the disposal. I heard the clank of the good china behind me and the sudden slippery rush of hot soap and water.

"Why didn't you tell us you were going to Atlantic City?" my mother said.

"Would you?" I asked. "It was important for the business. We have to compete with all these Internet sites and I need every possible advantage and contact I can to fight for us out there. And you know he would have said no."

She kissed me on the top of the head, which was unusual, while Helen lowered her arms into the soapy water up to her dangling triceps, which were loose enough to start a tidal wave.

"But you can't meet people on the Internet," Mom said.

"Where else? Chadwick's? I've dated everyone in Bay Ridge. And didn't you see how polite he was?"

"Ted Bundy was polite. How else are you going to get someone into your car before you dismember them?" Helen said, eating the last tiny bit of garlic bread off one of the plates.

"Mom, please, you know I've wanted to go to Africa since I was five and now I have someone to go with. You can't let Uncle Ray take this away from me. I earned it."

"I know you did, honey, but it's his business. In this economy, you have to be careful."

"I'm tired of being careful," I said, scraping harder.

"Well, that's pretty clear, meeting someone on the Internet," Helen said.

"He's perfectly harmless and exactly what he says he is."

"He could be killing your uncles right now," she said. My mother nodded.

There was a bloodcurdling scream. I dropped one of Mom's plates and we all went running into the den.

# Chapter Eleven

There was Roger, wrestling my Uncle Leon right under Gary, our bison head. My shortest brousin and Uncle Tony's oldest, Frank the cop, had his service weapon pointed at them. I ran forward just as Roger let Uncle Leon go.

"Wow," Leon said, reaching over and touching his toes, then swinging his torso from side to side. "I haven't been able to do that in fifteen years. I love this guy," he said, putting his arm around Roger. "He's a keeper, Cyd."

I turned to Frank and raised my eyebrows. He put his gun back in the waist of his khakis and shrugged.

"Why don't you spend the night, kid?" Uncle Leon said. "Our couch is comfortable as hell. That way we can all get to know you better."

No, no, no. Roger saw my face.

"No, I couldn't possibly. But I would love to take Cyd out for a coffee, if you don't mind? Cyd?"

"Absolutely, that would be great. Just let me freshen up," I said, running for the stairs. I thought about the Minettis surrounded by wild animals on their anniversary safari. I thought about Mrs. Barsky lying on gerbil pellets. I thought about Bobby Barsky, who'd been smart enough to make a run for it when he had the chance. It was time to take mine.

Still, if I was going to pull this off, I had to be quick and I had to be careful. I turned on the tap, as you could hear it all over the house, then ran to my closet. Of course I had done a "practice pack" for my Africa trip. I grabbed my "absolutely necessary" list and did a quick check of my bags. I could put the "absolutely absolutely necessary emergency" things in the carry-on once we were out of the house. I'd found the lightest indestructible luggage set I could afford at Luggage World. I double-checked my passport. I touched all my obsolete globes for luck, pushed my luggage onto the fire escape, did a fake flush of the toilet, and headed down the stairs.

"Ready?" I took Roger's arm and moved him to the door.

"You sure you won't stay for dessert?" Uncle Ray asked. "There's no need to run off."

"No, we'll be fine. Thanks for dinner, Ma, it was great."

"Lovely to meet all of you." Roger shook hands with my uncles and cousins and kissed my mother on the cheek. "Bridget."

"Be sure and bring her back." Uncle Ray said. "She's still our little girl."

I could have killed my uncle at that moment, but I figured what I was about to do would hurt him about as much, so I kissed him quickly, and finally managed to get Roger out the door.

"What was all that?" Roger said once we were outside.

"Do you have a car?"

"A rental."

"Would you mind taking me to the office?" I said, moving him behind a panel truck just down the street. He looked at me funny.

"Cyd, what is going on?"

"Shhhh," I said, pulling him further behind the truck. Finally, the front door closed and I looked him in the eye. "Did you really come back for me?"

"I came back because I couldn't do anything else." He kissed me.

"God, don't do that, I'll go all wobbly." I made him promise to stay there while I ran behind the Faragamos' hedge and into our backyard. It might seem hard to climb a fire escape in spike heels, but I'd had years of practice. When I got within five feet of the ground, I dropped the suitcase—it was guaranteed for two hundred pounds of pressure. It had wheels, but they would leave tracks, so I hoisted it into my arms with my carry-on and headed for the street. Happily, Eddie had just aerated the lawn, so my heel marks wouldn't show. I made it around the corner.

"Running away?" Roger said.

"It's not a joke. Where's your car?" He pointed at a Crown Vic. I took his keys and popped the trunk.

"Cyd, honestly, what is going on? You're acting like a crazy person."

"Just get us onto another street and I'll explain everything," I said. "I promise." He started the car. "Go right at the stop sign." I looked back at the house. If any of my brousins were going to follow us, we'd hear a car. So far, nothing.

"Okay, what is it?" Roger said.

"Left here and pull into the back."

The Redondo Travel sign glowed green in the dark street. Roger pulled down the alley into the parking lot and we headed in. I moved down the hall to my desk and turned on the computer, praying that Uncle Ray hadn't already deleted the travel vouchers.

"Cyd, honestly, stop and tell me what's going on."

"What's going on is that I'm going to Tanzania."

"I know, that's great."

"I mean I'm going tonight."

"Now? What's the rush?"

"I hope this doesn't jeopardize your faith in me as your travel consultant, but the truth is, I've never actually been outside the greater New York/ New Jersey area."

"What? You talked to me about Tahiti for twenty minutes. Did you make that all up?"

"Of course not. I know everything you need to know about Tahiti. Theoretically." I was already at my desk, searching for an e-mail from our partners, Adventure Limited. "Look. I've booked over five thousand successful trips, all from this desk and, except for a few mishaps beyond my control, have never had any complaints. We have a seventy-five percent return rate for our customers and it's only that low because some of them die before they can afford another trip."

"I still don't get it—why tonight?"

"My uncle says I have to cash in the trip and put the money back into the business."

"But you worked so hard."

"Exactly." There it was: "CONGRATULA-TIONS MS. REDONDO! YOU'VE DONE IT!" I gave a sign of relief. My travel documents were attached and correct. I looked up at Roger. "Uncle

Ray always does this. Now that he knows about Atlantic City, I guarantee he will guilt me into it."

"What's so bad about Atlantic City?"

"It's a long story. Roger, I swear, if I don't take this trip, I will die in that house. Theoretical is not enough. I've wanted to go to Africa my whole life. I want to stand on a clove plantation and I want to see a lion and I want to know what the hell I'm talking about when I tell my clients the squat toilets are fine." I thought about my ancient clients squatting over a hole with their walkers, and sped up my Internet search. "Also, my next door neighbor has been murdered."

"Murdered? I thought she had a stroke."

"Nope, murdered. And her son doesn't even know she's dead—I can't pass up a free ticket to his last known abode."

"The son is there? In Tanzania?"

"He was. Maybe someone there will know where he is."

"What about me? I thought I was your 'plus one.'" Roger said.

"I'd love for you to come with me. Of course I would. I just figured it was too short notice. Don't you have work?"

"Can I make a call?"

I nodded and kept typing while he walked

down the hall. He came back just as I had confirmed my flights. He was smiling.

"I'm in. I can postpone a few clients. I'd be crazy to turn down a free trip to Africa, especially with you." He was being so perfect, he was making me a little nervous.

"You don't mind that I have to do some work while I'm there?"

"Of course not."

Was this happening? I checked the system and saw I could make it work.

"Do you have your passport?"

He reached into his jacket and handed it to me.

I opened it and did a double-take. "What the hell is this?"

"Roger's my nickname."

"Roger is not a nickname."

"Would you have spent the night with me if I'd told you my real name?"

He was right: Seymour Pettigrew Claymore III was not a sexy name.

"Why Roger?"

"It's kind of stupid."

"Try me." I started filling in the two visas Adventure Limited had supplied.

"Okay. When I was little, I hated being an only child. So sometimes I pretended I had a brother and we both had walkie-talkies. I would take one in the yard and leave one in my room."

"And talk to yourself?"

"Well, yes. Lots of kids have imaginary friends, it's psychologically healthy."

Except me, I thought. No one ever left me alone long enough.

"Apparently, I said 'Roger that,' a lot, so my nanny started calling me Roger. It stuck."

Who could hate that story? He looked at me with those Raisinet eyes and I thought, what the hell? I hit confirm, e-mailed for a pick-up at the Dar es Salaam airport, and headed to the Tupperware cabinet. Roger followed me, then stopped in the hallway.

"Shit. Wait, Cyd. Don't we need a bunch of shots?"

"I know a guy," I said.

# Chapter Twelve

Six hours later, Roger and I were kicking our luggage through JFK, our arms aching and incapacitated by injections. Roger's sandals made a dull thud against the canvas of his World Wildlife Fund duffel bag, while my Charles Davids snapped against my purple polka-dot hard-shell case.

"You'll throw your back out. Let me get a porter," Roger said. "Come on, we're armless."

I rolled my eyes. "Waste of money. We're doing great. You just have to get a rhythm going," I said, alternating my carry-on and large bag, one kick at a time. He shuffled beside me and apologized as he misjudged his punt and knocked his luggage into an occupied stroller, edging it toward a moving escalator. I angled my next move in the direction of the British Airways First Class line. No kiosks for us. You couldn't use your relationship with a kiosk.

"This way." I tried not to scream as the punctures in my arm swung into a stanchion.

"I thought you said you traded our first-class tickets for coach."

"For coach tickets plus five round-the-world vouchers, good for three years. Then I used two of the vouchers to upgrade us back to our original seats."

Roger's eyes went wide. "You are a good travel agent."

"Well, I try."

As we waited for a family to check twenty-five bags, I thought about the last few hours: breaking up Dr. Kevekian's poker game, his warnings about the side effects of our "last minute" typhus shots, Roger fainting during the yellow fever vaccine.

I had left my personal cell phone in my room in case Uncle Ray tried to triangulate, so I had called my brousin Eddie from Doc's landline.

"Eddie Redondo, Redondo Imports," Eddie answered. I hesitated. "Cyd? How could you have a guy show up at the house? Are you nuts?"

"Come on. Have you ever seen Uncle Leon take to anyone that fast?"

"Yeah, well there's no accounting for taste."

"Exactly. Anyway, I really like him. And it's not many guys who walk into our dining room and not run out screaming. So, I'd like to spend the night with him." I held my breath.

"You barely know the guy, Cyd."

"Look, it's not like I'm going to marry him tonight," I said, "but I'm getting up there and things start to dry up."

"Echhh," he said.

"Anyway, will you cover for me until morning? Just tell them I called and might be late."

"No way. You are not dragging me into this. We're already dead for the whole Atlantic City thing. No. Sorry."

"You still owe me bail money." There was a long pause.

"Okay. Don't get pregnant."

"I'm thirty-two. I probably need in vitro."

"You're going to jinx yourself."

"Hey. Love you. Thanks for doing this."

I hung up, feeling awful. I hadn't actually lied to him, I'd just understated the truth.

Roger elbowed me. The pain in my arm returned my brain to the airport line. We were next. I kicked the big bag first, trying to leverage it onto the luggage weigher with my hip while I smiled at the ticket agent.

"Hi, Amy. Cyd Redondo. Redondo Travel." I handed her the tickets as Roger put his carry-on on the scale. "What are you doing?" I said.

"Checking my bag."

"But you can carry that on, easy."

"I'm happy to leave it to the professionals. Especially when I'm crippled."

"As your travel agent, I wouldn't advise it."

"It will be fine. I do it all the time."

He was a grown man, what could I do? I got us seats together in the bulkhead, then kicked my carry-on toward security, keeping an eye out for any Redondos or Redondo spies who might be trolling the terminal. My uncle knew a lot of people.

My lack of arms made security tricky. By the time we got through, some of the feeling had begun to come back—mostly in the form of pain. I could move enough to grab two bottles of Calvin Klein Obsession in Duty Free before we were at the gate and onto the jetway for my first-ever international flight. Once down the aisle, I wasn't quite able to get my carry-on over my head, so I grabbed the blanket and hid it underneath my legs.

"I still don't understand why you didn't just check it." Roger offered me the window seat.

"Eighteen-point-four percent of bags get lost on international flights. That's almost a fifth. And it goes up five percent with every connection. I recommend my clients always take the maximum amount of carry-ons with at least a few essentials on board. For example, Tupperware." I pulled out one of my nesting containers and grabbed the First Class goody bag. I dumped the contents—socks, an eye mask, lip balm, moisturizer, ear plugs the color of a Creamsicle, and a miniscule toothpaste—into my container and burped it.

"You might want some of that on the flight," Roger said.

"I know," I said, and told the flight attendant politely that they had forgotten to give me one. Roger glared at me. "They're promotional. Believe me, we're paying for it."

I was about to check my client message line when they gave the announcement to turn off all electronic devices. And delivered free alcohol.

"To this, our second date." I lifted my mini glass.

"Third date. I consider dinner with your family our second date."

"Oh, God."

He kissed me. I could feel the bubbles of the champagne mix with lust and almost paralyzing guilt. It was a heady combination. We were due for another malaria pill. Roger had packed his, so I gave him one of mine. Dr. Kevekian had warned us about the side effects, which included nausea, dizziness, hallucinations, and dementia, but if you paid attention to the possible side effects of drugs, you'd never take anything.

The captain turned on the "Fasten Seatbelt" sign and asked for flight attendants to prepare for takeoff. Roger watched me with some amusement, especially the part where I actually watched the entire safety film and checked for the flotation device under my seat. My stomach dropped to my heels as the plane shifted suddenly and we were airborne. I couldn't breathe. I opened my Balenciaga handbag—it was expandable—and put my head inside.

"You have travel anxiety? That's ironic. I could hypnotize you."

"What?" I pulled my head out.

"I could hypnotize you. I do it with my clients all the time. I'm licensed."

"Absolutely not. I may do a lot of stupid things, but I want to know I'm doing them and that they're my fault." He patted my hand, rhythmically.

"Don't even think about it," I warned.

"Will you try some deep breathing at least?" Roger gave me the drill and by the time the flight attendants brought us the warm nuts and olives, I felt better. I pulled out my Tupperware and put half the olives in it.

"For emergencies. Nothing is going to squash your sandwich in one of these." To prove my point, I put the container on the floor and tried to drive my heel into it.

"Well, I'm sold," he said. "Is Tupperware recyclable?"

"Who would know? They never stop working. I've still got the pink sandwich box I took to first grade." That made me think about Uncle Ray. I started folding the adorable salt and pepper shakers and teensy oil and vinegar bottles into my napkin and putting them in my purse. Roger took my hand.

"So, what's the deal with your uncle?"

It was the first time I'd had a chance to talk about this without the risk of it getting back to my family, so I told him everything—about my dad, my uncle, and about how none of my brousins really took to the travel business, so I was honor-bound to carry it on. Then, he asked about Mrs. Barsky. I caught him up on the newest developments, which took us past Iceland.

"Any idea who killed her?"

"Well, I doubt it was anyone from the neighborhood. Anyone local would have just asked her for a discount on a parrot or something and that would probably have done the job. Anyway, my brousin Frank is a cop and he's on it. The only thing I can do to help, really, is try to find her son—he's her executor and he's missing."

When we stopped in London, I turned on my client cell phone, but got no reception. I told Roger I didn't like being out of touch with my clients.

"I thought ninety-five percent of the time calls on the emergency line were nothing?"

"But five percent is a lot if someone's in trouble."

"It's your uncle's business, I'm sure he'll handle it." Yeah, and fire me. Well, what's done was done. I ate an olive from my bag. I tried the phone one more time just as they were telling us to turn them off. Of course it worked then.

I was only able to retrieve one message. It was from my brousin Frank, who said he was calling in an "official kind of capacity." I had to get down to the Precinct right away—I was the prime suspect in Mrs. Barsky's murder.

# Chapter Thirteen

Prime suspect? Come on. I wasn't even subprime. Was he serious? Or was this a new low in my family's obsession with keeping me in Bay Ridge? Before I could find out, we started down the runway and the flight attendant gave me a look worthy of Sister Mary Agatha. I hung up.

"What is it?" Roger said.

"Nothing." I'm sure my face disagreed.

"Tell me about our trip." Roger slipped his hand onto my thigh.

The plane lifted off. There was nothing I could do until I got to Tanzania. So I put on my best travel queen face and explained that for this package, we had partnered with Adventure Limited, an international company that specialized in offering help and expertise on the ground in exotic locations like Tanzania and Indonesia. Although normally I liked to organize everything myself, I had caved when they had offered me the free trip.

By the time I'd gone through our itinerary—starting with a boat trip to Zanzibar, two days in Dar es Salaam, and five days on an eco-safari in the Ngorongoro Crater—and Roger and I had both dozed a bit, we'd begun our descent and could see the Tanzanian shoreline underneath the wing. The city itself came right down to the very edge of the Indian Ocean, the waves actually bumping the cafés and warehouses. I spotted the red-and-white spire of the Azania Front Lutheran Church, flanked by new high-rises and low tin roofs.

"Dar es Salaam," I said. "'Haven of Peace.' Population 2.24 million."

Roger and I were first in line for the jet door when it sucked open. I stopped at the top of the stairs to take in the landscape and let my four aspirin kick in, then promptly slipped on the metal steps and slid into the melting tarmac at the bottom. Still, I was here. I took in a deep breath of Africa, all cloves and diesel and rotting fruit, but no trace of tomato sauce or subway. I might be an international fugitive, but I was happy.

The Julius Nyeyere International Airport, named after Tanzania's first president, had the sweeping, optimistic roof of a California diner. Inside, concrete columns, papered with ads, pointed us to the Customs line. I pulled out my phone to call Frank back about this whole prime suspect nonsense.

Roger touched my shoulder. "You can't use your phone until we're through Customs." Damn.

The Customs area had the tangy smell of overheated bodies and melting rubber. I had decided the olives in my bag were an appetizer, not a vegetable, so I wasn't lying when they asked me if I was bringing produce into the country. As we exited the restricted area, I looked up our luggage carousel and hurried toward it, trying to get a signal on my phone as I moved.

"Miss Redondo! Miss Redondo!"

Behind a large sign reading "Miss Cyd Redondo REDONDO TRAVEL AMERICA" was a tiny African man with knobby cheekbones in a neon pink Ralph Lauren polo shirt, pressed Gap jeans, and shiny brown Oxford shoes, pushing through the crowd.

He arrived, breathless and smiling, and held out his free hand. "*Karibu.* Welcome. You are even more beautiful than your passport photograph," he said. The lighting and makeup artist had paid off.

"I am Akida Nyondo, from Adventures Limited, your contact, liaison, and host in our beautiful country of Tanzania. I trust you are well. How was your journey?"

"*Asanta Sana,* Akida. *Habari. Mzuri,*" I said,

ignoring Roger's look. "It's a pleasure to meet you. Please call me Cyd and this is Roger Claymore."

Akida reached up to shake Roger's hand. "Mr. Claymore. Enchanted." He turned back to me. "Cyd Redondo, your Swahili is excellent, but of course I expected no less from such a travel agent as yourself. I have heard about your ability to get upgrades from a stone. I am delighted to meet you both. I trust your family is well?"

I had read that Tanzanians always had a long buffer of courtesies before they could get to the point so I tried to be culturally sensitive, even though I was dying to use the phone and retrieve our luggage. I approached the carousel, hoping we could trade civilities *en route*. I heard my phone beep on. Akida continued speaking over the brief siren and clunk of machinery that meant the bags were coming.

"I am hoping to learn much from you during your stay," Akida said. "It is my dream to travel the world and help others do so. I hope someday that you will show me your native land of Brooklyn and tell me your preference of CRS programs for booking internationally."

"I'd be delighted, anytime, Akida."

He proceeded to tell us about his family.

Roger saw the crease growing on my forehead.

"Perhaps we should look for our luggage?" he said. I shot him a look of gratitude.

"Most certainly, most certainly. Please, after you. May I carry your bag?"

"Thank you. How is everyone else? The Andersons and the Giannis?"

He looked down. "I did leave several messages about that."

"I'm so sorry, I couldn't get reception on the plane. They're all fine, right?" He was about to answer when we arrived at Carousel B. Just at that moment, the rubber panels shuddered. The carousel ground to a stop, empty except for a rotating goat in a large tub. I looked up the chute, just to make sure nothing was stuck.

"I don't believe this," I said. "I should have at least four trips before this happens."

"They'll come on the next plane," Roger said.

"The next plane is in four days. And you checked your carry-on. Your malaria pills were in there. You could die."

"I'm not going to die."

Akida offered to inquire.

"I'm sure he'll sort it out. He seems very enthusiastic," Roger said.

"So far. But anyone's only as good as their next emergency."

"Cyd, don't worry about it. I'm sure they'll

turn up. It's not a big deal." It was a big deal if I had to head back on the next plane.

"I booked your vacation. I want it to be perfect."

Akida came back, head low. "It appears yours and Mr. Claymore's bags have been lost. I apologize, sincerely. Unfortunately, this happens. With frequency. Most travelers recover their belongings eventually. It happened to the Andersons as well. They are lovely people."

"The Andersons' luggage got lost? Why didn't they call me?"

"That's more than eighteen percent. That's actually a hundred percent," Roger said.

"Roger, all I can do is stay on top of my most recent published figures. How was I supposed to know there'd been a spike?" I turned to Akida. "Did they get it back?"

"Not as yet, but the airline says it will arrive tomorrow."

"Tomorrow? They're leaving tomorrow. God, they must be furious." I started dialing the Andersons.

"I'm afraid they will not be able to answer the call."

"And why is that?"

"They are in jail."

# Chapter Fourteen

"Jail!" My legs gave out. I slumped into a hard plastic chair the color of vomit. Visions of *Midnight Express* flew through my head as I plugged in my charger. This was my punishment for running away. Or for not running away soon enough.

I hadn't even left the airport and I was already in over my head. I tried to breathe. What was it Mrs. Barsky's mynah bird always used to say? "Fake it 'til you make it! Fake it 'til you make it!" Right. Well I was going to have to fake it, for Roger's sake, as well as the Andersons'.

Jack and Barb Anderson, Bay Ridge dry cleaning magnates, had been the first couple to sign up for the package. Jack was a bit of a hypochondriac and Barb had serious osteoporosis. I could only imagine the imaginary diseases Jack had contracted overnight or what a jail toilet might do to Barb's fragile hipbones.

My phone beeped on to a host of new

messages, including two from Uncle Ray. The rest were from the 68th Precinct. I turned to Akida.

"What happened?"

"I believe they were apprehended for photographing the military."

"Dammit. I told them not to do that. It was in their instructions."

"You send instructions?" Roger asked.

"Of course I send instructions. For exactly this reason," I said. "When did it happen?"

"We received a call yesterday afternoon."

"They spent the night in jail? They're eighty."

"We are, of course, making inquiries."

"Inquiries?" I saw my sunset-drenched Zanzibar bungalow slipping away. Even Frank and Bobby Barsky would have to wait. I turned to Roger and looked at my watch. "You can still catch the ferry to Zanzibar. Go ahead, I'll meet you as soon as I can."

"There's no way I'm leaving you."

"I'll be fine. Really. This is not your problem."

He shook his head and sat down. I have to say, despite my brave front, I was relieved. I decided on a strategy. Obviously, I had to get to the embassy and to the jail, but I also had to file a claim for our luggage before I left the airport or British Airways wouldn't be liable. I decided to multi-task and get in the claim line while I made calls. I pulled up my Uncle Ray's number.

"Hold my hand," I said to Roger, then hit call.

This was going to be even harder than telling the Feragamos their Yorkie had been eaten by a Rottweiler in the cargo hold.

"Uncle Ray?" I said. There was a long silence.

"Where are you, Cyd? We've had the whole Precinct out looking for you. Your mother is worried sick. Well?"

I admit, I considered lying. "Dar es Salaam." I could hear his blood pressure rise.

"Fricking Africa? Are you crazy? What about the computer upgrade? And you know the Precinct wants to question you about Mrs. Barsky. Your fingerprints are all over the damn place. There are papers missing. You have to get on the next plane and come home. Right now."

"I can't."

"Yes you can. I'll fix the ticket from here."

"No, I can't. The Andersons were arrested. I have to get them out of jail. I was just leaving for the embassy."

"That's what Adventure Limited is for. Taking care of things on the ground."

"They haven't had any luck. Plus, they don't know our clients and our clients don't know them. Look, you're always telling me that customer service is the cornerstone of our business. If I'm here, I can get them out and serve as a liaison for the other clients who are on their way. If we don't handle this right, everyone else will cancel. It could ruin our reputation. And you know damn well that I didn't kill Mrs. Barsky. And so does Frank. If you want to fix something, fix that. I'll be fine." I hesitated. "Roger's here with me."

"Roger? That nincompoop from the Internet? I don't trust that guy, Cyd. There's something off about him."

"In your opinion, there's something off about everyone." We were almost at the front of the line.

"What do I tell Frank?" he said. "The detectives are pressuring him not to give you special treatment. He's up for a promotion, you know that."

"Tell him I'll call him as soon as I sort this out, but in the meantime they should look for the actual killer."

He was quiet for a minute. "All right. Be careful, Cyd. Really careful. It's not the neighborhood."

"I'm aware of that."

"I'm always here if you need me."

"I know. Love you, bye." Roger and I finally made the counter.

The agent was in Muslim garb, so I was glad I'd dressed conservatively in a navy miniskirt and a silk blouse with matching polka dots, topped by a white chiffon scarf. I wrapped my scarf around my head and after learning the details of how Agent

Hasari had dislocated his collarbone, I had a copy of the claim receipt and we were headed for the parking lot.

Akida bowed in front of the most battered Toyota minivan I had ever seen. At some point, it might have been white, but now rust was chewing through every surface, all the wheels had lost their hubcaps, and by the looks of it, the axle was the next to go. The front bumper had a dent the size of a baby. Akida explained that by night he was a *daladala* driver and that at twenty-five cents a ride, it was by far the least expensive way to get around Dar. I tried to imagine the Andersons' bony behinds on the wooden benches in the back and winced, holding on tight to my Balenciaga and my carry-on, since they now held everything I owned.

Akida drove like a sprinter, stopping for long intervals of rest, then shooting forward for a few feet at eighty miles an hour, the entire vehicle vibrating with exertion. At least I was traveling with a chiropractor, I thought, as the van swerved onto two wheels.

"Akida could drop me at the jail while you go to the embassy. It might speed things up," Roger said.

"It will help me more if you're there for moral support. I've never talked to an ambassador. And some people don't take women seriously."

"At their peril," Roger said. He was quiet after that.

The traffic finally opened up and the van kangarooed forward with a particularly nauseating crunch. We headed down the Bagamoyo Road, north of downtown, the sea on our right. Akida explained that this embassy had been built after the original U.S. building had been bombed in the nineties. Of course—the U.S. Embassy bombings. I was still training then; we'd had a lot of cancelled safaris.

As the van passed locals bicycling on the roads and green-painted stalls spilling fruit, Akida chattered on: the new embassy had been built on the site of an old drive-in cinema—he had seen *Die Hard* for the first three times there. "It is my favorite film. Except for *The Breakfast Club*."

I prepared myself as we got closer, working on my story and happy that I had worn such a classy outfit. I imagined a huge, dark-paneled building, fronted by banana trees. I couldn't have been more wrong. We turned off the main road into a long, ceremonial drive, lined with palm trees on one side and what Akida said were flame trees on the other.

"One of the jewels of our country" he said. "Twenty-two acres, completely secure."

He wasn't kidding. The white wall rose for almost two stories and seemed to go on forever.

I could just glimpse an American flag and a few modern, cream-colored buildings peeking above the concrete. As we got nearer, two armed guards at the entrance moved out from under their shaded post.

"Is it okay just to drive up?" I said. The van had suicide bomber written all over it. "I could wave my scarf out the window or something."

Roger started to laugh.

"They are expecting us. I will, however, stop a respectful distance from the entrance, just to be safe." Akida slowed down and the van choked. We waited while he started it again. "The grounds include ten thousand indigenous plants," Akida said, pumping the gas, "including shrubs which encourage meditation."

"Really?" Roger said, looking at me.

"That is what the press release promises," Akida said. "I myself have never been inside. I hope that your visit will be calm and productive."

"Even meditative," Roger said. I elbowed him.

The van did a quick jiggle, then stopped. I slid off the bench, landing a splinter in an inconvenient place.

"Are you sure you don't want Akida to take me to the jail?" Roger yelped.

"Are you on an Interpol list or something? Just come in with me."

Akida told us to text him when we were done,

then headed back down the asphalt, the van blending into the sandy landscape until it disappeared. I straightened my hair and skirt, looked down at Roger's sandals, sighed, then approached the guards. They checked our passports. We passed through a metal detector and into the massive atrium and, as Akida had predicted, were "pleasantly surprised by the brightness of the interior."

We were met by a short American, as preppy as a faded deck shoe and half as charming.

"Miss Redondo, Mr. Claymore. I'm Brent Winbourne, the Under Under Secretary. How can we can help?"

I had seen more helpful faces inside a subway information booth. I explained the situation and emphasized that my client Jack Anderson needed his diabetes medication. Jack didn't have diabetes yet, but I'm sure he would, eventually. "I'm sure no one wants a dead senior on their hands."

"Please follow me."

I turned and caught Roger checking me out. It seemed like five years since that hotel room in Atlantic City, but his eyes could still undo me. I imagined him kissing my back and ran into a pole.

The minion ushered us into the ambassador's modern, minimalist office—no indoor palms, no vertical blinds, no wild animal heads on the wall. So much for *Mogambo*. I had hoped to snap a couple of good examples of a rhino mounting for Uncle Leon. Sometimes it's hard to shop for a taxidermist. I explained my dismay to Roger.

"After the Siteez treaty, they could hardly have that stuff up," Roger said.

"After the what?"

"The 1975 Endangered Species treaty."

"My treaty knowledge is pretty much limited to Versailles. Wait, how do you spell that?" But the ambassador came in before he could answer.

"Claymore. Overdressed as always."

I turned to see a man who could have been Dick Cheney's younger brother: the thinning pate, the needle nose, the smarmy smile, and a dress shirt so white it was positively Antarctic.

"Harrison Belk at your service." He held out a palm the size of a cutlet. It even had the slightly damp feel of raw pork.

"Your Highness," I said. Roger snorted.

"Please call me Harrison. How are you, Roger? You should have told me you were coming. We could have put you up in the residence."

"Wait a minute. You two know each other?" I said. What the hell?

"We had something of a rivalry at Stanford, didn't we? Please have a seat. I've inquired about the Andersons. First, let me say that they are fine."

"He means still alive," Roger said.

The ambassador shot him a nasty look. "They are being held temporarily at the Remand Prison on Maendolo Street. It is a pleasanter place than our alternate facility."

"Less disgusting."

"Pleasanter, as I said, than Ukonga, where they may be moved at any time. Sadly, there's a limit to what we can do when the military is involved."

"You can't be serious. These are two eighty-year-old tourists who accidentally took a picture."

"If we sweep in and rescue every American they arrest, it sounds as if we're not taking the military seriously. It's a sensitive diplomatic issue."

"Well, it's going to be a major diplomatic incident if Jack doesn't get his insulin."

"Miss Redondo, please don't overreact. I've spoken to the lieutenant privately and I'm sure together we can sort this out. It's just that the consulate can't be officially involved."

"I don't understand. Isn't that what you're here for?"

"Not in these kinds of cases."

Roger squeezed my hand and stared at Ambassador Belk. "There are other avenues, I'm assuming?"

"There are always other avenues in Tanzania. If you go to the facility and speak to Lieutenant Panza, he might have some suggestions."

"Bribes," Roger said to me.

"I would be very surprised if someone with Miss Redondo's extensive travel background really requires an interpreter, Claymore."

"Everyone needs an interpreter for diplomatic doublespeak, Belk. Isn't that the point? Come on, Cyd, I told you we should have gone straight to the jail."

"Miss Redondo, I regret the embassy can't be more helpful, but if there is anything else you need, anything at all, during your stay, please don't hesitate to contact me day or night." He kissed my hand too long and gave me his card. In for a penny, I thought.

"Actually, Harrison, there is something else. I'm trying to locate a Robert Revere Barsky. He's a vet, originally from Brooklyn. His birth date is 9/21/53. His mother's been killed. If you could help me track him down, I'd be very grateful. Here's his last known address in Dar es Salaam." The ambassador and Roger shook their heads.

"What?" I said. "That's not something you do, either?" I could feel our vacation disappearing. Come on, was nine days and eight nights too much to ask? God, it was already down to eight days and seven nights and we'd lost our Zanzibar bungalow.

"No, of course. This is completely within my purview. If you'll leave those details and your local contact information, I'll make sure someone gets back to you. And may I just say on a personal note, it is rare that such an exotic specimen enters our domain. Africa pales in comparison."

Roger rolled his eyes. "Good-bye, Belk. I thought you'd be Senator Belk by now. Wasn't that the plan?"

"Plans change, don't they? Please give Alicia my best, by the way." Belk put his hand too low on my back and moved us toward the door.

It was barely closed when Roger swore. "What a dick."

"Roger."

I texted Akida as we headed down the stairs. "I'm so glad I'm traveling with someone who enjoys alienating the people who can help us."

"He was never going to help us."

"And who's Alicia, anyway?"

"Someone we went to college with."

Before I could ask any more, a cloud of dust exploded from the gate and Akida skidded to a stop. After we climbed inside, we passed under the flame trees and headed into town, hitting continental-sized potholes with regularity. Between jolts, I worried about my next move. I needed local intel. I asked Akida about the best way to handle the jail negotiation. Even in a bribe, you don't want to be ripped off. After all, it was coming out of my emergency money. He said it all depended on the greed of the person taking the bribe, but for this I should not pay more than seven hundred-fifty thousand.

"Dollars?" Holy crap.

"Tanzanian shillings."

I whipped out my thumbnail currency converter—three hundred U.S. dollars. I breathed again. "Will you come in with me, Akida?" He hesitated. "Please? I promise to teach you the new Hilton log-in system." He finally nodded. It was just my luck, to be in a foreign country surrounded by hesitant men. As we neared the jail I started to sweat through my chiffon. I had bailed my cousins out more than once, but this was different. I opened my Swahili guide and started cramming. Roger was staring out the back window at a town car behind us. I thought about the town car in our parking lot.

"Akida? In your country, is there any special significance to stabbing a parrot?"

"Oh, yes. Very bad. Heavy curse, worse than death."

# Chapter Fifteen

Great. "I don't believe in curses," I said.

Then I remembered Mrs. Barsky and the Andersons and crossed myself twice for good measure as we stopped in front of the medieval door of the prison. Let's just say the flat building, vaguely whitewashed and sagging in spots, lacked tourist charm. Two uniformed soldiers stood outside, staring at my legs with absolutely no expression. Suddenly I felt underdressed. They moved to open the door, four feet thick and groaning under its own weight as it swung out.

We went in. Urine was the top note of the Remand Prison bouquet, with touches of sweat, sour milk, mildew, and burned coffee. Barb Anderson had spent her entire life in a cloud of Glade Air Freshener and 409. I hoped she was unconscious. We approached the barred windows. I greeted the officials in Swahili, as a courtesy. I was just getting some pleasantries ready, when a uniformed Asian man with a pockmarked face and a nasty scar down one cheek came forward and held out an unnaturally small, manicured hand.

"Miss Redondo?"

"*Ndiyo.*"

He frowned. "I am Lieutenant Panza. The ambassador informed me of your arrival. Welcome to Tanzania," he said, in English.

"Thank you, Lieutenant. This is Mr. Claymore and Mr. Nyondo," I said, again in Swahili.

"You are here to inquire about the Americans?"

"Yes we are. Would it be possible for us to see them?" I said, stumbling over the grammar.

"I'm afraid that is impossible." He glared at me. "No visitors."

Akida pulled me aside. "Far be it for me to advise you, Cyd Redondo, but when a Tanzanian has taken the trouble to learn English, they find it insulting when you speak to them in Swahili. I fear you will not get far with this approach."

"Why didn't you tell me earlier?" I whispered.

"I was trying to be polite."

I shook my head at him and approached the counter. "I apologize for my inadequate Swahili, Lieutenant. Your English, on the other hand, is impeccable."

"We are not savages here, whatever Americans think."

"Americans have great respect for the citizens

of Tanzania. And for your authority. I appreciate that I may not be able to visit the prisoners. But would their attorney be allowed a conference?"

"Of course. As I said, we are a civilized nation."

"Wonderful. This is their attorney, Mr. Claymore." Roger stiffened beside me. I hoped the lieutenant couldn't see the sandals from his vantage point.

"Five minutes." The lieutenant gestured to Roger, who gave me a furious look.

I looked at the peeling Tanzania's Most Wanted posters on the wall until Roger and Lieutenant Panza were out of sight. One of the fugitives had a sad ponytail and Mrs. Barsky's nose. I missed her.

"How do we work this?" I whispered to Akida. I usually bribed people with services. Was there a secret handshake? Did you leave it in a paper bag? Could you ask for a receipt? "How do we know how much?"

"The money is usually exchanged while you are signing the release papers. I will watch for the sign. Do not hate the police, Miss Redondo. They are not well paid; they are just trying to feed their families." We heard screams. Finally, Roger came back.

"Are they all right?"

"A little shaken. And fragrant. But not hurt. They seem to have made some friends. And they're thrilled you're here. Helen also said you were marriage material."

"How would she know?" I snapped.

Roger grinned and said we were to come back in two hours. He wanted to buy a SIM card and some clothes, and Akida offered to help. Would I be interested in spending some time in the Kariakoo market? You bet I would. It was time for our medication. I handed Roger one of my malaria pills, hailed a *daladala,* and told them I'd meet them back there at three.

●  ●  ●  ●  ●

The moment the Toyota screeched to a stop beside a stall of waving blankets bright enough to see from space, I was in my element. First I bought a huge woven bag in turquoise, yellow, and green. I figured with my handbag and this, I could do some damage. The market had everything, from fruits big as mantle ornaments to jewelry stacked like onions in bins. Suddenly, everything in America seem faded.

Then I saw a wall of tortoiseshell. I had coveted the tortoiseshell hairbrush set my grandmother kept on her vanity my whole life, but it had gone to Aunt Helen, so I snatched up a few pieces. I bought enough bracelets to go up to both elbows, a bag full of scarves, and fifteen presents for less than I'd pay for a cut and blow dry at the Hairlarious Salon. Then, I set out to score some tanzanite.

My jeweler friend Ronnie had shown me how to spot the real thing. I picked my mark: a small stall squeezed in between a smoky grill and a stand of bottle cap earrings. The seller was short, with a barrel torso and a thick neck that didn't seem to match his pinched, suspicious face. His eyes were black as an Americano.

As I hoped, he had spotted my polka dots and my Balenciaga. I wanted him to peg me as a typical tourist. I arrived at the stall. We appraised each other.

He held out a stone. "Tanzanite. It is our national gem. Very rare. It is the most beautiful gem in the world because it holds three colors rather than one." In the hazy gray sunshine, the gems looked almost white, but I could see tiny bursts of potential in their reflection. I looked professionally bored. It was important never to show interest in the beginning, or they'd just jack the price up.

I asked him if he had anything more special? Extra special?

He reached for a carved, locked box. The smell of his desire to rip me off was even stronger than his sweat, which was laced with patchouli. He opened the box to reveal two rings. To the naked eye, one ring held up to Ronnie's criteria. Beside it was a flashier, but inferior piece. That's the one he offered, smiling.

"Very special price for such a lovely lady." He turned and said "Watch this" in Swahili to his friends.

"Watch what?" I replied, also in Swahili.

He jumped, then bowed. "You speak our language, Madam?"

"I try," I said with my most gracious smile, then pulled out my travel-size jeweler's loupe and a guide to precious metals and gems. I had the Swahili version, for emphasis.

"May I see?"

He hesitated, then handed me the inferior gem.

"*Ni bei gani*? How much?" A few people had gathered to watch. I guess hearing Swahili with a Brooklyn accent was tantamount to a Broadway show here.

"Five hundred U.S. dollars," he said.

"Really," I said. "For iolite?"

His face fell and a couple of the men who stood behind me laughed. I shrugged. "I'm only interested in real jewels, in something rare."

"Rare." He nodded. I waited for him to hold out the real ring. Instead he reached for another box, one with three locks. "You are a woman who knows the value of things." He winked. In case it was a cultural thing, I winked back. He winked again. I winked back. He gestured me closer, looked around and opened the box just enough for me to see. There was an ivory necklace with dozens of tiny elephants. Even the wrinkles of their skin were visible; the work was incredible. I remembered hearing something about not buying ivory, but it was too late for this tusk, so I decided to ignore it.

"How much?"

He whispered an amount I couldn't afford, but the thing was calling to me like a beached Siren. I shook my head and reached for the real Tanzanite ring. He lowered the ivory price, as I knew he would.

"Too much," I said.

He lowered it again and I focused on the ring. He was a pro, I'll give him that. He made me wait. But finally, he offered to throw in the ring with the necklace and I nodded, though I was screaming inside at this, the pinnacle of my bargain-hunting life.

I put both items into the secret compartment of my bag. I felt eyes on the back of my neck, then heard a clicking sound. Out of the corner of my eye, I thought I saw someone who looked familiar. I had seen that suit and sandy hair before. But the man who was photographing me had his camera up and I couldn't get a good look at him. I tried to follow him through the crowd, but I lost sight of him at a bushmeat stand. I looked at my watch. I was late for jail.

# Chapter Sixteen

Lieutenant Panza stood behind the counter, while Akida cowered by the door. There was no sign of Roger. I clutched my sunglass case full of three hundred emergency dollars and moved forward.

"The situation has changed." Panza said. "In preparing the prisoners' belongings for return, we found several pieces of illegal ivory. It is a very serious offense."

I went pale. "It must be a mistake. They would never knowingly make an illegal purchase They won't even cross against a light. Is there anything I can do? Considering their age and ill health? I know the ambassador is concerned."

Panza looked at Akida, then nodded.

"One thousand U.S. dollars," Akida said under his breath. Of course my "emergency" money was in my purse, right under my own contraband ivory necklace. I tried to use a cleavage distraction while I rummaged for my wallet. I finally found the secret zipped compartment I used for cash.

"What do I do?" I whispered to Akida.

"Leave it under the bell."

"You got all this from a nod?" He nodded.

I approached with some trepidation and put the money under the bell.

The lieutenant handed me several papers. "Please sign here. I am releasing these prisoners into your custody. If they violate even the smallest ordinance, especially if they are found with any more contraband, they will not be allowed to leave the country and I will be forced to arrest you as well. Do you understand?"

"I understand. *Asante*," I said. "I mean thank you."

I never saw him take the money, but when I turned around it was gone. Jack and Barb Anderson, owners of Andersons Sparkling Dry Cleaning, appeared, looking like they'd just climbed out of a dumpster. I ran to hug them both. My polka dot blouse would just have to be collateral damage.

"I just want to say, as a representative of Redondo Travel, that we will be giving you a complete refund on your package and anything else that you want. I am mortified and can't apologize enough."

Barb leaned over and kissed me on the cheek. "Don't be ridiculous, Cyd. What other travel agent would use her own money to bail us out?" Not

Peggy fricking Newsome, I thought. "Besides, we've had the trip of a lifetime, just like you said. We saw a whole family of lions."

"Pride," Jack said.

"Pride. And two giraffes mating. Jack has only had two malaria symptoms."

"Dizziness and sleeplessness. Of course, there's still time."

I asked Akida to help them to the van, while I turned back to Lieutenant Panza and put another two hundred dollars under the bell.

"I'm looking for a Robert Barsky, he's an American living here. This was his last known address. Could you recommend anyone who might help me find him?"

He looked at the address, hesitated, then said he'd be in touch.

By the time I got back to the Toyota, Roger had returned and we all piled in. On the way to the hotel, the Andersons told us they were just taking a picture of the National Museum and didn't realize two soldiers were in the frame. They had been scared at first, but Barb said they had met several fascinating people. They'd shared a cell with the local witch doctor who had several stains that, even with fifty years in dry cleaning, they'd never seen before. They couldn't wait to get the filthy clothes home.

"Barb loves a challenge," Jack said.

"It was fascinating. I felt like a local." They couldn't wait to tell all their friends.

Great. There goes Redondo Travel.

I had booked all four of us into the Movenpick Royal Palm Hotel. Roger and I checked in while the Andersons cleaned up. That night, we went to a restaurant the Andersons' cellmates had recommended and ate *ugali* and fresh fish with our left hands. On the way back, I managed to convince Jack and Barb to keep the jail episode to themselves, at least until the rest of my clients had gotten back to Brooklyn safely. I asked them about the ivory, but they didn't seem to know what I was talking about. Panza must have taken me for just another American sucker. I would make sure that didn't happen again.

I promised to take them to the airport in the morning and headed upstairs with Roger. He had been quiet since the embassy. For some reason, I suddenly felt shy and hesitated before putting on the emergency teddy from my carry-on. Roger stripped down to checked boxers and a t-shirt.

"Sorry about today. Once I get them on the plane, we'll really be on vacation. I promise."

"Don't worry about it, Cyd, it's fine. I'm just tired. We haven't slept in almost two days."

"Yeah. I know." That's not all we hadn't done.

He kissed my hand and seconds later he was asleep. It took me about two more hours. Was Uncle Ray right—was it too early to travel together? I vowed from that moment to make sure Roger had the best vacation of his life and begged God, or whatever entity was in charge, to please just let this relationship last to the end of our seven days. It didn't seem like too much to ask.

The next morning, I woke up first, did my hair, put on perfume, and went down to get us coffee. Roger was just making his way out of the covers when I got back. He took his cup gratefully and gave me that shy grin I'd fallen for in the first place.

"You look beautiful." He pulled me down. "When do we have to leave?"

"In about fifteen minutes. I'll take a rain check, though."

"I'll hold you to that."

See? Confusing. We met Jack and Barb downstairs. The airline had called and said their luggage had been found and would be checked back on their departing flight. Maybe ours would show up too. Akida dropped us off at Departures, and I said I would go deal with the luggage.

"It's already checked in." Roger said. "The airline said all they have to do is get on the plane."

"We don't know if anything's missing. If they don't check here, they can't file a claim."

"Cyd, just because it's Africa doesn't mean anything's missing."

"Africa Schmafrica, I would do this in Cleveland. The luggage's been missing for ten days. If you don't inventory and something's missing or damaged, you have no recourse. It's unprofessional. It won't take long. Okay? Just keep an eye on them, please." I headed to the British Airways desk, exuding my most professional travel agent aura.

"*Shikamu*," I said. This was the most respectful form of greeting.

"Hello," the clerk said. He was tall, with a pencil thin mustache and hair slicked back almost flat on his head. After the obligatory pleasantries, I made my request, in English.

He took the claim forms and moved to the door behind him. As it opened, I gasped: there was my purple polka dot hard shell case. I had pasted half of a Mets sticker near the bottom for easier identification. Roger's WWF duffel bag was right beside it.

"Excuse me," I said as the man disappeared behind the door. "Excuse me?" A couple of the soldiers turned to look. I asked the woman behind me to hold my place, then snuck behind the desk and pushed on the door.

I heard the crack of a rifle. I put my hands in the air as a soldier gestured me away from the door with the gun. I edged back toward the counter. I wasn't sure whether the stupid American or sensitive American was a better approach, but as I knew the words for "forgive me" and "sorry" in Swahili, I went for sensitive.

"*Nisamale. Pale.*" Just then, my clerk came back out. "*Nisamale,*" I said. "When you opened the door, I saw my luggage. It didn't arrive with us yesterday and I was just hoping you'd check on it? I didn't mean to violate any rules."

"That is a restricted area. Travelers are not allowed."

"I understand. Again, I apologize."

He handed me the Andersons' claim checks. "These bags have already been checked and loaded onto the aircraft. They are not available."

"There's been a mistake. You see, they must be checked in the port of arrival before being sent back."

"I'm afraid that is not possible."

The two guys with the guns were still standing there and Roger was hovering, gesturing for me to let it go. I saw the Andersons watching too. Every travel agent molecule in me knew letting those bags go unchecked was wrong. I was going to do right by the Andersons if it was the last thing I ever did.

"Perhaps I could speak to your supervisor?" I asked, banking on the fact that no one, in any hemisphere, wanted you to speak to their supervisor. Sweat broke out on his forehead.

"That is not necessary."

"Then perhaps we can try again. I respect that you are a man who believes in rules, so I am sure you will want to follow this one. I'm happy to wait," I said. He looked at the long line which was forming behind me, took the forms and went back behind the door.

"What the hell are you doing?" Roger asked, moving beside me.

"Let me do my job, Roger. I wouldn't try to diagnose sciatica." Finally, the man came back with two gray Samsonite bags. They looked like they'd been dragged behind a truck.

"These will have to be checked and pass through security again," the clerk said, significantly. "You are from Redondo Travel?"

"Yes."

"And you are sure?" He winked. What was it with the winking? Was he flirting, or was something else going on? Either way, I had to check the bags.

"Yes, and of course, we'll recheck them." I thanked him and moved out of line. The soldiers kept us in range.

"Okay," I said to Jack and Barb. "Just do a quick check of the contents, we'll recheck them and then we'll get you on that plane."

Roger came closer and leaned in. "Cyd, do you really want to open those bags here?"

"Of course I want to open the bags. What is wrong with everybody? This is standard procedure. Absolutely standard."

"What if their favorite possessions are ruined? Why don't you let me handle this and you keep them occupied?" he said, reaching for the bags.

"Roger, I am the travel professional here. You are my plus one. The plus one is not in charge." I gripped one suitcase in each hand. He tried to take one of the bags. I held on harder.

"You're horrible at this, you know," he said.

"What? At my job? I am not." I gripped the bags harder.

"At traveling. You are horrible at traveling, you…you orphaned Tupperware tart."

I was so startled and embarrassed, I loosened my grip. Roger grabbed both the suitcases.

He eased the first one open, looked at it for a minute, then closed it. The he opened the second one. His face went pale. He slammed it shut, picked up both bags, and ran for the exit.

# Chapter Seventeen

"What the hell?" Jack said as we watched Roger fly through the door and jump into a taxi. Several soldiers ran after him and got into a Jeep. I turned to the Andersons, horrified.

"I'm so sorry. I don't know what just happened. I promise I will get that luggage back."

"Forget the luggage. Go. Go after him Cyd. He might be a klepto, but he's cute and once you're over thirty, you can't be that picky. We'll be fine." BA was calling for their flight.

"Are you sure?"

"If not, we know who to call."

I hugged them both and ran for Akida's Toyota van.

"Follow that Jeep," I said.

"What has occurred?" he asked as he shot the *daladala* out into the road. I wished I knew. I had never been so humiliated in front of a client. What could be in the bag that had made his face go white?

Had Panza's men planted more ivory to frame the poor Andersons? And what would happen if Roger was caught with it? I didn't want Akida to see my panic, so I answered him as matter-of-factly as I could.

"Mr. Claymore has stolen the Andersons' luggage and the police are after him."

He swerved off the road on the right to gain on the Jeep. There were three or four taxis in front of us and I had no idea which one Roger was in. In true Tanzanian fashion, the traffic came to a complete stop. We were in the slowest chase in modern history. I jumped out of the van.

"Pick me up once you're moving." I ran as fast as I could past taxi after taxi, checking each one. Suddenly, I was right behind the soldiers. I stopped, not sure how to get around them but then Akida's Toyota was there, to give me cover. Once I was past, he stopped and popped the hood. Whatever we were paying him, it wasn't enough. I thought I spotted a familiar head of hair about two cars ahead just as the traffic started moving again. I ran back to the van and Akida pulled out, the hood slamming itself shut as we pulled forward.

I jumped out again and banged on Roger's window. He was looking the other way and ignoring my screams. I jumped onto the side of the cab, not a great idea in heels. Roger finally opened the door, and pulled me in.

"You shouldn't be here." he said, pushing me toward the floor. I pushed back.

"Tupperware tart? What does that even mean? Do you really think I'm going to let that go?" I edged over to sit on the bag.

Roger intercepted, gripping me on his lap. "Can't you see I'm trying to get away from you?"

"Not with my clients' luggage, you're not." It was hard to fight with him while I was on his lap.

"Are you telling me you really don't know why I ran?"

"I am telling you I have no fricking clue."

"You don't know what's in the bags?"

"If I had to guess, Depends? I'm kidding. It's clearly something bad. Did they have more ivory? What? What?"

He turned my face to his and looked at me for a long time, then kissed me on the forehead. "You're right. It's bad. There's something illegal in the Andersons' luggage. I don't think they put it there, but if anyone had seen it, especially after the previous arrest, they'd spend the next twenty years in that jail and so would you. The soldiers were right there, I couldn't explain it to you. There wasn't anything else I could do but run."

I took a second to process this, hoping the

Andersons were safely on their way home by now. "So that's why the soldiers are following you?"

"There are soldiers following me?" The traffic had stopped dead again. I looked around. The soldiers' Jeep had pulled out, getting ready to pass us on the right.

"Get down," I said, and stayed in the window, my back to them. The soldiers passed us and pulled back into traffic three cars ahead.

"Okay, we've got to lose them." I said. "Get out."

"If we're trying to lose them, why are we getting out?"

"Because they're in front of us. What price did you negotiate with the driver?"

"What are you talking about?"

I sighed and asked the driver the fare. He gave me an outrageous sum. I turned to Roger for the money, but he and the luggage were already gone. Why did I always attract cheapskates? By the time I had settled up, Roger was between two ramshackle houses. I ran after him.

"This doesn't mean I'm still not furious with you," I said when I caught up.

"I know. Look, I'm sorry about the Tupperware thing. I had to make you mad enough to let go. I'm sorry, really. I didn't mean any of it."

"Well, it sounded pretty thought-through. And, anyway, you said that before you opened the luggage. How could you know there was something inside?"

"I just had a feeling."

I didn't buy that for a minute. I was about to start screaming when the soldiers turned around and we both went silent. Finally, they inched ahead and away. Roger put the bag down. I was sweating through my La Perla. What didn't he want me to see?

"Stop screwing around and let me see it," I said.

"No. Look, right now, you can actually say 'I don't know what you're talking about' to the police. I'm trying to give you reasonable deniability."

"Roger, my brousin is a real cop and he doesn't even talk like that. These are my clients. If they've knowingly or unknowingly broken a law, I need to know. And if the local police have framed them, I need to report it to Fodor's at least. Let me see the damn luggage."

"It's evidence. We need a chain of custody."

"Roger, seriously, you're a chiropractor, not a secret agent. I have every right to see what's in there. It's client/travel agent privilege."

"If you just let me get this luggage where it needs to go, it will be better for you."

"And how is it that you know where it's supposed to go?"

We'd attracted an audience of street kids. A

chicken pecked the ground about five feet from us and a wave of charcoal wafted into my hair.

"I'm really getting tired of this. What is wrong with you? Show me the damn luggage." I must have stood there for a whole minute.

"Okay. It's your choice. But not here. We need a contained space."

# Chapter Eighteen

"You have to promise you won't overreact."

"When do I overreact?"

Roger rolled his eyes and laid the suitcase flat. We were both squatting beside the luggage inside the handicapped stall in the women's room off our hotel lobby, since, according to Roger, our room wasn't safe. On reflex, I stole a spare roll of toilet paper and put it in my purse.

"We might need it on safari," I said, when he looked at me. "Unless we blow up first."

"It's not a bomb. Calm, okay?" He eased the suitcase open.

Curled on top of a pair of Talbot's khakis was a bumpy lizard the size of a baguette, with three horns and marble-sized, bulging eyes set wide on either side of his head.

Roger's hand slammed over my mouth. I bit him just as the lizard's tongue shot out of the suitcase and right for my eye. I watched in horror as one of my eyelashes disappeared into the little bastard's mouth. Roger let go and I fell backwards, knocking my head on the toilet seat.

"Ow!"

"Isn't his tongue cool?" Roger said, rubbing his hand. "Imagine the years of evolution it takes to zap an eyelash. It's amazing."

I had my eyes scrunched closed and was feeling the bump on my head.

"Roger? Hello. Could you cool it with the PBS stuff? I'm probably going to lose an eye."

He held up the tooth marks on his hand. "There are a lot more germs in the human mouth than in his. He's not poisonous and he's not going to hurt you. It was just instinct. He's probably starving, poor thing. Who knows how long he's been in there. His tongue extends about fourteen inches. As long as you stay that far away, your other eyelash is safe."

God, Roger had seen me without matching eyelashes. He's never going to want to sleep with me again. Just my luck that I wound up with a reptile Gene Simmons.

As the scaly creature started to wobble across the clothes on his tiny mitten hands, his tail curled tight as a fiddle head, I had to admit he was kind of cute in a *National Geographic* kind of way. The lizard changed color as Roger placed him onto one of Barb's Polo shirts. He crawled onto a Chico's

Caribbean Explosion blouse and disappeared altogether.

"They've probably given it some kind of drug. Bastards. Oh, God."

"What? What does that mean, 'Oh, God?'" I said crawling onto the toilet seat.

"Parrot sausages. This is old school."

Parrot sausages? The stabbed bird in Uncle Ray's office flashed before my eyes. I stared as he pulled out a pomegranate red parrot, its beak clamped shut, its feathers pressed down like a closed umbrella, all squished in a stocking leg. Then he kept pulling. There were four parrots in each leg of a pair of panty hose, a knot tied between each one.

"Are they alive?" I asked.

"Barely." Roger shook his head, He found socks filled with baby tortoises, their tiny legs pumping, and under Barb's capri pants, there were two egg cartons and a clear takeout container duct-taped closed and filled with bright blue frogs no bigger than thimbles.

"Who would put animals in the Andersons' luggage?"

"Maybe Lieutenant Panza was right. Maybe they are smugglers. It's the perfect cover, you have to admit, harmless-looking senior citizens. I mean they did have the ivory."

"They were at my christening. There is no way. Obviously they've been set up, but why?"

"Seriously? Money, Cyd. I'm guessing there's a half million dollars' worth of endangered animals in this luggage."

"Well there's your proof. The Andersons are on a fixed income, how could they afford that? And besides, Mrs. Barsky charged like three dollars for turtles like that."

"Not for these turtles, believe me."

"What makes you such an expert?"

"I'm a member of the World Wildlife Fund," Roger said as I raised an eyebrow. "We have newsletters. We watch documentaries. Do you have anything sharp?"

I reached into my bra for plastic mini scissors. You never knew when a cuticle would go. I looked at Roger and hesitated.

"I'm not going to stab them, Cyd, for God's sake, I'm trying to keep them alive. I'm just loosening some of this so they have more air."

"Are we taking them to the police?" I said. He just looked at me. Right, I thought. "How about letting them go?"

"They'll die. They need to be returned to their natural environment. I'm pretty sure I can get a number for someone at the Tanzanian Wildlife

Service. I'll call them while you take these guys upstairs."

"What about 'the room isn't safe'? What about the soldiers?"

"They don't know who I am."

"Well, they know who I am."

"Oh, right. Okay. We should probably get new rooms under a different name."

Unlike Cyd Redondo, my alter ego Felicity Wallcot required extra pillows and a wake-up call. Luckily, there was a different clerk working at the desk. I got an additional room at a shocking price and came back to find Roger leaning too casually by the ladies room. He tried to hand me the suitcase. I hesitated.

"So now you don't want it?" He grinned, then told me he'd meet me later and not to leave the room.

"What should I do with, you know, the merchandise? Do they need food? Water?"

"They'll be okay until I get there. Don't open the frog container and be careful with the snake eggs, they're close to hatching." Snake eggs. Perfect.

Once I got upstairs, I put the suitcase on the bed. You're never supposed to do that, because of bedbugs, but let's face it, this luggage wasn't going home with anyone. It seemed better for the reptiles to be horizontal, somehow. I unlocked the clasp a sliver, just so they could get some air, and I went into the bathroom to check my face.

That was a mistake. My mascara had shifted to the bruised skin under my eyes and one of my eyelids was naked except for a few snowflakes of glue. I took one look at myself and burst into tears. I guess I was due. In the last forty-eight hours, I had betrayed and abandoned my family, taken a twenty-hour plane trip, lost my luggage, bribed foreign government officials, had rifles pointed at me, and lost an eyelash to a fricking endangered lizard. I deserved a good cry.

I splashed my face with bottled water and started over. I always have extra lashes, but I still needed other things from my carry-on in our old room. I figured Roger would think that was a bad idea, so it was just as well he was still downstairs. I put on sunglasses and my collapsible sun hat and headed up to room 411. I yelled "Housekeeping," waited, then slipped in my key card and opened the door.

Whoever had broken in had not been subtle. My "Africa" Chantelle boy shorts were hanging from a lamp. My emergency black sequined mini dress was balled up on the carpet, my plastic can of Mace under the dust ruffle, and my Tupperwares completely un-nested. It took awhile to do an inventory. Nothing was missing but the tiny airplane liquor bottles. Damn, I could have used a shot of Jack Daniels at that moment. It clearly wasn't a robbery, as Roger's wallet was still in the drawer. They must have been looking for the suitcase. Maybe Roger was right, the animals were worth something.

I reorganized my carry-on and picked up Roger's wallet. I probably shouldn't have looked, but honestly, who wouldn't have? There was a black American Express card, a driver's license with an address in San Francisco, fifty American dollars, and a picture of Roger, smiling wildly, with his arm around a tall, thin, blonde with what could only be called "yoga arms." They were standing in front of a house with a macramé light fixture and a stained-glass door. Maybe it was his sister? But he'd said he was an only child. Cousin? Even the optimist in me thought it didn't look good. Couldn't anyone just let me have a vacation with a plus one for two whole days? I knew I should ignore it. I headed downstairs anyway.

Roger was at the end of the phone bank in the lobby. He was tapping his fingers against the top of the phone. I moved into the booth on the other side and listened in. I wanted to hear what he said to the Wildlife Service. The acoustics were in my favor.

"We'll discuss it when I get back," he said, sighing. "Alicia, stop overreacting."

Alicia. I remembered that name. My heart dropped about three floors. I took the photo out of his wallet, stomped to the other side of the phone booths, put my hand on my hips and held it up. He went gray as wet cement.

"I'll, I'll call you soon. Thanks. Sir." He put the phone down.

"Who is this? Is it that Alicia person? Is that who you were talking to?" He tried to move me out of the middle of the lobby. I shook off his hand. "Who is she?"

"She's an old friend."

"How old?" I said, hoping I was wrong. His face told me I wasn't. "You're going to tell me exactly what's going on, or I'm going to have a full-on Bay Ridge roller derby scene in this lobby right now. And don't you dare tell me I'm overreacting."

"Okay. Let's go up to the room."

"No. I want witnesses."

The lovely, stoic Tanzanians were already staring. I had read they considered any kind of public confrontation or public display of affection extremely rude. I let him lead me to two sleek, uncomfortable chairs that overlooked the taxi rank. He ordered two Jack Daniels.

"Okay," he said. "You know that everything happened really fast with us. Which was great. Is great. But we didn't really have much time to talk about ourselves. About our pasts or anything."

"Are you implying I have some kind of past?"

"I didn't mean…I'm not talking about jail time or anything. It's just that we're both adults and nobody comes to a relationship at our age without some baggage."

"You told me you just had a carry-on," I said. "Let me guess. She's some vegetarian Pilates queen who wouldn't know a basement sale from a standing rib roast. Am I right, Mr. World Wildlife Fund?"

"Actually, she's a vegan. Alicia. She's a vegan."

Sitting I was too short. I stood up.

He looked around at everyone watching him, including Akida, who waved. "We lived together for fifteen years."

My knees stopped working. There was a collective gasp from the spectators as I fell back into the chair. "Fifteen years? And you never got married?"

"I was never sure."

"You weren't sure for fifteen years? Wow. So, when did you break up?"

"We met in college. She's a biologist. She's… she's nice. She recycles, she likes to hike. She's never really given me any reason to just, you know, end it."

"Roger? Roger, when did you break up?" The spectators leaned in.

"I was waiting for a sign."

"Roger?"

"I was waiting for you." He tried to take my hand, but I jerked it away. "It didn't seem fair to do it over the phone. After all this time, I thought I owed it to her to tell her face-to-face. I just haven't had the chance yet."

"You're on a ten-day, nine-night with me and you're living with someone?" I said. The whole lobby moaned. "What kind of plus one does that?"

"I'm sorry, I'm so sorry, Cyd."

"Well, I am too. Really sorry." I rose with as much dignity as I could, glad I had at least eyelashed up. I handed him his wallet and travel documents.

"Here is everything you'll need for the rest of your trip. Akida will take you to the plane in the morning. You can take the animals and keep room 411. As you said, they don't know who you are."

# Chapter Nineteen

Akida waited until Roger was in the elevator, then hurried over. "What can I do, Cyd Redondo?"

"Find me another safari. Serengeti, Selous—anything. Maybe someone cancelled."

"I will give it all my best effort," he said. "I know you are sad, but a man who steals luggage is not the man for a travel agent such as you."

The lobby crowd parted respectfully as I headed for the elevator. Of course Roger was living with someone. I should have known. Still, there was something about him. It wasn't just the sex. He'd stuck up for me in front of Peggy Newsome, he'd been nice to my nephews, he'd let Doc Kevekian give him eleven shots and still offered to carry my bag. By the time I got upstairs, all I wanted was to throw my arms around him. When he finally showed, two hours later, I was back to wanting him dead.

"Yes?" I said as I let him in.

"Cyd, the last thing I wanted to do was ruin your vacation. You should take the safari, I'll go home."

"Absolutely not." I closed the suitcase full of sleepy birds and reptiles with a click and lugged it to the door. "Redondo Travel honors its reservations." I held out the bag. "Mr. Claymore, as we go our separate ways, I hope that Redondo Travel has done everything possible to make your trip a pleasant, easy, and memorable one."

"Well, it's certainly been memorable," he said, leaning toward me. Two housekeepers appeared. He backed away. I slammed the door.

After eating some wrinkled airplane olives, I made sure the Andersons had gotten on their flight. I would explain the luggage, and Roger, later. I also checked on my other Tanzania clients, in case any of them were incarcerated. They were okay for now: the Giannis were sunburned but safe in Arusha, the Abercrombies were touring a clove plantation on Zanzibar, and my favorite anniversary couple, the Minettis, had survived the *QE2* and their flights and were mid-safari and had seen a baby hippo on their anniversary. They said they were having the best time ever. I told them I was in Tanzania if they needed me.

It was time to face my messages. I decided I needed a drink first and headed down to the lobby bar. The bartender, who'd witnessed the incident with Roger, bought my first shot. Once I'd downed that and ordered another, I called my voicemail. In addition to my family, there were four messages from my brousin Frank and four more from the 68th Precinct Homicide Division. Great. For a few hours, the Andersons, the animals, and the break-up had made me forget I was a wanted fugitive.

It was late in Dar es Salaam, but it was ten a.m. in New York. I downed my shot, pressed my speed dial and asked for Lieutenant Frank Redondo.

"Cyd. Where are you? We sent a squad car by the house about fifteen times."

"I'm in Africa."

"Africa? So you fled the country?"

"I didn't flee, I won my trip. I'm on vacation. Kind of."

"Look, Cyd, it's nothing personal, but the detectives need to talk to you."

"Who? Dick Di Salvo? He's known me since I was three. There's no way he thinks I did this."

"Think about it, Miss *Law and Order*. You had keys to the store, check. You were the one who found the body, check. Poisoning is usually a woman's crime, check. And the victim left you her apartment. Motive, means, opportunity, check. So for the record, they have to at least talk to you."

"Fine, but you know I didn't do it. First, I

didn't have the keys, they weren't in the drawer, so Jimmy must have had them. And if the apartment is their stupid motive, I won't take it. Joni can have it. Or Bobby. Have you found Bobby?"

"Not yet."

"Well, somebody needs to find him. He doesn't even know his own mother is dead. And if she was poisoned, check her cupboard. Even Tang's got to have a shelf life."

"It wasn't Tang." I heard him rustle papers, "Look, I know you didn't do it, but we have to follow procedure. Plus, you know I'm up for promotion and I'm not getting it if I can't even arrange an interview with my own cousin. When are you coming home?"

"Nine days and eight nights from now," I said. "I'm innocent and I'm not coming home early. For now, I need to know what kind of poison. And check out the CIA. They hire women too."

"I can't give you information on the case. You're a suspect. I could lose my job."

"And if Karin finds out about the little "fishing" trip I booked you to the Cape, you could lose your wife." Silence.

"Fine. But I'm giving the detectives your number."

"Fine, I'll ignore them while I'm doing their job and finding Bobby. Good-bye, Frank."

After we hung up, I sat for awhile, trying to figure out who could have actually wanted to kill Mrs. Barsky. Even if she had something on someone, she'd have forgotten it. She had a rotten short-term memory. None of it made sense. My phone rang. It was Akida.

"My deepest apologies, Cyd Redondo. There have been no cancellations. I feel that I have failed you."

"Of course you haven't failed me. We both knew it was a long shot."

"What would you like me to do?"

Roger or no Roger, I wasn't going to miss my free safari. We'd just have to sit on opposite sides of the Range Rover. But I did need to try to find poor Bobby Barsky before I got on the charter flight.

"Call Phoenix Tours and see if there's any way to get separate rooms at the eco-resort. And will you book me a later charter and let them know I may be late? Do you mind taking Roger to the airstrip?"

"It will be my pleasure, despite my hatred of him."

"Good. Keep me posted. Thank you, Akida. You've been very kind."

"It's my career and my pleasure," he said. "Perhaps tomorrow will bring another outlook."

I headed upstairs. Looking in the elevator mirror at my sagging eye makeup and limp hair,

I thought about how much I had wanted to be a world traveler, to be cosmopolitan and non-plussed and flexible and glamorous at the same time. It was harder than it looked.

When I got to my floor, the hall lights were out, which I took as a bad omen. I swiped the key card, holding my mini travel flashlight in front of me, so I could blind anyone waiting in the room. After I'd made as much noise as possible, I turned on the lights and found everything pretty much the way I'd left it, except for a slight rustling sound. It was more bug-like than human, probably roaches.

I knew from living in Brooklyn that the roaches didn't actually want anything from me— they would only cross over me on the way to something else. I crawled into bed. Then, I turned and saw a shadow the shape of a Three Musketeers' hat move behind the bureau lamp. I grabbed a spike heel and inched over, only to find the chameleon from the Andersons' luggage casting a bizarre hand puppet on the wall. He had turned the dull yellow of the lampshade. He must have crawled out when I unlatched the suitcase.

As the lizard started to lope along the edge of the lampshade, grabbing the edge with his little Kermit hands, his red tongue snatched a cockroach the size of a Mars bar. Well, at least it was eating bugs. I wasn't too keen on picking him up, so I unplugged the lamp and eased it into the bathroom and closed the door. I would get him back to Roger in the morning. Finally, at about four o'clock, I fell asleep.

The next thing I knew, it was ten in the morning. I downed two bottles of water while I called Roger's room. The desk clerk said he had already departed for his safari. Damn. What was I going to do with the creature? I needed coffee before I did any thinking. I stole some garnish lettuce off the breakfast buffet downstairs and put it in the bathroom sink, where the chameleon had taken up residence. I had to admit, he was growing on me. Maybe it was because he was all alone in an alien environment, like me. Maybe it was because he reminded me of someone. I realized, suddenly, it was Barry Manzoni. They had the same bug eyes and ambling walk.

What should I wear? Khaki washed me out, so I chose a linen shirt in rose that tied at the waist, a white denim miniskirt and some low (i.e. three-inch) nude Sofft heels, since I'd be hiking. After one look at my calves in the mirror, I replaced them with Stuart Weitzman stilettos.

Then I tried to figure out what to do with Barry, the chameleon. I didn't want the maids to sell him on the black market. He was currently lurching on top of the desk chair. I still had some lettuce, so I put it on the edge of my carry-on in hopes he'd go for it and fall in. No such luck. He just shot his tongue out and took it right off the zipper. I edged the bag closer, until it was right under him. Was this a bad fall for a lizard? It was only five inches. Just as he got to the edge of the chair, I scooped the bag down and kind of batted him in. He landed on top of my taupe bra and immediately started to disappear.

I realized how easy it was going to be to lose a creature who specialized in blending into his sur-roundings, so, just to be safe, I wound a fuchsia scrunchie around the bottom of his tail. I left him more lettuce, hoping it didn't have e-coli. After all, he was now my plus one. I put the carry-on on the top shelf of the closet, put my Do Not Disturb sign on the door, and left the TV on.

I picked up my Balenciaga and headed down the hall, Bobby's last known abode in my hand. It was always a good idea to establish a relationship with the concierge, so I handed the address to him, along with a generous tip.

"Cyd Redondo, Redondo Travel," I said and asked what price I should negotiate for the fare. He looked at the address, frowned, and excused himself. Five minutes later, he'd personally arranged for a taxi and escorted me outside. There was a late model Mercedes by the curb, which I hoped was my ride, but instead, he handed me into a small white sedan with a green stripe, spitting white smoke out the tailpipe. It probably had a coolant leak.

I gave the cabbie the address on Dosi Street in the Mbezi Beach area—apparently a haven for expats. We'd been driving about five minutes on the crowded Morogoro Road when the cabbie turned down an alley and slammed to a stop.

"Is someone after you, Miss?" he asked.

"Of course not." I saw the Mercedes pass the alley. "Crap. Any chance we can lose them? There's another ten U.S. if you do."

"Perhaps one hundred?"

"Thirty. It's all I have in cash," I lied.

He shrugged and made a U-turn worthy of Vin Diesel. We flew down a series of dusty, rutted streets and alleys until we reached a neighborhood of tiny wooden bungalows and finally arrived at the address on Dosi Street. It was hard to see the house behind the tangerine and turquoise blankets hung on the laundry line that stretched across the yard. Instead of stopping at the curb, the cabbie tore under the blankets and into a hidden garage.

"What are you doing?"

"Getting you to your destination safely," he said, jumping out and closing the garage door. That was when I saw the gun.

# Chapter Twenty

"You've got to be kidding," I said.

"They offered me fifty."

Damn. Hoisted by my own thriftiness. "Who's they? Is it too late to renegotiate?"

"Come on, Miss, inside," he gestured with the gun. It looked like a Sig Sauer combat revolver, which was not great for me; according to Eddie they rarely misfired. After he jerked me out of the cab, the cabbie shoved the gun into the small of my back, then rammed a greasy makeshift blindfold down over my eyes as he pushed me toward the house. I felt my eyelashes unhinge. He opened a door and pushed me forward. The place smelled like the Elephant House at the zoo, times a hundred.

"I'll wait out here."

"Inside."

I calculated the cabbie's height and weight and figured he was about my brousin Jimmy's size: five-nine. I just needed a solid surface to hold onto and him directly behind me. When I touched what felt like a counter, I put both hands down and waited until I could feel his breath on my neck and the gun pointed down, bumping my hip.

I leaned forward and kicked my stiletto heel backwards and up, directly into his balls.

I'd perfected the one leg kick years ago when Sal and Jimmy used to sneak up behind me on a daily basis. It was one of the few times when my shortness was an advantage. As expected, the cabbie didn't have balls of steel. Like most men, his seemed to be made of something resembling chicken livers. He went down and I swung wide, knocking him out with the full force of my Balenciaga. Just when I jerked the blindfold off so I could grab the gun, I heard the hiss.

A cobra swayed back and forth on the counter, five feet from my head. I tried to concentrate on him and block out the dozens of cages of other snakes and squirmy reptiles that filled the room. What was I, a reptile magnet? This was no time to faint, as Roger wasn't here to catch me.

I reminded myself that I had a snakebite kit, but the last thing in the world I wanted to do was sit on a filthy kitchen floor in my white miniskirt and suck poison out of myself. Plus, it looked like my head was the snake's most likely target and I defy pretty much anybody to suck venom out of their own head. If we could do that, there'd be no therapists.

I kept as still as I could. I had no idea how far the thing could reach, but after the chameleon, I wasn't taking any chances. I figured it could strike faster than I could aim the gun, if it were loaded. I needed some kind of shield. My Balenciaga was my only option—high and wide enough to cover my head and neck and the very top of my cleavage—but I loved this bag. Still, Bay Ridge Leather was great with stains. Surely cobra venom couldn't be worse than barbecue sauce? I tried to calculate where the snake's direct strike might go and said, "Please don't let me die." Then I gently cocked the revolver, threw my purse up in front of my face, jammed my eyes closed and pulled the trigger.

Everything got quiet. Then something slimy hit my arm. The screaming reflex forced my eyes open. The snake had made a dive for my bag and apparently the bullet caught it in mid-air. Half of it was hanging by its fangs from the thick red leather of my purse and half of it was twitching on the floor by the cabbie's head.

I eased the purse down and watched to see whether the head, curved like some satanic hood ornament, was still alive. Something thick dripped down the purse, turning the dark red leather black. Finally, the head stopped twitching. Now, how to

get the snake's head and fangs off with the minimum damage to the bag?

I had mini travel tweezers, but they wouldn't
handle the weight and I really didn't want to drop
the bloody end of the snake on my new skirt.
Breathing through my mouth, I surveyed the
area, keeping the gun handy. Across the room, a
burlap sack was wriggling. I didn't consider burlap
secure. I needed to get out of here. I checked that
the cabbie was still breathing, took his keys, then
secured him with plastic tie handcuffs courtesy of
the 68th Precinct.

"Who doesn't have tongs?" I opened drawer
after drawer: nothing but matchbooks, dried-up
ketchup packets, takeout chopsticks, and sporks.

I opened the fridge just in case, only to find it
filled top to bottom with frozen pink/white mice,
squished together in zip-locks like mutant jumbo
shrimp. In the end, I decided on the chopsticks.
Eddie had taught me how to use them when I
was six. Eight thousand General Tsao Chickens
later, I wasn't bad.

Remembering to hold the bottom chopstick
like a pencil and pretending this reptilian hunk
of poison was just a slippery dumpling, I closed
the wooden ends around its hood and lifted carefully, up and back, to disengage the fangs. At that
moment, I heard the solid thunk of a car door

closing. Two more seconds, I thought. I had just pulled the fangs free, when a door opened in the front of the house. By the time I stood up, there was a tall man with a military haircut and twice-broken nose, heading right for me. If he had a gun, it wasn't out.

When he was about three feet away, I flung the snake head at his face and scrambled for the back door, out and into the garage, shoving the gun into my bag. I had just gotten to the cab when the door rolled up, revealing two more guys: one short and ropey with bow legs and slicked-back hair, and the other bald, with a gut that poked through his suit like a boil. They both pulled guns. This was my vacation, damn it, where was my frosty drink?

The man inside yelled with a heavy South African accent, "Get that bitch in here, she butchered the bloody King cobra."

I was considering the chances of reaching my gun when the guys shoved me through the door. The tall man looked down at the top half of the cobra, then at the cabbie.

"Well, you're not getting paid," he said to the prone figure, then turned to me. "You idiot. Don't you know how much this snake was worth?"

"How much?"

"A hundred grand at least. Bunty sent you a price list."

Who was Bunty? And who did they think I was? "Bullshit. Besides it was him or me," I said.

"What was it going to do—bump you to death? Its mouth was stitched shut."

"The hell it was."

The man turned the snake head over, revealing the fangs. "Dammit, Moe" he said, turning to the fat man. "You were supposed to do this last night. You know one that size can kill a man in three minutes."

"Exactly my point."

"Shut up. That's still no excuse for killing a perfectly good product. You should know better. And what in the fuckity universe was it doing loose?" Fuckity universe? "You know we're supposed to ship these out today. Did you do the other ones?" Moe looked down.

"He had a hot date, Henrik," the other guy said. "Stewardess."

It was clear the tall guy, Henrik, was in charge. He was the one I had to take out.

He turned to the ropey guy. "You're supposed to keep an eye on him, Jock. Jesus. Bunty is going to go berserk. You know what happens when the shipment is light." Moe reached protectively toward his privates. "What a waste," Henrik said, looking down at Moe's crotch, then punching him in the face.

"Maybe we can sew it back together and they'll

just think it died on route. We lose most of them anyway." Jock the short, ropey one said.

"Well, where are the other five?"

Moe and Jock looked across the room toward the wriggling burlap sack. Yikes.

"You guys are fuckity unemployable. Let me guess, you didn't duct-tape those dart frog containers either, did you?" They were still looking at the floor. Henrik scowled at me. "And you. What kind of slag throws a snake head at a complete stranger?"

"The kind of slag who's been kidnapped and attacked by an unstitched fuckity cobra." I tried to open the outside pouch of my purse without their noticing. "Who are you, anyway, and why am I here?"

"Like you don't know. If you had left that luggage alone like you were supposed to, we wouldn't have had to arrange this meeting. You should know better than to bypass the middle man. Where's the shipment now?"

While he was distracted, I slipped my hand in my bag and almost had a hold on the two things I needed. If I could distract them, my plan might work. I looked down and pointed. "Ahhhh! Cobra!"

As Henrik turned, I shot him, winging his arm. When Jock and Moe tried to grab me, I did a jujitsu turn, maced both of them in the face, then bolted for the door.

# Chapter Twenty-one

I heard them yelling as I jumped in the cab and started it up. Luckily, the garage door was still open. I reversed too hard, swung into some trash bins, then headed back out the alley and hoped for the best. The first order of business was to get as far away from this house as possible.

Once I was a few blocks away I ducked down a tiny alley and hid under some hanging laundry. I kept my eye on the rearview mirror. My heart stopped when I saw the Mercedes fly by. I waited for them to back up. The alley was a dead end. Who were those guys? Smugglers, obviously, but why did they think I would know about cobra prices? And who was this Bunty character? Had the cabbie actually taken me to Bobby's old address or somewhere else? Could they be the ones sending reptiles to Mrs. Barsky? I'd have to check a map. Later.

Finally, I inched the cab out. No sign of the Mercedes. I surveyed the area. The St. Jerome

Church was on my right, so I was heading north. If I could keep the steeple on my right, I was pretty sure I could remember how to get to the embassy. Clearly the thugs thought I still had their animals and they weren't going to let that go. I started the car and concentrated on driving, breathing easier once I saw the flame trees and the flapping stars and stripes. I slowed well away from the entrance and waved. Happily, the guards recognized me and didn't shoot. Maybe my luck was improving.

The completely uncharming Under Under Secretary Brett Winbourne, clad in slightly damp Brooks Brothers, asked me what my visit was regarding. I said I preferred to tell the Ambassador Belk in person. While I waited, I tried Akida and wondered why he wasn't answering. I paced for awhile. Finally, Winbourne returned and took me upstairs, entering the ambassador's office behind me.

Belk rose from his desk and kissed my hand, gesturing to a massive couch. Maybe men in Tanzania measured their penises with couches instead of cars. He was wearing another pristine shirt, this time with a deep lavender tie and silver tie clip. He smelled of Aqua di Parma with a tiny hint of Dr. Scholl's anti-fungal foot powder.

"Miss Redondo, what a pleasure. No more clients in jail, I hope."

"No, this concerns a different matter, Ambassador."

"Please, call me Harrison. What can we do for you?"

"I just wanted to inform the embassy that I was abducted at gunpoint and threatened with venomous reptiles earlier today." I took him through everything that had happened in the cab and in the house, trying to keep the Andersons out of it. Of course, without them, it didn't make any sense.

"Miss Redondo. Cyd. You're among friends. It's really best if you tell me everything. Your comments will remain in complete confidence."

"Okay. Someone put animals in the Andersons' luggage—I guess to smuggle them to the U.S. I think maybe the men were after the animals."

"I see. Where are these animals now?"

"Roger has them. He's supposed to turn them into the Wildlife Service."

"Do you think you could identify any of these men if you saw them again?"

"Absolutely."

"Good. It sounds like a horrible ordeal. Would you excuse us for just for a moment?"

"Of course."

While Belk and his underling were gone, I poked around his office. I mean, why else did he leave me alone? I'd just sat back down when they returned.

"Cyd, we'd like to offer you a room here until this is sorted out. I don't mean to alarm you, but it seems ill-advised for you to return to the hotel."

"But I need my carry-on. I'm leaving on safari this afternoon."

"I will send someone for your bag." Belk gave the Winbourne my room number. Shit, I thought. Barry. The chameleon.

"My carry-on bag is extremely fragile. Please ask them to be careful with it."

"Of course. I've also had the cab returned." After the Under Under Secretary had left, Belk sat down beside me again, closer this time. "We're having a gala this evening and I'd love for you to come as my guest. We can fly you to the reserve in the morning."

A gala sounded pretty great after the day I'd had. And it would serve Roger right if I went on a date with his arch rival.

"That would be lovely. Thank you."

"Excellent. We have a collection of formal wear if you don't have anything with you."

"Oh, I have something with me."

Belk handed me over to a barrel-sized man in a sports coat, who took me down a series of complex hallways before he unlocked a large, paneled door into a sunny, beautifully appointed room, complete with romantic mosquito net and an adjoining turquoise-tiled bathroom with a jacuzzi. My tax dollars at work.

"Did Hillary Clinton ever use this room?" I asked.

"State secret," he said and winked. "Perhaps you could meet the ambassador for a cocktail at six? Your luggage will be here within the hour."

"Thank you." Wow. I was going to sleep in Hillary Clinton's bed. Alone. I pushed the thought of Roger out of my head and explored the room. The French doors looked out on the courtyard, where caterers were preparing for the party.

What I wanted now was a bath. I ran the jacuzzi, careful not to let any of the water splash into my mouth. Once I was clean and lotioned up, I pulled the black sequined mini dress out of the side pocket of my purse. Debbie said that I was crazy to carry it around "just in case," but yet again, I had proved her wrong. The dress was my favorite combination of glamorous and slutty: it hit me about a third of the way up my thigh, had a high boat-neck front and was cut down to what Roger had called my "coccygeal vertebra" in the back. I put on some fresh eyelashes and was just turning on my battery-operated curling iron, when I heard a knock.

I opened the door. My carry-on sat on the plush, moss-colored carpet. I brought it inside, closed the shutters, and unzipped the top. There was the plastic bag and a shred of lettuce, but no Barry. I emptied it completely. He wasn't there. The thugs must have gotten to my room before the courier did. I don't know why this made me so sad. After all, if the reptile guys had him, they wouldn't be after me anymore. Still, I wouldn't wish those guys on anyone, even a lizard. I had to tell Belk right away.

Having learned not to let any bags out of my sight, I left with my Balenciaga and was instantly lost. I saw a door ajar and looked in, hoping for directions. The room was empty, save for a large desk and a dolly filled with diplomatic bags and pouches of various sizes and shapes, but all made of dark green vinyl with "Property of the United States of America: Tanzanian Embassy" stamped on their sides with block numbers. A stack of way-bills sat on the desk beside them reading BA flight 1756 with a set of documents that looked just like the ones sent to Mrs. Barsky: CITES label, Latin names, "Captive Bred" stamps, the works.

I have to admit, my curiosity got the better of me. The first bag held folders in Swahili. The next one had what looked like about a hundred thousand in U.S. dollars. Holy crap. I could understand dollars coming into the embassy, for petty cash or whatever, but why would dollars go out? The hall was still quiet, so I took a chance on one more, shaped like a man's toiletry bag. At first it seemed to be empty, but when I looked closer, there, glowing like a fluorescent beacon, was a fuchsia scrunchie.

# Chapter Twenty-two

Barry, curled up and "diplomatic bag" green, looked about as unhappy as a reptile could. He swiveled one eye away from me, then the other. I felt horrible. There was no way I was leaving him here. I heard a toilet flush nearby. I unzipped the extra compartment of my Balenciaga, which doubled its size, and slipped the diplomatic bag inside, making sure not to squish Barry.

I grabbed another bag from a shelf and looked for something that might be about a chameleon's weight. I settled on a half-empty Perrier bottle and put the scrunchie around its neck for good measure. I thought I heard someone on the other side of the open door. I swiveled backwards, to look like I was coming in rather than going out, and yelled.

"Hello? Hello? Anybody here?"

"May I help you?"

"Oh, you scared me." I said, whipping around. A man of about twenty with a five o'clock shadow and an ill-fitting suit stood there, reeking of smoke. "I didn't know smoking was allowed in the embassy." He looked guilty. "I'm so sorry to bother you, but I'm a guest of Ambassador Belk's and I'm lost. Can you direct me back to the guest quarters?"

Clearly more concerned about being caught smoking than guarding diplomatic secrets, he gave me directions and closed the door.

Someone in the embassy was in cahoots with the reptile guys. Neither Barry nor I were safe here. With any luck, I had at least an hour before anyone would notice me missing. Once I was inside my room, I pulled out my phone and called Akida again. Still no answer. So much for "in country" help. My phone rang. It was my brousin Frank. Maybe he'd found Bobby. Maybe I could stay with him.

"Hey, Cyd, you didn't see a dart or a needle lying around Mrs. Barsky's body, did you?" Frank said.

"A dart?"

"Yeah, I know it's a weird question but this whole thing is weird. It turns out Mrs. Barsky was injected with the poison from a…shit….a *D.E.N.D.R.O.B.A.T.I.D.A.E.*" My years of Latin failed me. I blamed the nuns. "A poison dart frog. I kid you not. They're little blue things with enough poison on their skin to kill about ten people."

"Wait, it's on the frog's skin? Maybe she just touched one. Maybe it was an accident?"

"There's an injection site. Definite murder. Plus those frogs are totally banned in Brooklyn. Whoever killed her had access to the poison or to the frogs."

"Obviously that rules me out."

"I don't know. You're a travel agent, you could smuggle anything in."

I remembered the Latin on the FedEx package. "Frank, maybe you can check on something. Mrs. Barsky got a FedEx the day she died—I signed for it. It had some weird documents with Latin names. I tried the phone number on the waybill but it was disconnected and they just had a P.O. Box. Maybe it's a clue."

"Great, where are the documents?"

"I kind of have them." I pulled them out.

"Jesus, Cyd. You tampered with evidence, too? WTF?"

"If I killed her, would I be sending photos of them to you right now? As you see, the P.O. Box is in Tanzania. And I'm in Tanzania. If you get the address, maybe I can check it out. It's a long story, but there's definitely stuff going on down here."

"Cyd, you shouldn't be more involved than you already are."

"Gotta go, I have fifteen minutes to flee the embassy. Call me later."

I hung up and turned off the phone to save battery. I thought about poison dart frogs—hadn't the smugglers mentioned them? Then I remembered the tiny blue frogs in the takeout container from the Andersons' luggage, the ones Roger had taken on safari. Shit. I tried Roger's phone and Phoenix Tours. Nothing. I needed to get to that safari before Roger poisoned himself. Or anyone else.

By agreeing to stay at the embassy, I'd missed the flight Akida had booked for me. And he wasn't answering his phone. I decided to call one of the Flying Doctors, an emergency rescue team available as add-on coverage for our safari clients. Dr. Dennis and I had been phone- and e-mail-flirting for years. I had convinced every client we'd ever sent to East Africa to sign up, so he owed me. Plus, he had said on more than one occasion that he'd come pick me up anytime, anywhere and take the fee out in trade.

I dialed Dennis' number as I multitasked, catching a beetle for Barry and misting perfume. Dennis said he couldn't helicopter into the embassy, but there was a rooftop landing pad about two miles away. Damn. Belk had said he'd returned my cab to the company. How was I going to get into town without anyone at the embassy knowing?

The French doors were locked, but any Brooklyn girl could pick with them with a bobby pin. I looked out at the party preparations. At least some of the people setting up were in formal dress, so I wouldn't look out of place. I grabbed my bag and carry-on, popped the lock, and tried to walk normally in the direction of the nearest catering truck, where I took cover. Being no stranger to catering, I knew this truck wasn't going anywhere. So who would be leaving soon?

I heard an engine start up. I ran for the vibrating panel truck, jumped in the back, and hid behind a wall of bagged rice. I heard voices as they loaded one more dolly, then pulled the truck door down. The gears ground into reverse and the truck started, throwing two huge bags of rice which barely missed my head. The truck slowed down, then we were through the security gate.

The truck jerked ahead, boxes flying, then swerved to the side. I emitted an involuntary scream. The vehicle stopped, throwing me and Barry's temporary hotel against the wall. I had just gotten back on my feet when the door opened and a blinding sun knocked me backwards. A silhouette stood in the doorway, waving what looked like a machete.

# Chapter Twenty-three

It was a machete. Holding it was a girl, about five-six, in a Bob Marley t-shirt, baggy shorts, and the ugliest pair of Birkenstocks I had ever seen. She couldn't have been over nineteen. She was sunburned all over, with a Connecticut nose that turned up at the end and had clearly been peeling for weeks. I put my hands up.

"Up against the...the side." Up close, she smelled like zinc oxide, Secret deodorant, and feet. "Who the hell are you?" Her hands were shaking, never a good thing with a machete.

"Cyd Redondo, Redondo Travel. Hi. I'm sorry I scared you. Gerald at the embassy said I could catch a ride out with you. I'm from Brooklyn."

She looked me up and down. "Oh, my God, are those Stuart Weitzmans?"

"Yeah, got them at cost," I said, modeling like Dorothy in Munchkinland.

"I'm so sick of wearing sandals I could die."

She dropped the machete, sat down on a box beside me, and started to bawl. I understood. Sometimes it was easier, even preferable, to cry in front of strangers. They couldn't hold it against you for fifteen years. I put my arm around her, taking the opportunity to move the machete out of range and check my watch.

"Sorry. I just wanted a gap year where I could feel like I'd done something worthwhile, you know, and it would look good on my résumé. Now, all I want is to walk into a mall that has Victoria's Secret and the Gap and Restoration Hardware and have a smoothie. I'm a horrible person."

"No you're not. You're just homesick."

She was still looking at my shoes. "How much were they?"

"It will just upset you."

"I'm already upset."

"Fifteen bucks."

"Get out."

"For serious. Century Twenty-One, seventy-five percent off the regular and forty percent off with another ten on coupon." She started to cry again. I thought about Roger and Barry. I had to make a tough decision. "What size are you?"

"Eight," she said. Damn.

"I'll swap you if you can get me to this address."

"No problem."

Forget laughter. Shoes are the language spoken round the world. I took a deep breath and reached for my stilettos, handing them over slowly. After all, earlier today those shoes had saved my life. I took her Birkenstocks, the color of congealed oatmeal, and put them on. She said I could ride in the front. I stood up and promptly fell backwards, coming back up with my exposed back peppered in raw rice. How did people walk in these? Five minutes later she had deposited me in front of the Tanzania National Bank and I headed up the elevator to the roof.

Dennis was waiting at the top, in khakis so worn they were see-through and a faded denim shirt, unbuttoned one button too many. His thick blond/gray hair was shoved under a baseball cap. He wasn't as cute as his voice, but I was so glad to see him it didn't matter.

"Can we make it?" I asked, worried about Roger and the poison frogs.

"Just," he said. "Let me throw your stuff in the back."

I had taken Barry's diplomatic bag out of my purse for safety, as for once in my life, I didn't want instant reptile death.

"I'll keep these up front with me." I hiked up my dress to get into the copter.

"Nice dress."

"I was going to a party, but I had to make a quick getaway."

"With a diplomatic bag, that goes without saying. Don't worry, I'm not going to ask."

"Thanks," I said. "You're pretty much, literally, saving my ass."

"Pleasure to have your ass in one piece."

He was tanned and buff, he was flirting with me, and he was a flying doctor, for God's sake, but he wasn't Roger. What had happened to me? How could one man ruin my entire future love life in three days?

The minute we jerked upward, I felt seasick, or what I imagined seasickness would be like if I had ever been on a boat. I tried to look straight ahead and hoped Barry wasn't a nervous flier too. I could feel him skittering around in the bag. Dennis lived in Africa. Maybe he knew something about animal smuggling. I asked.

"Are you thinking of taking it up as a sideline?"

"Just curious. I've heard some things."

He said the slaughter was horrendous—over a hundred thousand elephants had been killed in the last few years—even Al Qaeda was using ivory to fund operations. They'd taken to firing missile launchers at the Kenyan Wildlife planes to keep them away from the poachers. And there was an eco-disaster going on in Madagascar with endangered tortoises, snakes, and chameleons all being poached or killed. I checked Barry's zipper.

"Half the time the animals are worth more dead than alive. Christ, some rhino horns go for fifty, a hundred grand.

"No way."

"Yeah, people grind them up for aphrodisiacs. The Chinese say it increases sexual performance."

"Does it?"

"Of course not. But they kill them anyway. That's why there's only a handful left."

"So my nephews are going to live in a world without rhinos for the faux Viagra of China?"

"Pretty much. Then there are all the tortoise-shell headbands and the snakeskin shoes."

We made a dip that almost brought up my breakfast. At least I had a seat belt. This must be like the Coney Island Cyclone for Barry. I should have strapped him in with Band-Aids. To avoid guilt about my ivory necklace, headband, and most of my shoes, I asked him about Phoenix Tours.

"I know Cassandra, the woman who runs it."

"Know her, know her?"

"Well, it's a small country," Dennis said. I could identify with that. Was Cassandra Roger's type? "She's a do-gooder, you know. Everything on the tour is really green and she's pretty militant about it. If anyone even wears perfume, they're off."

He looked over at me; I had doused myself with Calvin Klein's Obsession before I left the embassy.

"She's going to hate me."

"Yeah, it should be fun." He grinned.

Perfect, I thought. The sun was low, the tall grass going golden orange, and the flat, wide baobab trees dark against the sky. All I needed was a flock of flamingos. I got a herd of giraffes instead. Oh, my God. Giraffes, skin like chocolate chip ice cream, legs long as Jersey pines, galloping over the plains. It was really something, to see them run. The giraffes in the Bronx Zoo barely had room to stroll. I noticed a couple of babies at the back, trying to keep up. I gasped.

"Real Africa," he said. "Or it will be if something eats it in the next ten minutes."

"Stop it," I said, "leave me a few illusions."

I pressed my face to the window and scanned the horizon. Somewhere out there were lions. And lionesses. And elephants. And lumpy, huge-mouthed hippos. I forgot about the reptile kitchenette and the guns and the Andersons. Just for a minute, I was a tourist, on an actual vacation. What day was this? My third. Only six left. I wanted to see a lion. As the helicopter hovered above the camp, I saw people prone on the ground, their asses in the air.

"What the hell?"

"Downward dog," Dennis said.

"I beg your pardon?"

"Yoga."

"That's pretty damn undignified," was all I could say. As we got lower, the group began to scatter. We finally landed. The rotors slowed to a low roar, then stopped. Dennis turned to look at me.

"Here it comes," he said.

# Chapter Twenty-four

Striding toward us in the clearing was a woman about five-foot eight and "willowy," with, of course, yoga arms. She wore a tank top, cropped green Abercrombie and Fitch pants that ran about three-fifty retail, and delicate golden leather sandals; apparently there were pedicures available in the jungle. She had almost unnaturally green eyes and her long, honey hair was loose and wavy. That, at least, I knew wasn't natural. We Bay Ridge girls could spot a Golden Sunrise rinse from eighty paces. She hugged Dennis and I gave one of those sheepish waves, the kind you make when you've knocked the mannequin over at Bendel's, and took a deep breath, determined to win whatever competition I was in with this dye-job anorexic green freak.

I scanned the crowd for Roger. The eco-tourists were all wearing something ugly and expensive: cargo pants, which were never going to dry in this humidity, and shirts with multiple pockets, which always added five pounds—ask anyone. I was glad to be in my sequined dress, Birkenstocks or not.

Dennis came around to help me down. "Keep it professional," he winked.

"Naturally," I said, holding onto my purse and Barry's bag and letting Dennis grab the carry-on. I attempted to get down without flashing the nature lovers, then turned to Dennis. In these shoes, I was too short to kiss him. Even on tiptoes, I could only hit him somewhere on the neck.

"I really appreciate it," I said. "I understand that next time I'll have to be injured to get a ride."

He looked over at Cassandra and the other campers. "That doesn't seem beyond the pale. Just be sure and ask for me, will you? Dick would smash right into some wildlife if he saw you in that dress."

Dennis gave me a small pat on my ass and jumped into the helicopter. Maybe in another vacation, I thought, and waved as the huge rotors flattened everything within fifty feet, including my hair. I tried to push it back up, heard a cough, and there was Roger, with zinc oxide on his nose, staring at me. Cassandra stepped between us. I held out my hand.

"Cyd Redondo, Redondo Travel." She had a limp handshake. I could take her.

"Hello, Miss Redondo. I'm glad you're not going to forfeit the fee," she said. "I hope you've brought appropriate clothing. It can be cold at night."

"Oh, this?" I did a quick spin for Roger's benefit. "I had to make an appearance at an embassy function. That's why I'm late."

Cassandra sneezed. "Are you wearing perfume? It's strictly banned on this safari. I thought I made that very clear in the literature."

"Well, I'll be happy to take care of that if you'll show me to my room." The big stone lodge was just up the hill.

"Yes, of course. We'll get you to your tent so you can change for dinner. We meet for organic cocktails in an hour."

Tent? "Excuse me, I had reserved a room in the lodge."

"I'm afraid arriving late, you lost your suite." Bugs, I thought. Bugs. "Our tents are four-star. Even travel agents like them," Cassandra said.

"I assume my client, Mr. Claymore, received what he was promised?"

Cassandra smiled. "Mr. Claymore is getting the full package. Faraji will help you with your things."

Faraji was a tall native man, also in Abercrombie and Fitch, with a tattoo on one side of his face. I introduced myself and he took the carry-on while I held onto my purse.

"I have to talk to you," I whispered to Roger as we passed. "Right away. Don't touch the frogs."

Cassandra moved to Roger's side and took his arm. It was on. I didn't care if he had a girlfriend in America, he was not going to have one here. She was dead tofu.

I did my best to revive the normal sway of my walk, but it was impossible in these shoes. No wonder the aid worker had been in tears. I had to admit it was a little easier to manage the bags, though. Maybe I should look on eBay for a pair of those Chanel flats with the little bow. Outside the tent, the crickets were louder than a Maytag spin cycle and I heard the high-pitched cries of something that might be monkeys.

Faraji, his pecs pressing open the pockets on his cargo shirt, lifted the flap. There was a real bed with a mosquito net, chest of drawers, an eye mask, and a bathroom. Everything was white. There seemed to be running water and a toilet, though it was probably chemical. Still, the place smelled more like ginger than sewage, and now, at least, I could tell my clients I had roughed it.

"If there's anything else you need, there's a walkie-talkie by your bed," Faraji said. The walkie-talkie was the same creamy white as the bed. Did Barbra Streisand do their decorating? "Drinks in half an hour at the lodge. There's organic bug spray in your bathroom. We're trying to keep toxins out of the environment."

Screw that. With the size of these mosquitoes, I needed pure DDT. "Thanks very much, Faraji. Look, I need to speak to Mr. Claymore about his travel arrangements. Do you know where I could find him?"

"I believe he's with Cassandra. He'll be at drinks."

"Thanks. Where can I charge my cell phone?"

"No cell phones at Phoenix. We want you to achieve the peace of an earlier time."

"What about emergencies?"

"Cassandra would evaluate the situation."

In the boroughs, people moved at the speed of light just to get a cannoli or some stamps. Here, no one was in a hurry, and if you were, they just pitied you.

As I sat down on the perfect bed, I wanted Uncle Ray. I wanted a Jack Daniels. I wanted to crawl up in Roger's arms and forget everything. Instead, I checked on Barry. He had no visible scars. As I lifted him out, I saw a paper folded in the bottom of the bag. I didn't have time to read it, so I put it in my bag, found Barry a few bugs, and shoved down the three malaria pills I had forgotten to take over the last twenty hours. I figured they were the same as birth control pills—you just took more if you missed a couple. Afterwards, I took a sponge bath, basically, in bug spray.

I considered changing, but I didn't want to give Cassandra the satisfaction, so I donned my second best pair of heels and hurried to the huge stone lodge, which was covered in vines thick as pine trees.

The A-line lounge looked out on the plains. You could just make out a sliver of sun above the horizon, the sky above it orange, pink, and Yankees blue. The room was built around a fireplace that would hold about four linebackers. Three other guests stood by the Colonial bar.

"Cyd Redondo, Redondo Travel," I said, with my best professional smile. Every traveler was a potential client, even if they were wearing hemp. If you were going for a distinctive fragrance, hemp mixed with human sweat was the ticket. We went through the introductions as I reached for the hardest liquor I could find. Unfortunately, this was an organic cabernet from Zimbabwe. Sam and Helene Arnold shared matching Magellan safari suits and wrinkles. The other guest, Jason, wore rimless glasses and a pedometer on his beefy, undeveloped arm.

"What did I miss?" I asked, offering them wine.

"Mostly environmental instructions. At home green isn't this…well, green," Sam said.

"Didn't your travel agent brief you?"

"We booked online."

"Ah." I gave them a pitying look and offered my card. "I never send my clients anywhere I haven't tried myself."

"Thank you," Helene said. "I like your dress."

"Thanks. Sale." Two other people came in.

Helene pointed to a drab brunette. "That's Emily. She has a lot of allergies. A lot."

Emily sneezed on cue. Sam looked out the window. "Helene," he said, "zebras."

"I'm talking, honey."

I almost spilled my wine when Cassandra walked in on Roger's arm. What was this, the nineteenth century? She was wearing another see-through outfit that flowed around her praying-mantis frame. It was so easy for tall women to have a flow. On me, things just sort of sat.

Emily cornered Cassandra. I could hear the high-pitched whine of her allergic voice from across the room. I saw my opening and took it, following Roger to the window.

"Hi. I was worried you wouldn't come," Roger said.

"I wasn't going to. But some things came up. Do you think you can keep yoga girl away for a minute?"

"It's not what you think." He took me by the

elbow and moved me out onto the veranda. The sun was gone now, replaced by a deepening blue and the soundtrack from a PBS Nature show. Roger turned me toward him. "Okay, I know you're upset with me, but you have to understand that when you…well, happened to me, it wasn't something I planned. And it may not have been convenient, but that doesn't mean it wasn't real." He looked down at me and I turned to jelly. This was ridiculous. I was a grown woman with a long and varied boyfriend history. This was stopping, now.

"Let me tell you about the last twenty-four hours I've had since I found out my plus one was a lying, cheating shit heel, okay? I found out my neighbor, Mrs. Barsky, was murdered by poison from a dart frog—I think the same kind that are in the suitcase—are they still in there?" Roger nodded. "Well, be careful. Then, I was kidnapped at gunpoint and tied up in a house full of unstitched reptiles."

"That's why Magnum P.I. brought you in his helicopter? You were kidnapped? Come on, Cyd."

"Will you let me finish?"

"Not willingly," he said.

"That's not the point. Courtesy is hardly ever voluntary. Then, the embassy couriers stole Barry and we had to hide in an aid van, where a nineteen-year-old refugee from Outward Bound shoved a machete in my face and took my favorite shoes."

He started laughing. "Come on, Cyd, just forgive me. I really am sorry. You don't need to make up a bunch of stuff to make me feel bad."

I had perfected the "whip around" by age twelve. Not being believed was a very sore subject for me. I planted my heels about ten inches apart, and put my hands on my hips.

"First, I am not interested in you or anything about you except as it regards your travel plans. Second, I would never make up a story involving reptiles or guns to get attention from any man, especially one from California. Third, I have evidence."

He was still laughing.

"Fine. Where the hell do you think I got this?" I said, as I jerked the revolver out of my bag. At least that took the grin off his face.

"Gun!" Emily croaked from inside. The pedometer guy dove behind the bar.

# Chapter Twenty-five

"Ms. Redondo, put down the gun." I turned to see Cassandra holding a .357. I held mine steady.

"It's not real," Roger said.

"It is too real," I said. "I cut a cobra in half with it this morning."

"Cyd, please. There's no need to keep up the pretense. We're among friends."

"Maybe you are."

He stood right in front of me and shook his head. Finally, I loosened my grip and he put the gun in the back of his cargo pants. His belt was hemp, of course.

"Sorry everyone," he said to the guests gathered in the doorway. "Just a little good-natured African gun play, Hemingway style."

Cassandra rolled her eyes but lowered her gun. Roger reached for that one too. "It's my fault. I told her never to admit it wasn't real. No harm, no foul?"

Cassandra smiled at him, then turned to me.

"Ms. Redondo, it seems you are not entering into the spirit of our lodge. Perhaps in the morning, as you are a travel agent, you can make other arrangements for yourself."

Although I had every intention of doing just that, there was no way she was winning this fight.

"Ms. Phoenix, frankly I'm shocked that you would pull a live weapon on an unarmed guest. It's a good thing I was able to document your behavior," I said, having used my last shred of phone battery to snap a photo of her with gun aloft, looking completely deranged. Everyone nodded soberly when they saw the clear digital image of the gun pointed right at me.

"As Mr. Claymore always says, I'm just an orphaned Tupperware tart from Brooklyn, hardly a threat to someone with a loaded weapon. It is loaded, isn't it Roger?" Everyone watched as he checked Cassandra's gun and nodded. "I have prepaid an extremely high premium for this safari," I lied. "I am a member in good standing of every major international travel organization and have twice been the president of The Bay Ridge Third Avenue Businessperson's Association. I have acted in good faith and yet have already been denied the upgrade I paid for. And now, within an hour of my arrival, and while having a personal conversation with one of my clients, you have threatened me with live ammunition. I'm sure *Fodors*, *The Rough Guide*, *The Lonely Planet*, and *Let's Go! Africa* will be grateful for this documented information, should this argument go any further. Now, I'm sure dinner will be delicious. Let's eat, shall we?"

Cassandra gave a small nod and moved toward the table, apologizing to the other guests on the way. Roger and I followed.

"Gun, please," I said.

"No."

"People are after me," I said. He kept walking. "People from the government." He ignored me. "I'll start screaming." Finally, he handed it over.

"Keep the safety on, for God's sake. I'll find you after dinner."

We all sat down. I was starving. In fact, I could have used an enormous piece of undercooked meat, but this was, of course, at Roger's request, a vegetarian tour. I muttered an obscenity under my breath and reached for the mashed yams.

As I bit into the chewy, bitter potatoes, I tried not to make eye contact with the pedometer guy on my left, whose name was Jason and who was staring at my breasts. Asthmatic Emily gave me several dirty looks. Jason said the trip had been a present from his parents in hopes he'd not spend so much time on the Internet. He was about to explain how many steps he'd taken today when Cassandra saved me by standing up and tapping her glass. We all looked up from our mangoes.

Under other circumstances, I might have admired her guts. After all, to come to Africa and start a camp like this and make a go of it was no small feat. I couldn't even keep my clients out of jail or keep a guy for four days. Who was I to judge?

"The joke's on her," Jason said, pointing to Cassandra. "You can't keep people from the Internet. It's our inalienable right."

"Wait, you have the Internet here?"

He nodded. "You could come to my tent," he said. Oh boy, here we go.

"Great. I'll come by later." He must have a power source and my phone was completely dead. It was going to be tricky, but I'd been a longtime virgin and knew how to keep men at bay without anyone getting violent. Too bad I hadn't done it with Roger.

After dinner, Cassandra told the group Faraji had sighted a pride of lions near one of the watering holes, so we were heading there before first light. She reminded us to drink water, take our malaria pills, and pull the mosquito net down fully. Faraji accompanied us back to our tents.

The trail was gorgeous at night, shimmering with mosquito torches every few feet. The tents were as see-through as Cassandra's blouses. I didn't know what was worse, dressing in the dark in the jungle or having everyone know the kind of shapewear I needed to make this dress fit. I opted for dark.

Mosquitoes the size of travel umbrellas buzzed and bumped against the tent flap. I was just down to my Spanx when there was a knock on the tent. God, was Roger here already? I grabbed a nightgown and long peignoir I'd brought for just this kind of occasion. It was a very light pink chiffon with marabou trim and matching mules. I'd gotten it at a fire sale at La Petite Coquette in the West Village. I put all my new bronze bracelets on at once, creating a solid shimmer all the way to my elbow. How was my hair? Did I need my gun? I looked out of a slit in the tent. It was Jason.

"I know you wanted to use my charger and the Internet, so I thought I'd bring everything over. You shouldn't be wandering alone out here at night."

I could smell his aftershave from three feet away. This was bad. "That's very kind of you," I said.

"Can I come in?"

"I was just changing clothes. Give me a second." I threw on my leopard print rain poncho over the marabou and let him in. He unloaded his bag: aside from his laptop, nothing looked bigger than a pack of Camel Lights. Then he held out a tiny black box.

"Solar-powered generator," he said. "I got it for contributing to NPR."

"The Charlton Heston guys?" I figured playing that dumb might scare him off. Sadly not, as he just moved a little closer. "Any chance I could charge my phone?"

"Sure, do whatever you want." Still staring at my breasts, he handed me the charger. My phone made a comforting little chirping sound. It showed multiple messages. I reached for it.

"No, don't." He grabbed my hand. I disentangled it carefully. "You have to wait for it to charge at least half an hour. It's no problem. I'm happy to hang out."

"Okay. Can we check CNN International?"

"Sure." He sat down on the bed with his laptop. I locked my knees together, just like the nuns taught me. "You're really pretty," he said. "Most of the women I meet doing eco-tourism are, well, hairy. But not you. You look great, whatever you're doing. That dress you were wearing earlier. Wow."

"I was worried people would judge me because it's synthetic."

"It is? I thought pretty much everything came in natural these days."

"Nothing that fits really well," I said. "CNN?" Out of the corner of my eye, I saw a dark shape outside the tent.

"I see what you mean about tourists in trouble." Jason pointed to the box on the left of the screen. "There's dysentery on a cruise ship and these old people just got arrested for smuggling snakes at Heathrow."

I gave a small scream. There, on the front page of the CNN International website, were two more of my clients from Bay Ridge—the Giannis. They had flown out of Dar es Salaam the day before Roger and I arrived. Mrs. Gianni was the kind of person who wouldn't even stand in front of the yellow line on the subway or cheat during Lent. There is no way she had brought an endangered monitor lizard through Customs. The story featured their mug shots: Mr. Gianni's wispy comb-over was unsettled and, without makeup, Mrs. Gianni's eyebrows and lips had all but disappeared. The looks on their faces pierced right through my underwire and straight into my heart. What the hell was going on? I needed my phone.

Jason was staring at me. "You know them?"

"Since I was eight," I said. "I booked their trip. Can I check my messages yet?"

"Another few minutes, to be safe." Then he grabbed me and shoved his tongue down my throat.

"Hey." I kicked him hard in the shin until he loosened his grip. He yanked his charger away, sending the phone flying across the wooden floor, and threw everything into his bag.

"I thought you were different, but you're just like every other green bitch in the world." He stormed out, knocking one of the tent pegs loose.

Shit. I didn't mean to upset him. I decided to offer him upgrade vouchers and ran out of the tent, marabou flying in my wake. I stopped mid-flight, arrested by the sight of Roger walking down the path with Cassandra.

There was a loud hiss, then impact.

# Chapter Twenty-six

Something red and sticky was all over me. Was it blood?

"Murderer! Fur wearer! No furs! No skins! No synthetics! Save the Earth!"

Emily stood in an unflattering nylon poncho. She pointed the spray can at me again. I felt the weight of the bracelets on my forearm and aimed all of them right for her runny nose.

"Tahhhh," she screamed, the yelp full of phlegm. "Violence is murder."

Jason had appeared behind her and several other travelers were gathering.

"This is marabou, you moron," I said. "They shed. No birds died for this negligee. And by the way, hasn't anyone told you you could do something with yourself if you wore a little blush and a two-inch heel?"

"I don't want to be a whore like you, chasing the only eligible man here." She gazed at Jason, who'd moved beside her.

"Yeah. Prick tease," he said.

"She's nothing of the sort." Roger was suddenly behind me. "Let's all calm down." He moved between me and my attackers and pushed me into the tent. Emily made another lunge with the can just as Roger pulled the main flap shut. Outside I heard Helene scream, "Atmosphere killer! Chemicals suffocate the planet!" and a large thud. Honestly, was this what vacations were like? Maybe I needed another profession. I caught sight of myself in the mirror and did a silent scream.

"It's just paint," Roger said.

"I know that," I said, "I know it's paint and it's never, never going to come out. Would you excuse me a minute?" Although the poncho had taken most of the hit, my peignoir still looked like the victim of a blender accident. I lifted the clothes off, trying not to get paint on anything else, then dropped everything in the tub. I walked back in, wrapped the duvet around me, and sat down. A few drops of paint fell onto the creamy organic cotton.

"I'll wash my hair later."

He shook his head. The melee outside seemed to have died down, but there was still one willowy shape outside the tent.

"Roger? Should I wait for you?" Cassandra and I both waited for the answer.

"I'm going to get try to get some sleep. I'll come by in the morning, before I leave," he said.

"Fine." I knew that particular delivery of "fine." It was a classic of my mother's and basically meant "screw you, you jerk/daughter/mechanic/ gynecologist."

First round to me, but probably not for long, in the state I was in.

"Thank you for getting me out of there," I said.

"I'm sorry about before. You have to admit the story sounded pretty unbelievable."

"Everything is believable sometimes."

He sat down and patted my hand. When men patted me, it was hard not to knock them senseless. I had actually done that with two of my brousins, when they patted me and told me "all girls got Cs in physics." My response, just before I connected my book bag with their heads was "all boys get stitches."

I took my hand away. "Look. In addition to being the prime suspect in a poisoning, I just found out that two of my Tanzania clients have been detained for smuggling at Heathrow. I've got to get out of here so I can do something. Will you help me? Obviously, I can't go back to the embassy."

"Why not?" Roger said. I pulled the diplomatic bag out from under the bed. "You took a diplomatic bag?"

"I had to. Look. Be careful, though."

He unzipped the bag and there was Barry, eyes swiveling up at him. "You have the chameleon?"

"I did, before the embassy couriers stole him and put him in this, marked for Heathrow. That's bad, right?"

"Harrison Belk's always been a privileged douche, but I didn't think he was actually a felon."

"It's probably the creepy Under Under guy. He's the one that took my room number."

Roger went to the tent door and looked out, then turned off the lamp.

"Roger, you are not forgiven yet," I said, hopeful.

"It's just a precaution." He sat across from me. "Okay, start from the beginning." He wrote some of it down and kept shaking his head and swearing under his breath as I explained.

"Roger, do you think the smugglers murdered Mrs. Barsky? Maybe they were laundering animals in Brooklyn. The frog thing seems like too much of a coincidence."

"I don't know, but you need to keep out of it."

"How? I'm a suspect. The only way to stay out of it is to find out who really did it."

"Well, at least give me the gun."

"No way. I earned that gun and I still might need it. You should get one too."

"Why would I need a gun? Cyd?"

"When the guys at the embassy asked me where the animals were, I told them you had them. How was I supposed to know they were after Barry?"

"Barry? Who the hell is Barry?"

I pointed at the diplomatic bag. "Barry."

"You named the chameleon Barry?"

"You're more than welcome to use his scientific name if Barry is too ethnic for you. Look, are you going to help me? Please don't make me call Uncle Ray." He reached over and I leaned into his shoulder, smearing paint on his scratchy beige shirt and breathing in almond shampoo and sunscreen.

"Okay. Okay. Just let me think for a minute."

I didn't know how he could think while we were hugging this way. I certainly couldn't. I turned toward him and it looked for a minute like he might kiss me. Then, he didn't. Instead, he took me by the shoulders and moved me back about a foot.

"Cyd? It's really over with Alicia. Now that you know about her, could we start over? And go slower this time, maybe?"

I knew it was a bad idea, but I nodded anyway. He kissed me on the forehead and stood up. Wow. When he said "slower," I guess he meant glacial. Still, it was better than a pat.

"Why don't you get a good night's sleep? I have to go meet some people from the World Wildlife

Fund in the morning to deliver the animals. They're sending a truck for me. I'll be back tomorrow night and we'll figure out the rest."

"Tomorrow night will be too late for my clients."

"Why not call the family?"

"I am their family. I mean, their twins died in a car crash. They're seventy-five. They don't really have anyone else. It has to be me. Take me with you."

"No, I can't. Absolutely not."

"Why not? I won't be in the way."

"Yes, you will. You can't help yourself. Besides, I don't want you more involved than you already are. Look, the guys I'm meeting will at least have satellite phones. I'm sure all the wildlife control guys know each other. Heathrow might listen to them. Give me all the information."

I did.

"You look good in red," he said. "Just have a good time on the safari tomorrow. It will give you a chance to check lions off your list." He started to go, then turned. "Oh, I'd better take the chameleon."

"Why?"

"He's not a pet, Cyd, he's a wild animal."

"I know that. Can I say good-bye at least?" I walked to the tent wall and picked off a huge moth with my fingernails. It turned out acrylic nails were really good for this kind of thing. I held the bug up and Barry's tongue came out, grabbed it, and went back in. He was a kind of magenta at the moment, like the torches. "Bye, Barry," I said. "Don't ever change." Who can resist a little chameleon humor?

Roger told me to be careful and I told him not to touch the frogs. He took the diplomatic bag and left me in the dark, the jungle noises louder, now that he was gone.

I heard the familiar sound of hemp on jungle floor as he walked away. Why didn't Roger want me to come with him? And why was he taking notes about the embassy? How did he really know the guys at the Wildlife Service? And could I trust strangers to save the Giannis? He may have braved my family and rescued me from an environmentalist, but there was no way I was going to put my clients' future, Mrs. Barsky's murder, or Barry in the hands of a womanizing chiropractor, however cute. I had to get to a working phone myself.

It was too bad about the lions, but I was going to be on that truck in the morning.

# Chapter Twenty-seven

I spent the next hour getting paint out of my hair and trying my phone. It still didn't have enough charge to retrieve my messages. I paced for awhile in my paint-flecked mules, then repacked to calm my nerves. I counted my malaria pills; I had given most of them to Roger and I didn't have many left. I didn't want malaria; my olive skin already looked a little yellow in the winter. Jaundiced, I was going to be positively fluorescent. Out of habit, I picked up a cockroach with tweezers. Was I actually going through lizard withdrawal? Was there such a thing?

I decided to reorganize my bag and found the embassy document. I pulled Mrs. Barsky's waybills out of my carry-on to compare. The embassy papers also had the word CITES and lots of Latin. Then I saw the words "importation certificate" and *Chamaeleonidae*. Had the embassy been planning on importing Barry the chameleon? And if the documents went with the animals, why did

Mrs. Barsky's documents come by themselves? Or did they? And was the embassy connected to the "fuckity" guys? They must be. And if so, how did Brooklyn fit in? And where was Bobby Barsky? None of it made any sense. Maybe the Wildlife Service guys would have some answers.

I didn't sleep. How could I? Around four I gave up and decided to get dressed. As I was going undercover, I chose a light green chiffon shirt with a leopard print bra underneath, my metallic green snakeskin skirt, and my kitten heels in pony skin. In this outfit, I could fade into any jungle landscape.

It was still dark when a rusted green pick-up rolled in, about fifty yards from the camp. I kept my lights off, and finished my makeup by propping my emergency mini flashlight in the sink. Let's face it, no one looks good lit from beneath. I carried my shoes and snuck out the back.

The truck was parked next to a stand of baobab trees. I double-checked that I had my return e-ticket, my passport, my moisturizer, my Spanx, the waybills, and my phone charger. All set. I angled around the side of the vehicle. There were some burlap sacks and a few cages right behind the cab. So much for my outfit. I hoisted my purse and carry-on up, then put all three of us under the scratchy bags.

I heard Roger's voice. Footsteps moved around

to the back and I watched the driver take the suitcase and place it behind his seat. He reached for
the diplomatic bag, but Roger kept it.

"Suit yourself," the driver said in a four-pack-
a-day voice. With his sweaty red bandanna, he
looked more like a Hell's Angel than a conser-
vationist. I heard one truck door slam, then the
other. The engine started like a jackhammer and
the force of it threw me against the back wall as it
reversed. Behind us, I saw Emily sneaking out of
Jason's tent. I felt better.

Travel bloggers had clearly underreported the
severity of the African pothole. No wonder tourists
wore helmets on the bus. I needed some kind of
seat belt or I was going to fly out of the truckbed
altogether. I dug around in my carry-on and found
a scarlet satin ribbon belt from J.Crew that I used
as a headband when I wanted to be jaunty. I tied
it around my middle and hooked it to one of the
cages. It wasn't that secure, but it would at least
keep me from bouncing into the driver's eye line.
I worried about Barry. If this felt like a bouncing
castle to me, what was it doing to something his
size?

As soon as the sun was more than a fingernail's width above the horizon, it became almost
unbearably hot under the burlap and the road got
worse. I was going to hurt for weeks. I wondered

how good a chiropractor Roger really was, or if he could recommend one in the borough? Maybe he could get me a colleague discount.

I tried for the fortieth time to get comfortable, and then, as the road narrowed, I hit the cab so hard I actually yelled. The truck jerked, then stopped. Both doors slammed. Roger sounded upset. The other guy was grunting and I heard them moving toward the back. This was bad. I waited for someone to uncover me.

"Be careful," Roger said. "He may just be stunned." He?

"He's going to be dinner later, so what difference does it make? This one's mine, fair and square, a clean kill," the driver said. I wasn't too familiar with the World Wildlife Fund as an organization, but I couldn't really imagine the words "clean kill" were in their literature.

"Yeah, you're right. Okay, heave," Roger said. Heave what?

I stayed as still as I could when they pulled down the tailgate and threw something massive and smelly on top of me, then got back in the truck.

I waited until we were moving to see what was poking me in the neck. I found four warthog tusks about an inch from my face, the creature's spiky hooves digging into my ankles, its breath like a landfill. Let's just say, these animals had an extreme makeover in *The Lion King*. I did my best to roll out from under it.

Was it dead? No. I could see its ribs rising. Then, its eyes opened and it looked right at me. I didn't want to touch it, but those eyes killed me. They closed again and it gave an alarming shudder. As the truck sped up, I did my best to stay positive, lying under itchy burlap, sweating through my chiffon, and trying to avoid impalement.

Eventually, we hit an even narrower and bumpier road, if that were possible. By now, pain was my "resting" state. At least it distracted me from the itching. I didn't even want to think about what the roller coaster ride was doing to my shoes, which were slapping the metal truckbed in a frenzy. I not only loved these shoes, I needed them, after losing my Stuart Weitzmans to the weepy aid worker and my marabou mules to the whining animal activist.

Finally, the truck slowed down, waking the warthog. It began slamming its head and kicking its hooves way too close to vulnerable parts of my anatomy, like my brain. I rolled as flat and close to the edge of the truckbed as I could, as the animal went more and more berserk, giving me a good kick in the thigh.

As soon as the truck rolled to a stop, the warthog jerked upright and tried to jump out of the back. Its legs were a little too short and it could only get halfway over, its bristly behind still in the truck. I heard a yell and what sounded like a rifle cock. Geez, were they going to shoot it in front of conservationists? Trying to stay under the burlap, I moved over and gave its haunches a shove up and over. I heard a thud and then hooves scrabbling on leaves. There was a huge blast beside my head, then a curse. I was genuinely starting to feel for these animals, just out of the sheer number of things they seemed to be up against.

I quickly reorganized myself into a bag shape and wiped my hands on the burlap, not sure exactly which part of the warthog I had touched. I waited for the sound of the tailgate, but instead, heard feet moving away. The *eau de warthog* gave way to dung and dead mouse. The World Wildlife Fund wasn't much on cage hygiene. I could barely breathe.

Then I heard something that made me gulp down a whole mouthful of fetid air.

"How in the fuckity universe could anyone miss that shot?"

# Chapter Twenty-eight

My former captor, Henrik the Reptile Guy, yelled something else, but it was buried in high-pitched, hiccoughing squeaks, castrated turkey gobbles, and something that sounded like a saw going back and forth. The gunshot had set the animals off. Clearly the smugglers who had kidnapped me had tricked Roger into coming here. He needed help. I had already shot the fuckity universe guy in the arm, so he couldn't be too effective, but the other guys I'd only bumped and maced. I found the gun in my bag and checked the ammunition. I had four bullets left. It's not like I was a great shot. In fact, if the cobra were any indication, I did better with my eyes closed. The bad guys didn't know that, at least.

I edged the burlap off my face and tried to look through the back window of the truck. It was so filthy, I could barely see the keys in the ignition. I used a corner of the bag to clean a small hole. The truck had stopped inside a large compound ringed with acacia trees, scattered like open umbrellas around the buildings. There were a series of worn pathways, fenced pens, barbed wire, metal gates with padlocks, small huts, and one long, low concrete building with barred windows.

At the far left of the property was a Colonial-style house with a wide, sagging porch and peeling white trim. That must be where they had taken Roger. I would have to stick to the trees and try to work my way around. First I freshened up with Obsession and put my carry-on under the burlap. I grabbed my purse, climbed over the side, and used my emergency mini lint roll to remove an alarming amount of warthog hair from my blouse.

I could see a native man with a gun roaming the property, so I stayed low, limping to a small stand of gum trees and ducking into the closest hut. I squeezed myself between two stacks of cages filled with tiny monkeys crammed against each other and covered in filth. One row over were hundreds of birds in the same shape. Compared to this, the cobra hotel was practically a spa.

I heard the guard go by, waited a second, then snuck out, trying to shake feathers and bird shit off my shoes and ducking behind one of the huge clay urns that seemed to be all over the property. They were certainly big enough for a person my size to hide in if I scrunched down. When he turned away for a minute, I started to push the heavy lid aside, only to have a black snake, thick and slimy as an Italian sausage, start to crawl up my arm. Luckily, I was startled into speechlessness. The whole urn was full of them, tangled like earthworms and squirming right up to the top. I shook it off and slammed the lid. It made a loud crack. The guard turned around.

The urn was still in front of me. I didn't want to waste a bullet on him or alert the men in the house. I was just pulling the Mace out of my purse when he moved away. I fled for the cover of the concrete building and peeked in through the bars.

The walls were stacked to the ceiling with cages and wriggling bags. Workers moved back and forth between the cages and long, low tables. At the table nearest me, two men stood beside a mountain of tiny, squirming tortoises. One of the men had a roll of masking tape in one hand. The first man was picking up a baby tortoise and hitting it, hard. When it pulled its heads and legs into the shell for protection, the second man rolled masking tape twice over every opening, turning it into a neat, round tortoiseshell compact. They stacked five or six "compacts" each into pairs of thick white athletic socks and rolled them up, stacking them on the end of the table. How were the turtles supposed to breathe?

A man in a leather apron yelled, then pointed a hose at three cages full of some of the most beautiful birds I'd ever seen: they had electric yellow wings and scarlet heads, with beaks thin as pins. I gasped as the man sprayed black paint into the cages, turning the exotic creatures into common crows in about ten seconds. How awful to have paint in your eyes. Then I saw something so much worse.

I could make out three men with needles and thread, sewing parrot eyelids together.

At that point, I almost fainted. I knew I had to keep it together, but the idea of sewing eyelids on anything, even a doll, made me queasy. It was like I was in a bad Tim Burton movie. These people were monsters. God, what might they be doing to Roger? I had to get to the house.

As I passed by the next hut, I heard a loud hiss. I turned, ready to Mace another snake, but the second time the hiss sounded human. I cracked the door and saw a cage with three lion cubs and another with a large cheetah pacing in a tiny circle. I heard the hiss again and turned. There was Akida, sitting on the filthy floor in yet another Easter egg-colored Ralph Lauren polo shirt, with his hands and feet tied. He had worked part of the duct tape loose around his mouth.

"Oh, my God," I said, reaching for my emergency plastic cuticle scissors. I hadn't even gotten half the tape off before he started apologizing. Behind me, the cats started yowling.

"Cyd Redondo, I am so sorry. Are you all right? Is Mr. Claymore all right?"

"I think Mr. Claymore is inside the house," I said. I kept chewing at the rope with my scissors. It was pretty much hopeless.

"We must help him. I am very fine. I'm delightful, don't worry about me," Akida said, trying to smile. "Really. How can I be of assistance?"

"How many men are here? Do you know?" The cheetah started a low growl, while the lion cubs purred and rolled around, reaching their miniscule paws toward me through the bars.

"Approximately ten, I believe," he said. "Five in the workroom, one guard, and the other three men. Sometimes they bring in extra workers for the packing. And him."

"Who's him?" I asked, trying to undo a knot that was beyond my Girl Scout capability.

"Very dangerous man. Very dangerous."

"Well, I'll just have to trust the element of surprise. I'll be back to get you out," I said and headed out the door. It's always easier to do something stupid when you're morally incensed. I saw the guard head into the trees to relieve himself and started for the house. I found a small shrub beside a window on the left side and ducked behind it.

The screened window was open. The outside of the house might be bedraggled, but the front room looked like an Ikea showroom. In fact, there were at least two items from the Fall catalogue, plus a huge flat-screen TV, and several trophy heads on the wall, including a rhino's head that would have made Uncle Leon drool. There was a tiger rug on the floor. And someone had thrown a pile of tusks in the corner, like used gym clothes. This was clearly where endangered animals came to die.

The two other flunkies from the reptile kitchen, Moe and Jock, sat on a black leather couch beside fuckity Henrik, who was dressed down in an AC-DC t-shirt and cargo shorts, a sling on his injured arm and a tattoo of a plump mermaid on his good one. Moe had a black eye and his face was still red and blotchy from the Mace. His football shirt barely covered his watermelon belly and the lumpy layers on his forearm. He was wearing jeans, so at least I was spared seeing the flab valance I imagined hanging over his knees. Where was Roger?

I took out my folding makeup mirror and angled it to see the rest of the room. The truck driver was rolling a cigarette on the glass coffee table and Jock, the skinny criminal, was wearing an outfit worthy of Bay Ridge—a tight silk shirt and even tighter polyester pants. Both items looked stiff with dried sweat. The bastard was handing Roger a beer.

# Chapter Twenty-nine

A beer? Why were they handing Roger a beer? Was it poisoned? I raised up to get a better view and saw the fifth man. He was about sixty and steroid large, with a grizzled, ineffective ponytail, a ski-jump nose, and the red cheeks of a drinker. His filthy safari shorts exposed a prosthetic leg the color of Silly Putty. There was something familiar about him.

Then Roger smiled at him and lifted his Budweiser. "To a mutually successful enterprise," he said. They clinked their bottles. I couldn't process what I was seeing, especially when Roger opened the Andersons' suitcase and lifted out the parrot sausages. He shared a weird, macho chuckle with the other men.

"We owe you, my friend," said the peg-legged man, his accent more Coney Island than Cape Town.

"Yes you do, Bunty," Roger said, the diplomatic bag at his feet. "Let's talk about my finder's fee."

So this was Bunty. The boss. This was the man responsible for planting those parrots and turtles in the Andersons' luggage in Dar es Salaam. And probably the lizards in the Giannis' luggage too. The bastard.

"What's to keep us from killing you and just taking the animals?" Henrik said.

"I don't think you want to complicate things with Mr. Chu. He's grateful I prevented the luggage from being examined at the airport. Besides, you'll still clear two hundred grand. The chameleon alone, with these unusual markings, is worth half that," he said, bringing out Barry. I yelped, but no one seemed to hear.

Oh, my God. I was such an idiot. My plus one was a conniving, beer-swilling, chuckling, animal smuggler and I'd given him the perfect cover. He hadn't come for me, he'd come for the wildlife. How could I have been so stupid? Not only had I gone to him for help, I had given him Barry. As soon as I got my hands on that diplomatic bag, Barry and Akida were coming with me. I only hoped the keys were still in the truck.

First I had to get Akida loose. I looked around the yard for something to cut his ropes with and found a machete leaning against the side of the house; it seemed to be the go-to gadget of Africa. I didn't know if I could cut the ropes off Akida without amputating something, but it was better than cuticle scissors. Plus, it might make the guard think twice before he shot me.

I ducked behind the house as Bunty, Henrik, and Roger walked out the front door. Sadly, Moe and Jock stayed behind. Henrik lugged a case of Budweiser toward a pond at the back of the property. Bunty followed with a wire cage. I got out my mini binoculars and saw, to my horror, the pond was full of crocodiles. Suddenly, Bunty's missing leg made sense.

Bunty handed out beers, then reached into the cage and started flinging live rats into the water. The reptiles knocked back the squealing rodents like M&M's, their jaws cracking with every bite. The men laughed. It was time for me to make my move. I ducked into the hut.

"Did you save Roger Claymore?" Akida whispered.

"Those guys can keep him," I said, holding up the machete. Akida whimpered. "Shhh. I'm not going to hurt you, you idiot. This is to cut the rope."

"Oh," he said. "Do not cut the ropes. You must leave me here. Otherwise, I will lose my job."

"Your job? Shit. You, too, Akida? Really?" This one hurt.

"I am so ashamed. I am the breadwinner for my whole family. I did not know anyone might be hurt. Please leave before they know you are here. It is best for you and for me. Re-book your reservation and go home. There are no change fees or penalties. Put the tape back on my mouth, please. And good luck, Cyd Redondo."

I re-taped his mouth and shook his bound hands. Back outside, I saw Moe and Jock had joined the others at the rat massacre. I ran for the house.

The living room reeked of cigarettes, beer, and stale luncheon meat. I found the diplomatic bag. Barry was intact, so far, but he needed more protection. It killed me, but I was going to have to sacrifice some Tupperware. Once Barry was safely armored and "air-holed" inside my purse, I put a few parrot sausages and some sock tortoises in the diplomatic bag, then made a mad dash for the truck and jumped into the front seat.

I turned the key and, miraculously, it started. Then Moe spotted me and yelled. Just when I hit my first pothole, a bullet flew in the back window and out the windshield. I heard an engine.

Seriously? Was I going to die for a lizard? I had just wanted a simple Atlantic City fling, and to go on vacation like a normal person. Was that so wrong? For once, I wished my family were here to overprotect me. I tried to imagine what Eddie would do in this situation.

I saw a stretch of straight road ahead. Maybe

I could aim the truck and jump out with Barry? They'd follow the truck and I could hide. It wasn't a brilliant plan, but it was all I had. I could see dust gathering behind me. I was just about to take off my seat belt when the truck made the decision for me. The engine stopped dead. I turned the key again and again as it rolled to a stop. Nothing.

A filthy Range Rover screeched up behind the truck. I didn't know what was safer—to barricade us in the truck or run for it. Then I heard Roger's voice. Or a version of his voice.

"Out of the vehicle. Slowly. And no talking."

The vehicle? Really? I did as much of a whip-around as I could, given I was still wearing my seat belt. I kept one hand on my purse and started to roll down the window.

Roger looked back. The guys were out of the Rover and fully armed. Roger pointed his gun in my face.

Needless to say, this pissed me off.

"Assault with a deadly weapon? Is that really necessary? We had sex four days ago," I said, releasing the seat belt. God, had it only been four days?

"Just get out of the car and you won't be hurt."

"Too late. You might have mentioned you were an animal smuggler when we promised to 'start over' last night."

Roger leaned in with the gun barrel and

lowered his voice. "Cyd, please get out of the car so I can save your life. I barely stopped them spraying the truck with bullets as it was. And don't act like you know me, or it's going to blow everything."

"Believe me, it's blown."

"Now." Roger opened the door.

I stepped down, gripping my bags. It was a big drop for a short girl in heels. He jerked my arm to help me down and grabbed the diplomatic bag out of the truck.

"Hey. The chameleon is in there," I lied.

"I know. They know that too. Just move forward slowly and act pissed."

"Oh, that'll be hard." I shuffled forward, trying to keep one eye on Roger and one eye on the guys in front of me, which wasn't easy. I wished I had Barry's three hundred-sixty-degree eyes, as I saw how, when you were endangered, they would really come in handy. Bunty was leaning on his good leg and blatantly staring at my chest. Maybe the leopard print bra had been a mistake.

"I'll take care of her." Roger kept the gun on my back.

"Yeah, you just want her for yourself," Jock said. They all chuckled.

"Yeah, maybe," Roger said, chuckling too.

I seriously considered the "upwards ball kick" at that moment.

"Well, she killed our king cobra and shot me, so I think we get a fuckity go at her, too," Henrik said. "Right, Bunty?"

Bunty scratched his plastic leg. He was evaluating me in a way that wasn't entirely sexual, more like he was considering me as a food source. "We might be able to use her." He turned to the driver.

"Chip, fix the truck. What happened when it stopped?" he asked me.

Like I would help him. Henrik cocked his pistol. "It just stopped," I said. "The lights came on and when I tried to start it again, everything died."

"Alternator," the thugs all said, simultaneously.

"That gives us at least a week with her," Jock said.

"In your dreams, moron."

"I like 'em feisty," he said.

"I like them with a penis larger than a Vienna sausage."

He came toward me and Roger jerked me back. Jock flicked his tongue.

"You're all morons," I said. "It could just be corrosion on the battery." I hoped it was—I needed that truck.

"She's right. Check the terminals first," Bunty said. "Karl, take her back."

Who was Karl? Roger grabbed my arm and pushed me toward the compound.

"Karl?" I hissed. I tried to jerk my arm away, but he pushed the gun into my side.

Ten yards later, his normal voice came back. "If you hadn't followed me, neither of us would have a problem. What the hell were you thinking? I will get you out of here, but you need to play along or you're going to ruin everything."

"Ruin what? Your international smuggling ambitions?" He pushed me onto the porch as the Range Rover pulled up. "If you're going to tie me up, can you at least do it somewhere near an outlet?" I was still worried about the Giannis. "After all, you have been inside me, you bastard. Three times."

"Four," Roger said and sat me down next to a surge-protector. He stayed in front of me, gun out, while I plugged in my charger.

I looked to my right and saw a glass case filled with dozens of tiny, multi-colored frogs. Were they all poison? Was Bunty Mrs. B's murderer? I mean, how many people had access to poison dart frogs? The men walked back in, this time with Akida, still tied up. Jock tossed the diplomatic bag on the table. These people were idiots. That gave me hope. Bunty sat down, slamming his fake leg onto the glass coffee table with a crack worthy of a hockey puck.

"All right, doll. What's your name?"

Doll? He couldn't be from Africa. I got up, holding out my hand and hoping my bra would keep his mind off the outlet.

"Cyd Redondo, Redondo Travel."

Bunty grabbed onto my hand and didn't let go. "Wait! Not Cyd Redondo from Bay Ridge? Fuck me. No way. No fucking way. You're not Johnny's kid? Cyd the Squid?" Honestly, even in Africa? "I used to work on your dad's car. Moe—get the lady a beer. Here, sit down, sit down. Whatever happened to that car anyway?"

"The Galaxie? I still drive it," I said.

"No shit? Bitchin' ride. Killer suspension on that baby."

Okay, I was on *Car Talk* with a rat-killing, peg-legged animal smuggler from the neighborhood. Then it got worse.

"You don't recognize me, do you? Why would you? Bobby Barsky. Down here they call me Bunty. Do you want some salami? I have it sent down from Mike's."

God, Bunty was Bobby Barsky. And Bunty had sent the waybills to Pet World. Had he killed his own mother? He held out the salami.

"Thanks," I said, to be polite. I was also starving. I broke off a piece and took a long pull on my beer. I could feel Roger and Akida staring at me.

Had Roger known Bunty was Bobby all along, and never told me?

"Hey, guys, this is Cyd from the neighborhood. Last time I saw her she was about a foot high."

"She's not that much taller now," Jock said.

Bunty slapped him and turned to me. "So, how's my mom? You see her, right?"

Wait, he didn't know? What did that mean? Was he screwing with me? "Um, almost every morning. She usually came over for decaf."

"Good, at least it wasn't that Russian tea crap. That stuff'll kill you." Bunty looked me up and down. "Little Cyd Redondo. Ma always liked you. She used to joke that if I didn't behave, she was going to leave the apartment to you. Crazy, right?"

Shit. "Bunty? Has the embassy been in touch?"

"That fucking moron? Somebody needs to string him up by that stupid school tie."

"I meant about your mom?"

The room got silent. Bunty took one look at my face and threw his bottle against the wall. Henrik, Jock, and Moe ducked.

"What about my mom?" Bunty started tapping his artificial foot. "What about her?"

"God, Bobby, I hate to be the one to have to tell you this, but she died. About ten days ago. Joni's been trying to reach you. You're the executor."

He tapped his foot harder. "I know I'm the

fucking executor. What happened?" He leaned closer. Should I lie?

"Don't fuckin' lie to me."

I guess not. "Okay. Um. She was murdered."

"Murdered. The motherfucking CIA," he said. "I knew it. They never let up. That woman was a saint. How? What happened?"

"The Precinct said the killer injected some weird frog poison."

Bunty stood up. I tried not to look at the aquarium, but it was hard not to when he grabbed Jock's throat and shoved him against it, creating a frog ballet. "Morons. I told you not to send the frogs. How many times did I tell you? I must have said it a million fuckin' times, no frogs. No frogs!" Bunty punched Moe in the stomach and the fat man went down. Then he smashed Henrik against the wall.

"We didn't send any frogs, Bunty, I swear," Henrik said. "Mr. Chu's guys must have. Besides, we always duct-tape the frogs within an inch of their fuckity lives. We understand about the frogs. We've never had an accident with the frogs. Somebody on the Brooklyn end screwed up. I swear. That Brooklyn moron screws up all the time." Bunty let go and his henchman slid down the wall. Bunty limped to the couch and started to cry. I had a bad feeling about that Brooklyn moron.

Bunty wailed for a minute, then excused himself and went into the kitchen. He came back out, wiping his eyes with a bar towel

"What are you lookin' at?" he asked Jock, who was still frozen by the aquarium.

"Sorry, boss. Like you always say, it's the circle of life, right?"

Bunty punched him again, then turned to me.

"So, Squid Redondo, where the hell were you going in my truck?"

"I didn't know it was your truck. This guy Karl took my merchandise, I wanted it back." Bunty sat down. Then he laughed. "My mother always said you had Bay Ridge balls. Good for you. So you're buying your way in? Saying they're your animals?" He raised his eyebrows at Roger. "How much you asking? Considering I'll be carrying all the risk?"

"And taking into account the cobra," Henrik said.

I racked my brains for the numbers I'd heard in the last few days. Roger had said the animals in the luggage were worth half a million. Was that the street price? And where was the endangered animal street, anyway? Bunty was staring at me, waiting. He would want at least a three hundred percent profit. Plus the cobra. I did the math. "One hundred thousand for the bag."

"Minus any en route losses," he said.

"Cost of doing business," I said, shrugging for effect.

"I'll go for fifty," he said. "They were mine in the first place."

"I can't go lower than seventy-five."

Roger glared. He'd obviously never been to a flea market.

"Sixty," Bunty leaned forward. His acrylic ankle squealed against the glass table. "Henrik, get her bank details. The money will be in your account tomorrow."

I was so nervous, I actually wrote down the real numbers. I'd call the bank and cancel the account as soon as I could use my phone.

"Can we still tie her up in the shed for a few days?" Jock asked.

"No. Cyd from the block is not going in the shed."

Outside, I heard the truck's V-8 pull into the compound. The driver, Chip, glared at me as he came in and headed into the kitchen with Bunty. Henrik, Moe, and Jock followed. I managed to grab my phone before Bunty and the driver came back.

"You were right about the battery. Your dad would be proud. Come on, Chip will take you and Karl back to the camp."

Akida rose. "May I return with them as well, sir?"

"No," Bunty said.

"Karl" aka Roger moved me toward the door. I felt really guilty leaving the animals there, but what could I do? At least Barry was still in my purse. Akida whispered something to Roger just before we went down the steps.

"You both ride in the front," Bunty said when we got to the truck. "It's been a pleasure doing business with you. Tell your Uncle Ray I said hello."

"I will," I said. "Sorry about your mom. I'll really miss her."

"Don't worry," he said, "I'll get the bastards who did this."

"Will you call Joni?" I asked. He nodded.

Chip opened the passenger door. I gestured Roger in first. I wasn't interested in being squished up against three-day-old sweat, tobacco, and cumin. The other men were smiling at me, which was creepy. Chip put the truck in gear. I looked through the back window and waved at Bunty. At least I'd found Joni's brother and he was alive. That was something. I'd probably leave out the rest.

Despite the fact that Roger had a common-law wife and was a blatant liar, a criminal, and a general bastard, it was still hard to sit next to him without wanting to climb into his lap. I hated myself for feeling this way, but attraction wasn't really a logical emotion.

The truck had just hit a straight stretch when Roger leaned toward me and whispered, "Get ready."

Ready for what? He reached behind him, pulled a gun from his waistband, and conked Chip a very sound one on the side of the head. He was unconscious instantly, falling over on Roger and pinning him near the floor. The truck began to swerve.

"Steer," he said.

"From here?" I screamed, then put my leg over him and over Chip's head, and grabbed the uncooperative steering wheel. My hands were slick with sweat and slid around the wheel, making me bump and grind pretty much everything and everyone between me and the seat. This was not the kind of lap dance I had in mind. I struggled to miss the potholes, and tried to pull the truck over while Roger wriggled under me, trying to hold Chip up. But the unconscious man kept falling, all dead weight, and finally his lower half slumped down all the way, trapping Roger's foot on the gas and me with my legs in a cheerleader split over Roger's back. We went careening through the trees, decimating everything in our path, then stopped with a horrible crunching smash.

# Chapter Thirty

The truck had gone full-on into a baobab, turning the tree trunk into a giant question mark. I wasn't sure for a minute if we were still alive, and I was pretty sure Barry couldn't be. I heard the steady hiss of steam escaping, or at least I hoped it was steam. Somehow, I was still gripping the steering wheel. Apparently Chip's torso had kept me from flying through what was left of the windshield. The impact had finished the work the bullet holes had started: glass peppered the hood like kosher salt. Lucky for us, the massive V-8 engine block had taken most of the blow. I was sore, but mobile, but Roger just lay there under Chip's leg, completely still.

"Roger?" I touched his shoulder and moved around to see his face. He had a nasty gash on his forehead that was bleeding pretty freely, but he seemed to be breathing. I figured the first order of business was to bind his wound. I could be furious with him once he was conscious. My purse was wedged between Chip's legs and the floorboard. Barry.

I managed to inch the strap free and pull it gently toward me. I took a long breath before I opened it. All things considered, I had been through too much with this chameleon to have him wind up as a stain. But there he was, twitching inside the Tupperware, the Terminator of chameleons. I edged past him for *Lion King* Band-Aids, a bottle of water, and a handkerchief. Just as I finished bandaging Roger, he moaned. I crawled down to look him in the eye and called his name. He moaned again, but didn't open his eyes. I brushed the wound above his eye with my lips.

He started to blink, grimaced, then did his best to give me half a smile. "Cyd. Am I dead?"

"No such luck."

"Are you okay?"

"Are you actually expecting me to think you care? After you smashed up our only form of transportation?"

"I understand you're upset."

"Do you? Really?"

"There were reasons I had to lie to you."

"I bet."

"Look, are you okay or not?"

"I'm fine. So is Barry, I think, as if you care."

"Good. Can you help me up?"

I was torn. As a former boyfriend and smuggler, he didn't deserve my help, but as a client, I was obligated. The job always came before my personal feelings. Or at least I kept telling myself that. The "he was just another client" part.

"Are you sure you should move?"

"I guess we'll find out," he said.

I reached under his back and hoisted him up. "You could have a concussion. You have to try to keep moving and you can't sleep for sixteen hours." He gave me a questioning look. "Disaster training after 9/11," I said. "You never know when a client might land on your lawn."

He laughed and put his hand to his head, feeling the bandage. "Did you do this?" I nodded. "Thanks. We need to get out of here before he wakes up or the truck explodes." Happily, the accident hadn't frozen the doors. We both eased out onto the hard, dry dirt below. Roger winced when he straightened up. The gash on his head was leaking a little.

"Stand still," I pressed another bandage on top of his wound. We looked at each other too long and I backed up, reaching into the truck for my Balenciaga. "Roger? I don't mean to be impolite, but can you tell me why the fuck you had to attack him when he was driving us back to camp?"

"He wasn't driving us to the camp. Akida

heard Bunty tell Chip to drive out five miles and kill us.”

“No way. You saw how upset Bunty was about his mom. I mean, I know he's a criminal, but he wouldn't kill someone from the neighborhood. I mean, he didn't let them put me in the shed, right? He was friends with my dad. It's Bobby.”

“According to Akida, Bunty said ‘Leave her pretty for the casket, out of respect.’ The guy's wanted for multiple murders; he's second in command of a smuggling ring that goes from Jakarta to Belgium. If your friend died from a poison dart frog, whatever he said, I guarantee he had something to do with it. Honestly, Cyd, sorry about the wreck, but it was pretty much best-case scenario.”

“Did you know Bunty was the man I was looking for?”

“Can we talk about this on the run? We have maybe an hour's lead before Bunty's guys come after us. Of course, if they figure out you stiffed them on the chameleon, it might be sooner.”

“There's no way I was leaving Barry there. And don't even think about smuggling him.”

“Suddenly you're an animal activist?”

“Compared to you, yes.”

“Well, you might want to reconsider the snakeskin skirts.”

“Screw you.”

We both stopped at the sound of a small creak. Chip had shifted. That wasn't good. Roger reached into the cab to retrieve his gun, then hit the driver on the head again.

"That will buy us some time," he said.

"What the hell? I guess chiropractors don't really abide by the Hippocratic Oath. Oh, I forgot, you're not a chiropractor." I pulled my warthog encrusted carry-on out of the truckbed, put my purse over my shoulder, shook some fire ants off my shoes, and started for a stand of trees. I thought I saw Mount Kilimanjaro in the distance. Or maybe it was just a knoll. Whatever it was, I was headed for it.

"Where are you going?" Roger asked.

"Somewhere away from you."

"You can't go off by yourself. Bunty's guys will be after you."

"No, they'll be after you. I have camouflage," I said, indicating my outfit. "And besides, you're different from them how?"

"What about your clients? What happens to them if you get eaten or caught?"

# Chapter Thirty-one

Shit. In the middle of all the guns and car wrecks and maimed animals, I had forgotten the Giannis. I was furious at myself and furious at Roger for reminding me.

"Cyd, really, let me come with you."

Honestly, I wasn't that keen on being on my own after nightfall. I shrugged.

"We're not too far from the camp, maybe a day's hike."

"Won't they look for us there?"

"Well, they're less likely to mow us down in front of a lot of pacifists."

"Isn't that the safest place to do it? What are the campers going to do, write a letter?"

"Can you call your Casanova of the skies?" Roger said.

I reached for my phone, which had charged about a fourth of the way. Of course, there was no signal. The image of the Giannis in a Victorian jail cell eating gruel—whatever that was—kept running through my mind.

"We might be able to get a signal on the way." He looked around. "Of course, it would help if we had a map. Or a compass. Or water."

"We have all those things. Who travels without a compass?"

I reached into the most hidden pocket of my Balenciaga and untied a small suede bag, then pulled out a 1929 Wilcox Crittenham compass, its needle still shiny, and found true North.

"Wow. Where did that come from?"

"It was my dad's. Well, my Grandfather Guido's and then my dad's." Roger held out his hand. I'd kept the compass under my pillow every night since I was four and I was loathe to let go. He gave me a questioning look.

"My dad gave it to me on my fourth birthday. I had eaten too much cake and gotten sick. He came and sat on my bed and told me I was destined to be a great explorer. As long as I had the compass, I would never be lost. A month later, he was dead." I gave Roger the compass.

"Oh, Cyd. I'm sorry. Really. Are you okay?"

"Fine," I turned away to pull out my laminated map of Northern Tanzania and put it against what was left of the hood.

"Where are we?" Roger asked.

"Here, I think," I pointed. "Ready to go?"

He looked askance at my carry-on. "Do you really need that?"

"Yes," I said. "If you want the compass and the water, I do." I started looking for bugs for Barry. I put some water in a leaf and held it out to him. I figured even reptiles needed to hydrate. Then I doused myself with Obsession—a girl should always try to be fresh.

Roger whipped his head around. "Do you have to do that?"

"Do what?"

"Smell so good," he said.

I ignored him and started toward the gum trees. "Carry-on," I said over my shoulder. He sighed and picked it up. "Don't sigh. It's two pounds under the limit," I said, as a branch hit me full in the face.

"Here, let me go first." He moved in front.

"How chivalrous," I said. "What a gentleman."

We went in and out of wide swaths of plains and watched for lions in the grass between. Occasionally, Roger would turn back and look at me, but I managed to keep my mouth shut, unless he let a branch fly in my face, at which point I swore, loudly.

"Who's Mr. Chu?" He didn't answer. I had a pretty good idea, but I didn't like it.

I heard several high-pitched yips that I hoped weren't hyenas. Hyenas freaked me out. Finally, the sun began to slide toward the horizon. This seemed to be the universal "all clear" signal for bugs. We both started slapping our arms every four seconds. I saw a particularly obese mosquito on Roger's back and smashed it. I might have hit it a little harder than I had to. I tried to figure out what day it was. It seemed like a week since I had climbed into the back of that truck and seen tortured animals and had two car wrecks and found out Mrs. Barsky's son was the bad guy, but it was still Day Four. Five days left. I still wanted lions, but maybe not when we were on foot.

"Have you been taking your malaria pills?" I asked.

"Of course," Roger said. "You heard what the doctor said would happen if we didn't."

Yeah, I had. I was hoping he'd been right and the last two days had just been one long hallucination. I should be so lucky. I had given Roger most of my pills and only had a few left. I bit one of them in two and took half, checking on Barry in the meantime.

"Rog, do you think he's all right?"

"Who?"

"Barry." I moved up a bit so we were side by side.

"I'm sure he endured worse in that suitcase."

"Yeah. Well, I guess you would know all about that. I know it's a bad economy, but how low does someone have to go to smuggle reptiles for a living? I guess that's why you were in Atlantic City, right? That snake show?" He wouldn't look at me. "Are you going to answer me? I arranged a free trip for you, not to mention the sex. I deserve an explanation," I said, struggling to stay beside him. He sped up. So did I. "Really, why are you doing it? Is it just for the money?"

"Conservation through confiscation."

"What?"

"If we don't get these animals out of places like Madagascar, their habitats are going to disappear and they're going to become extinct, anyway. If we can get the rare animals into the hands of people who'll care for them and breed them, we can save them."

"People like Bunty? Are you out of your mind? Did you see that torture lab? They make Michael Vick look like Gandhi. Besides, I thought that's what zoos were for."

I passed under a vine and stopped. In front of me was a clearing and a small water hole about a quarter of an acre wide. I grabbed Roger's hand and stopped him. Three hippos lolled in one corner and a lone crocodile was submerged on the other side. His yellow eyes and horny head sat just inches above the filthy water. There were herons and gazelles there too, just out of the crocodile's range, I hoped.

A few monkeys came down to the edge and sipped. I'd read that at the end of the dry season, natural enemies were forced together around these water holes for survival. I didn't let go of Roger's hand until we moved on. I felt a rock in my shoe and I leaned against a tree that smelled like an unsanitary spa resort.

"Cyd," Roger said, his voice low the way it was when we first turned the lights off in Atlantic City. I stopped. A pang went through me for the fiftieth time that day, heartsick that I could have been so wrong about him. Was I ever going to make an intelligent decision about men? I put my shoe back on, but when I went to go forward, I couldn't move my feet. The soles of my shoes wouldn't seem to budge. Roger tried to take a step and almost fell backwards, stuck too.

"What the hell?" I said.

"Looks like bird lime."

"Bird what?"

"Bird lime. It's a special native glue. Poachers use it to catch birds. They usually use it on tree limbs. Well, we'll just have to lose our shoes."

"Another pair of shoes?" I whined.

"You need a special potion to dissolve it." He bent over to take off his sandals and wham, we were jerked, shoes and all, up into a massive, thick woven net. Roger was thrown on top of me and we swung there from the wide branch above, like a bag of oranges.

# Chapter Thirty-two

Great. We were stuck in net in the jungle at least ten miles from Phoenix Tours and not nearly far enough from Bunty's compound.

"It's him, isn't it?" I said.

"Bunty? He doesn't trap things himself. Most of the villagers around here work for him, though," Roger said.

"Great. Could you move your leg a little?"

"I can try," he said, squishing me more.

"Ow."

"Do you have anything sharp?"

"Down there," I said, looking wistfully down at my bag on the ground. I had broken the cardinal rule of the bag—never lose physical contact.

I asked Roger to grab my shoes, thinking I could work the heel through the fabric, but they were stuck to the net and the heel was on the wrong side. Finally, after he'd spent five minutes reaching through my legs to grab a heel, we gave up. Imagine playing Twister in a macramé plant holder.

"You're a guy, don't you have a Swiss Army knife?"

"Every guy doesn't carry a knife."

"Every guy I know does. Even I have a knife, it's just in my purse."

"We could try to swing toward the trunk and see if I can get a branch loose."

"A branch? Really?" In the distance, a sawing sound started up, the same noise I'd heard at the compound. "What's that?"

"Nothing."

"What?"

"Nothing. But just in case, stay still and try not to look like food."

"When have I ever looked like food?"

"You looked pretty edible the night we met."

I made my best effort to knee him in the groin and only hit his thigh. "Stop it. Are you actually flirting with me, after all this? You are unbelievable. I can't believe I slept with you."

"You don't mean that."

"Of course I mean it. What did you think was going to happen when I found out?"

"I guess I didn't think you'd find out."

"Right. You assumed I was an idiot."

"You're not an idiot, Cyd. At all."

"Yes, yes I am. I was totally wrong about you. Totally. I'm thirty-two. It's humiliating. My uncle was right about me. I should spend the rest of my life as a geographically challenged spinster." I was not going to cry, dammit.

Roger patted my leg, then took a breath. "Look, if I tell you something, will you promise not to tell anyone or reference it or accidentally mention it, ever?"

"That's a pretty tall order, smuggler boy."

"First, I had no idea you were going to stow away in that truck."

"My stowing away is not the issue. I was just trying to get cell reception. Your lying about going to the World Wildlife Fund and then trying to sell Barry, that's the issue."

"I wasn't trying to sell Barry, not really."

"Roger, I heard the whole thing."

He looked at me for a long time. I heard sawing.

"It was a sting operation."

"What?"

"I'm a federal agent."

"Please. You think I haven't heard that one before?"

"Really. I'm with the U.S. Fish and Wildlife Special Operations Unit."

"Come on. Like that exists."

"Of course it exists. Look, I'm on loan to Interpol, Customs, and the FBI—they're trying to figure out how Bunty and his guys are smuggling animals into the States. I called Interpol when I found the animals in your luggage and they asked if I could do a little bit of undercover work while I was here."

"Undercover? Well, you're certainly good at that."

"Okay, I deserve that. I'd appreciate it if you could try trusting me, since I'm trusting you. If you blow my cover, I'll lose my job and a lot more animals are going to die."

"And this would be my problem, why?"

"It's not, I know. But I can help you with something that is. I can notify Heathrow that someone is planting animals in the luggage from your tour and get your clients out."

"It would have helped if you'd called last night. Why didn't you tell me then?"

"Because I'm not supposed to tell anyone. Ever. That's the whole point of undercover. It's supposed to be a secret, no matter what happens." Roger rolled closer to me.

"No matter who you have sex with, you mean. What about when we met? Were you working then?" I said, trying to move away, but only getting more squished by the net.

"No. Kind of. It's a long story."

"Well, that's reassuring." I tried to think about the Giannis instead of myself. "I won't tell anyone if, the instant we get reception, if you are who you say you are, you call Scotland Yard and tell them my clients were framed by Bunty and this Mr. Chu guy."

"Agreed."

Then there was a whiskery sensation on the bottom of my thigh that didn't feel like Roger. In fact, it couldn't be Roger—I could see both of his hands. I looked down.

"What is it?" Roger said.

I could only nod my head toward the ground.

# Chapter Thirty-three

Underneath the net, sniffing my thigh, was a leopard the size of a St. Bernard. From an aesthetic standpoint, he was gorgeous, his buttery coat splattered with spots the color of a Hershey bar; he would have made any Central Park East matron drool. From a practical standpoint, the cat looked hungry. He made a couple of low growls in short, rhythmic bursts. I tried to lift my ass, but it was impossible. If you don't believe me, try doing a butt-lift in a hammock. The leopard nudged my behind and rubbed the top of its head up and down my legs.

"Roger? Can you please do something?" I was trying to keep the hysteria out of my voice.

"Shhhh! Just stay still. He isn't hurting us."

"No, just tenderizing us. Or me," The leopard butted my left flank.

"If he wanted to bite you, he would. I'm sure that cobra might have left you alone too, if you'd let it."

"Are you kidding? He had his full hood up. He was intent."

"It was endangered. There are antidotes."

"Antidotes? You are unbelievable. You really do care more about animals than people, don't you?" The leopard sat down under us and started a low purr.

"I have an equal respect for all living creatures."

"Except if they're from Brooklyn. It's fine if a U.S. citizen is fanged."

"In the bigger scheme of things, I don't think people are more important. That's all."

"Of course they are. Of course people are more important."

"Well, where are all those very important people going to live once you destroy the entire ecosystem? Have you thought about that?" Roger asked.

"Yes. Yes, I have." Actually, I hadn't thought about that at all.

"And where is that?"

"Indoors."

At that moment, the leopard leapt up onto the branch above us. His purr had the low rumble of a Harley-Davidson and when he yawned, he displayed an amazingly healthy set of teeth. His breath was another matter. I guess that's what happens when you eat raw animals and don't have access to Listerine. He kind of bopped me on my nose with his paw and settled down right over me.

"Roger, I'm not kidding. Do something. What are you looking at?"

"It's just weird. They're mostly nocturnal, leopards. They usually rest during the day." The leopard was looking right at me. Roger had managed to turn over and now we were kind of lying on our sides, face to face. Roger started sniffing me.

"What the hell are you doing?"

"What was that perfume you bought in the airport?"

"Calvin Klein Obsession. Why?"

"Jesus, Cyd. Of course. That's it. Obsession. It attracts big cats."

"Come on." The leopard butted my head again with his chin, like a mutant house cat. "That's ridiculous."

"I'm serious. There were a couple of articles about it last year. Some of the zoos and a bunch of conservation groups are using it to keep track of all the big cats."

"So I'm wearing leopard catnip? Great. They might want to check to see if it attracts reptiles, too, as that seems to be the other pattern that's emerging. Does this mean he does or doesn't want to eat me?"

"I'm not sure."

A series of chirping alarms and frantic squeaks started up. The leopard gave a low growl and tried to get up, but now he was stuck too. His circular saw rumble went on overdrive. I wasn't sure what was worse—an angry, stuck leopard or a calm, loose one. Suddenly, a net flew over the leopard, and Roger and I dropped unceremoniously to the ground.

# Chapter Thirty-four

I landed ass over elbow on a deep blue blanket which had magically appeared below the net. It was hard to be dignified in this situation while wearing a skirt. Still, compared to the natives standing over us I was seriously overdressed. Their outfits consisted of loincloths, a few scattered skins, and the native equivalent of "man bags," though there was a boy who looked about ten dressed in a shredded red soccer shirt and a faded pair of LL Bean swimming trunks. He smiled and I thought of Akida. I hoped he was okay, even if he did work for the bad guys.

The men set down their cages and cloth bags on the blanket. One of the bags instantly tried to crawl away. The oldest boy nudged the wriggling bag back with his narrow foot while two smaller kids shot up the tree trunk and started to wrangle the leopard. They poured a thin liquid on the branch, the other men held the net beneath. Finally the leopard jumped loose, only to be caught in the net. It didn't take long to go from predator to prey around here. I tried to look submissive while I attempted to pull my shoes off the net, until I saw one of the boys reaching for my Balenciaga.

"*Kuwa makini*," I blurted—"be careful" in Swahili. The boy stopped. They all looked at me. I tried "Sorry," but I didn't know if I was speaking the right dialect. I figured they were probably the Luo tribe I'd read about, but I wasn't exactly an anthropologist.

The eldest man had an Abraham Lincoln face and wore a necklace full of large, yellow teeth and small gourds. He reached out his hand and pulled me up. Once I was up and okay, Roger got up too. The man continued to hold my hand. I had heard this was a tradition in Tanzania, so I let him. This went on for almost as long as a commercial break. We nodded at each other and he gestured for the boy to bring my bags. I gave them my best smile and handed the carry-on to Roger as I took my purse. We all stood awkwardly for a moment, mostly because I was stuck again. I prayed for the pony skin while the boy in the soccer shirt applied the dissolving liquid they had used to free the leopard. By the time my shoes came loose, part of the sole was missing. Bay Ridge Leather was going to have a banner year. The men and boys packed up the leopard and started moving past the trees.

"*Kuja*," the elder man said.

"What?" Roger whispered to me.

"Come. It means follow them." We'd gone about a quarter of a mile when my phone beeped. "Roger."

"What?"

"Reception. Call Heathrow now."

"I don't think it's a good time to stop."

"You don't have to stop. You just have to talk."

He took the phone and walked ahead, out of earshot, which was irritating. I just prayed the charge would last long enough. He stayed on the phone for maybe four minutes. I didn't manage to talk to him again until our rescuers spotted a bright blue parrot and ran off. We ran to keep them in sight.

"Well?" I said.

"I've done what I could."

"What does that mean?"

"It's Special Operations-ese for don't worry about it."

"Well, that's not gonna happen."

About an hour later, when the sun sat low and fat behind the acacia trees, we arrived at a village set in a clearing and full of small huts with thatched roofs like Chinese hats. Pens of goats and chickens and the odd piece of Western detritus surrounded the enclave. The village looked familiar. Then I

realized it was the one in the Phoenix Tours brochure, the "cultural tourism" aspect of the safari.
Maybe lost tourists were a regular thing.

The smiling boy in the soccer shirt led us
toward a group of native women and girls standing in front of the largest hut. Many of them were
dressed in the traditional Kangas—large, brightly
covered rectangles of fabric—and a few in Western
dress. They smiled and put out their hands. I took
as many as I could reach and smiled back.

"*Jambo*. Cyd Redondo, Redondo Travel," I
said.

"Cyd Redondo? Cyd Redondo?" the boy said,
turning. He said something to the women and I
recognized the word "Akida." They murmured
among themselves and nodded at me. The boy
bowed.

"We are delighted to have you in our village,
oh Queen of Travel," the boy said. "I am Bopo.
Akida is my uncle. You are his hero. He will take
me to Dar one day to book international senior
groups," the boy said, grinning. I could almost hear
Akida in his voice.

"Well, Bopo," I said, "if you are as good with
clients as you were with that leopard, you will be
a great success."

"That is very kind. Would you like to clean
yourselves?"

"Yes, please." I followed a tall woman with the best posture I had ever seen into a nearby hut.

I thanked her in Swahili, but I could tell she didn't want to leave. She fingered my skirt and looked down at me. I wracked my brains to think of something to give her that I could live without. I was, after all, down to emergency clothes rations. I pulled out the scarlet ribbon I had used to tie myself to the truck and held it out to her. She took it shyly, then ran out the door. There were no mirrors, so I did what I could to sort myself out and checked on Barry, who looked irritated. I gave him a couple of bugs and let him crawl around a little, to calm him down.

When I came out, all the women stood waiting for me with eager faces. What the hell. They had taken us in; they deserved some fashion. I started handing out my clothes and by the time I was finished, I could only survive one more emergency. Still, I could replace most of it at Century Twenty-One. Where on earth were they going to get a Donna Karan belt at cost out here? I noticed Roger watching me from across the clearing, his hair damp and shining. Once the women had run off with their presents, he pulled me behind a hut and kissed me on the top of the head.

"What was that for?"

"Knowing Swahili," he said.

We were about a half an inch and one deep breath from a real kiss when a vehicle roared up around the corner. We peeked around the hut. It was Bunty's Range Rover.

# Chapter Thirty-five

The Rover threw up cascades of dirt, blasted its horn, and came to a screeching halt. The villagers froze, waiting. Stringy Jock, still wearing his Saturday Night Fever attire, jumped down first, then Bunty clambered down from the passenger side, swearing when he missed the running board. He was sweating through his khaki shirt and his socks sagged down his pale plastic leg and onto his work boots. His "good" calf was Slim Jim tan and covered in welts. He had a walkie-talkie on the side of his belt and a hunting knife tucked in above his substantial ass. I was still having trouble accepting that this abomination was Mrs. Barsky's offspring. He waved and several of the villagers gathered around. None of them were smiling. Roger jerked me down and started to pull me away.

"What are you doing?" I said.

"Cyd, he can't find us here."

"I know, but we can't just disappear. They've been so nice. It's just rude."

"Who are you, Miss Manners? Bunty wants us dead. It would be a lot ruder for them to have to deal with our mutilated bodies. Or for them to have to lie. If we're gone, they don't have to." I knew he was right, but it felt awful to leave without saying good-bye to Bopo.

"Okay, but don't you want to know what he tells them? In case there's a direction we shouldn't go?" I leaned by the wall to listen.

Bunty asked in Swahili about two *bwanas*, which I explained to Roger meant us. Then he held his hand palm down, indicating at least five inches below my height.

"Bastard," I whispered, while Roger jerked me back behind the hut. We started moving, wall by wall, toward the acacia trees at the other end of the village.

Then we heard the leopard. This time, Roger was the one who peeked out first. I ducked down under his arm to watch as Bopo proudly carried the leopard cage to Bunty, who gave it the kind of calculating, reductive look someone gives a rump roast, then nodded for Jock to put it in the jeep. It was all I could do not to run out and smash both of the men in the eye with my detached kitten heel.

"Oh, God. It's our leopard, Roger. They can't give him our leopard. He might stitch its eyes closed." I turned to Roger, expecting an argument.

"Maybe we can do something about it." Roger took out a camera the size of a flash drive. Maybe he did work for the government. "At least six or seven of those species are on the no-hunt list and two are highly endangered. If we can get him actually handing them money, we have him," Roger said.

"So that means we're not running?"

"That means I'm not. You should."

"Like hell."

Roger held his tiny camera around the corner and filmed Jock taking cage after cage full of birds and lizards and putting them in the back of the truck. Once the animals were loaded, the boys began unloading huge bags of rice and stacks of canned goods. Finally, a mangy goat tumbled out of the back and tried to run away. Two tiny girls caught him.

"Damn," said Roger.

"They do it for food?"

Roger slammed his hand over my mouth and jerked me back. Jock was coming our way.

We ducked into the nearest hut. There was no bed to hide under or closet to get inside: just pallets and some cooking utensils. I picked up a long knife and handed Roger a metal pot as we got on either side of the entrance. I heard Jock stopping at the huts on either side and then ours. We held our breath and our weapons, ready to knock him out or stab him, depending on our mood. At least in terms of survival, Roger and I worked well as a team. It was just the relationship stuff that was tricky.

Jock shoved his head in about five inches from mine. Roger had the pot right over the bastard, but the henchman just looked straight ahead and ducked back out. My heart was going about a thousand beats a minute. As I heard him walk away, I fell against Roger in relief, accidentally stabbing him in the thigh.

He screamed. Jock's footsteps stopped and headed back our way.

"Shhh," I whispered to Roger. "Don't be a baby."

We went back to our positions. Roger grimaced when he moved his leg. I rolled my eyes. We held our breath as footsteps stopped outside the entrance again. The door began to inch open, pushing into Roger's thigh. "Don't you dare scream" I mouthed, weapon at the ready.

"Mr. Jock?" Bopo yelled from a distance. Run, Bopo, I thought.

The door kept opening. Roger's mouth was opening in a silent scream. Then, an insistent hand grabbed the smuggler's sleeve.

"Mr. Jock! How much for these eggs?"

Jock looked once more, then closed the door.

We heard him walk away with Bopo. I didn't want to know what kind of eggs had saved our bacon, as it were.

This time, I stayed where I was until I smelled a horrific blast of exhaust and heard tires bounce out of a pothole. I pulled out my mini first aid kit and told Roger to take off his pants.

Roger stared at me. "Don't you want to say something?"

"Please take off your pants?"

"How about I'm so sorry for stabbing you and almost getting us killed?" He unbuckled his belt. His pants slid to the dirt floor.

"Please." I was furious that he was right. "I barely broke the skin. I've had worse waxing accidents. Stand still." I cleaned the small puncture wound and covered it roughly with yet another *Lion King* Band-Aid, glad I'd gotten them at Costco. I knelt down to put away the first aid kit. That was when the Chief and Bopo found us, with Roger's pants around his ankles and me kneeling between his knees.

I don't know who was more embarrassed. I stumbled to my feet, Roger jerked up his pants and the Chief and Bopo backed out of the tent, all simultaneously. Roger and I emerged, blushing, and the Chief nodded, solemnly, looking down at the ground.

"She stabbed me," Roger said. "Tell him in Swahili."

Instead, I used every apologetic word I knew in any language, while curtsying and making various "it's not what you think" hand gestures. Finally, the Chief looked up, while Bopo grinned. The Chief began speaking. I asked Bopo to translate.

"He says that Bunty will be back. You may stay tonight, but then you must go. The tour will come in the morning and you can return with them."

"Of course. You saved us, thank you. Thank you so, so very much," I said in my best Swahili, though I wasn't sure my dialect or accent would make sense. You are never more aware of your complete inadequacy in a language than when you want to convey real emotion and all you have are words like "toilet," "embassy," "bus station," and the same "thank you" you would give to a bell hop. As usual, theoretical blew. It was like trying to make cheesecake with Velveeta. All I could do was shake hands fervently and hope he understood. I vowed in that moment to expand my phrases to things like "thank you for saving our lives," "may all your children be blessed," "you are my favorite man/woman in the world," and "I owe you beyond measure."

The Chief spoke, and Bopo translated. "He says he is the grateful one. You brought the leopard."

"Just like catnip," Roger said. I elbowed him.

Bopo explained that they would have a feast that night, and handed me over proudly to a tall woman who took me to her hut. She was wearing one of my microfiber shirts over her high, pear-shaped breasts. It looked great with her native skirt and endless bracelets. It turned out she was Bopo's mother and Akida's sister, Shawana. She spoke a bit of English and asked if I had seen Akida. I didn't quite know what to say. Instead, I fudged, pestering her with questions, as she offered me a skirt like hers and a few necklaces, which she placed around my neck. She coiled my hair and by then, it was dark and time for the party. I told her I would be right out and sat for a minute in the hut, almost over-come with all the unfamiliar smells: the cinnamony pomade Shawana had used on my unruly hair, the tang of damp straw, the sweetness of roasted yams, and the note of animal dung that seemed to under-line everything. It was a heady mix and I took one more deep breath before I opened the door.

I eased out into the smoky African night. The only light for miles came from the bonfire. I took a minute to look up. Growing up in the boroughs clearly limited your idea of what the sky could be. Here, it seemed every star, even the tiniest and furthest away, was visible, scattered like glitter.

Here, the sky was everything. The people were the afterthought.

I had traded sirens and car alarms for a whole new kind of high-pitched beeping—the yips of wild dogs, the bellows of hippos, and the caffeinated gobbles of vervet monkeys—at least Roger said they were vervets. I wouldn't know a vervet from a Pop-Tart. I felt tiny and ignorant and breathless and full of wonder. Even if Bunty put a bullet in us later tonight, at this moment, it all seemed worth it. All my years of playing senior Bingo, all my years of saving unused frequent-flier miles, all my years of dating Bay Ridge blockheads—it was all worth it, if it had led to this, to being here on this pungent, star-infested night. All the things I had promised my clients about traveling were true.

When Roger came up and took my hand, I squeezed back. We headed for the feast our gracious hosts had decided to give us instead of turning us over to heinous felons.

The goat Bunty had brought was not so lucky. He was digging in his hooves and pulling on the rope as a bowlegged villager, who resembled a human wishbone, neared the creature with a machete and smiled at us, presenting the goat like a prize on *Wheel of Fortune.*

"How do you say 'no' in Swahili?" Roger said.

"Roger Claymore, don't you dare. You can't

reject their hospitality. It would be incredibly rude. This isn't San Francisco. These people saved our lives today, and if they're kind enough to serve us one of their precious goats, then we're going to eat goat, period."

"All right, this goat is on you," Roger said.

I couldn't look as the man brought the machete down. There was one, brief sad bleat from the goat, then the sound of blood dripping onto dirt. Roger went pale. I felt faint. The man had the courtesy to take the goat away to skin it.

Then Bopo led us to seats on the dirt of honor beside the Chief. Roger and I looked at each other through the spitting sparks of the fire and it was almost like we were back in Atlantic City. We drank a gourd full of baobab seed soda that tasted vaguely like Orangina mixed with charcoal. Everyone around the fire was smiling. I wasn't used to a large family meal where everyone was smiling. My reverie was interrupted by the arrival of a large wooden tray arranged with what looked like…well, intestines.

Roger gave me a significant look, which I chose to ignore. Even I might have to come up with a religious reason not to eat raw goat intestines. The Chief began to manipulate the twisted guts with a carved stick. The villagers all leaned forward in anticipation. Finally, he rose, turned to Roger, and bowed. He spoke in Swahili, so I had to translate.

"He thanks you for bringing such good fortune to the village. So, now he will—wait, now he will read your fortune in the guts of the goat." I looked at Roger and shrugged. We both bowed to the Chief.

The Chief said Roger was a man of great judgment who would have many children. That part, I translated properly. But when he said "and many wives," I limited it to one, figuring I could have easily misunderstood. Then the Chief said something really strange.

I leaned toward Bopo. "Did he just say 'Beware of stuffed animals'?" Bopo nodded. Roger stared at me while I translated. Again, I shrugged. "Stuffed animals, that's what he said."

"You are in danger. You will be tested and betrayed by a great evil that seems a friend," the Chief said, nodding sagely at Roger. "But you will overcome this evil and live a long and healthy life."

"And become head of Fish and Wildlife," I added, just because Roger was looking pale.

"Really?" he said.

"The guts never lie." I smiled at him and we both bowed again to the Chief. I waited for my fortune, but the Chief threw the intestines into the fire. We wound up only having to eat the rest of the goat. And I mean the rest.

By this time, the carcass rotated on the spit over the fire, looking particularly spindly, stringy and red, like an oversized tandoori gone wrong. This was the first time I remembered having a passing acquaintance with my dinner. It was a strange feeling. I'd consumed plenty of things my brousins had brought home from quail- and pheasant-hunts, but I hadn't seen those animals when they were alive. I felt a strange kinship with this goat and thought of how he'd just had the bad luck to be traded for a leopard and to land here on the night they had guests.

Roger and I ate our *compadre* cooked in spices. I have to say, it was completely delicious. The meat was tangy and moist and dripping with fat, which helped the fried grasshoppers and the monkey bread go down. All of it came with *ugali*. Roger and I laughed and ate happily with our fingers, red meat notwithstanding. Sitting there on the edge of the game reserve, with undeserved kindness all around me, and Roger smiling again, I thanked whatever Gods had gotten me here and just prayed they'd get me back in one piece, with my clients intact and without being excommunicated from my family.

Bopo entertained us with stories about Akida as a boy, and asked if I would let him work for

Redondo Travel if he could get to America. There's no way I was telling a ten-year-old no, especially since by that age I was already booking hotels. He made me shake on it and stayed near us until his mother sent him to bed.

When the feast wound down, the women led me and Roger to our respective huts. I was bunking in with the single women, so I didn't really get a chance to say goodnight to Roger. I looked behind me as he walked away. He looked too.

I might have spent more time thinking about this if I hadn't needed to go to the bathroom so desperately. I had been holding everything in all day, in fear of the slightly scary squat toilet shack at the edge of the village. I decided I was being a ridiculous American and headed out with my emergency toilet paper and my mini flashlight. I was sure the roaring I heard was just my imagination—until I saw a zebra's ear on the ground. Yikes. Needless to say, I hurried like hell in the dark, my heels sinking in what I hoped was mud and aiming at what I hoped was the hole.

My heart was still pounding when I got back to my bed. Finally, I fell asleep to the sound of mosquitoes and the occasional yowl of what Roger had said was a hyrax, as if that were the name of something. I dreamt of chasing a crocodile down Fourth Avenue.

Roger woke me early, too early, as I had just figured out how to corner the crocodile. I had slept in a slip and threw a shirt over it as I tiptoed around my roommates. Outside, the morning smelled like old wood smoke, eucalyptus, and leftover goat skin.

"Cyd? I'm going back to Bunty's to try to get some evidence, so the mission won't be a complete wash."

"No you are not. They've already tried to kill you once."

"I'm just going to photograph some of the animals, that's all. Bopo said he heard Bunty and his crew say they will be in Dar."

"That's still insane."

"Yeah, and I thought you were insane to jump in the truck, but we're both just doing our jobs."

It killed me to say it, but I had to. "I'm sorry I messed up your deal."

"Don't be. They probably weren't buying my cover anyway. I might be in that pile of slaughtered animals right now if you hadn't shown up. Besides, if I'd been able to be straight with you, none of this would have happened."

"If you had evidence, could you skip the compound?" I dug Barry's document out of my bag and handed it to him.

"Where the hell did you get this?" Roger said, reading it.

"It was in the diplomatic bag."

"Jesus." He took a picture of it with his flash drive-sized spy camera.

"What is it?"

"It's a fake 'captive bred' certificate. Smugglers pay off officials to take a poached animal and stamp it 'captive bred' so it's legal to import. A couple of countries are notorious for this bullshit."

"Like the United Arab Emirates?"

"Yes. How do you know that?" I told him about Mrs. Barsky's FedEx package. "Dammit, Cyd, why didn't you tell me that in Atlantic City?"

"I don't know, because I thought you were a chiropractor? Because the sex kind of took precedence over paperwork?"

"I'm sorry. You're right. Where are the waybills now?" I dug in my bag and pulled them out. "Jesus. It takes a lot of bribe money to get those documents—whoever sent them wouldn't be happy about losing them. And they were addressed to Mrs. Barsky?"

"No. To Pet World. Does that mean she was in on it?"

"Not necessarily. If Bunty's her son, it would have been easy for him to use the pet shop as a front without her knowing. Still, he would have needed someone on the ground. Did anyone else ever open her mail?"

My stomach fell to my knees. Jimmy. Of course Jimmy was in on this. He must be the "Brooklyn end." He would certainly fit the "moron" bill. That's why he was always in Pet World. This would kill Uncle Ray. I couldn't tell Roger. He would just have to figure it out for himself—with any luck, after I'd gotten home.

"Any chance I could have the documents? It would give us probable cause to arrest the slimy Under Under guy at least. And maybe get Belk reassigned to Iran" Roger said.

I thought about it, but I might need them to save Jimmy. "You can have the Barry one, but only if you let me keep Barry. He and that document need to be separated."

"You can keep him for now."

"You don't need to go to Bunty's now, right?"

"I still don't have enough evidence on him."

"Can't I come with you?"

"Absolutely not. I'll grab some photos and the Interpol guys will pick me up. I have backup if I need it. I'll be fine."

"So you're not coming back?"

"That's up to the boss. You'll be okay either way. Faraji is bringing the tour to the village this morning and he'll take you back to the Phoenix complex with them."

"What about the Giannis?"

"They're fine. They've been released." My shoulders came down at least two inches.

Bopo shouted to Roger. He nodded. "I have to go."

"So that's it? I have to go?"

Roger looked down at me and pulled me to him. I could feel the snaps on his shirt digging tiny round impressions into my skin. The kiss was like a thin strip of fire that flicked down my spine and the inside of my thighs and made it hard for me to remain upright. I breathed in Roger's sweat and the faint remains of herbal aftershave and iodine.

"Do you need my compass?" I asked.

"Yes, but I'm not going to take it. Good-bye, Cyd. Be careful."

# Chapter Thirty-six

I stood in my overshirt outside the hut, watching Roger and Bopo disappear. I realized there were about fifty questions I'd forgotten to ask. Would Bunty gun me down one day in Brooklyn? Did Roger leave me my gun? The other forty-eight were basically different versions of "are we over?" I was so distracted, I almost didn't hear the Phoenix Tours jeeps approaching. While Faraji and my fellow travelers piled out and toured the village, I said a formal good-bye to the Chief and a friendly one to Shawana. She'd put the gift I'd asked for in my two-cup Tupperware bowl. By the time the tourists were ready to leave, so was I.

"Faraji?" I said. He stiffened. "As a travel agent, I truly appreciate how difficult it is when someone doesn't stick with the itinerary. I sincerely apologize for any inconvenience I've caused you and the tour. I hope you'll forgive me."

He nodded and gestured toward the second

jeep. I went pale. The last place I wanted to be was in a confined space with Jason and Emily, who were both giving me death stares. I responded with my most dazzling smile, climbed into the backseat and kept my purse in a defensive position as I waved good-bye to the village. It made me feel like a fashion ambassador to see some of my outfits scattered among the women. Shawana nodded to me as we turned a corner, and then we drove out of sight.

I wasn't looking forward to seeing Cassandra, especially since I needed her help. She stood at the entrance in loden green cargo pants that must have cost five hundred dollars. I barely suppressed the desire to tackle her and pull out hanks of her carefully colored hair. Faraji gestured to my original tent. It was hard to believe I'd only been gone one night.

Once I was inside, I had the distinct feeling someone had been there. I decided it was just paranoia and stashed my carry-on, then put Barry in the sink. With all the low buzzing in the tent, I was hoping for a lizard smorgasbord. What was going to become of him? Could I keep him? Would he like Brooklyn? Did he eat bedbugs? Maybe Roger could arrange it. But that would probably make me just another sleazy smuggler.

I cleaned up, then put on my last emergency outfit: creamy silk/nylon blend palazzo pants with a pumpkin-colored boat-neck top. I was reaching for my eyelashes when Cassandra raised the tent flap.

"Someone from the embassy flew in looking for you."

Shit. "Is he still here?"

"He left rather suddenly."

I could hear the tiny slap of chameleon tongue against some unlucky insect's wings. I casually closed the curtain to the bathroom.

"Look, Cassandra, one businesswoman to another? I'm going to leave the tour, as you requested. But it would really help to make a few phone calls first. Is there anything I can do for you, as a travel professional, that might make up for bending the rules a tiny bit?" I knew she would say no, but I had to try. I heard Barry slurp up another doomed insect.

"Fifty-thousand Marriott Rewards points and two British Airways upgrade vouchers," she said.

I calculated my relationship with Sally at the Marriott desk. British Airways was a no-brainer.

"Done. Of course I'll need phone and Internet to arrange it."

She sighed. "Follow me." She walked me through the camp and into the lodge, delivering me to a room far away from the guests. For a green, *au naturel* safari owner, Cassandra's private quarters were strictly American consumer. I guess at this point, she figured I wasn't in a position to judge her. She was wrong, but I couldn't say anything—her diesel generator was too loud. She had not one but two flat screens, a full computer setup with desktop and laptop, and inset halogen lighting.

"Please lock the door when you leave, Miss Redondo."

As soon as she was out of sight, I plugged in my phone and booted up her laptop. She had a picture of herself with an elephant as her screen saver. It explained the halogen lighting: in regular daylight, she was due for some organic Botox and she knew it. First I did some quick online research on Madagascan chameleons to make sure I had Barry on the right diet. Note to self: he needed more ants and fewer wings. Then I went straight to Google.

I found a tiny article in the *London Times* online, saying a Brooklyn couple had been cleared and released by Customs. I breathed a sigh of relief, and blessed Roger. Beside the story about the Giannis, there were several links on "smuggling" and "airports." Eager to avoid a call to Joni to say her brother was a wanted, potentially matricidal psychopath, I hit a link, figuring there might be one or two stories: there were hundreds.

There was a woman who had a real tiger cub mixed up with some stuffed animals in her luggage, and a man who blurted out "I have a monkey in my pants" at LAX. One businessman had eight hundred-seventy endangered tortoises in his suitcases, rolled in socks—eight hundred-seventy. Two men with "visible erections" were stopped at JFK when the erections started squirming. The thought of snakes in any kind of proximity was terrifying enough, but down there? Really? The stories went on and on. I felt validated when I read an envoy from Indonesia had been caught with a chimpanzee in his diplomatic bag, and Dennis had been right about the Chinese using rhino horn dust as an aphrodisiac. Why couldn't they just use three margaritas like a normal person?

Finally, I found an article about a long-term undercover operation called Jungle Trade, where U.S. Customs joined up with Interpol, Scotland Yard's Wildlife Crime Unit, and U.S. Fish and Wildlife to take down smuggling kingpins in fifteen countries. Maybe Roger was telling the truth. And I found several stories about pet stores as fronts for smuggling rings. God. I thought about Jimmy's recent jewelry purchases and the stabbed parrot. He could be a jerk, but surely he was too lazy and incompetent to pull off smuggling, much less murder. My money was on this Mr. Chu as the murderer. I hoped Bunty thought so, too.

My phone was finally charged. My hands

shook as I punched in my voice mail code. There
were thirty-four messages. The first was from Uncle
Ray: "Thought we'd have heard from you. Everyone
is fine here. Love you." You know how every family
has a secret language? For example, whenever my
mom said "Okay, go ahead," she meant "I'm so
angry I could smash your face in—you are a complete and total disappointment to me." My uncle's
"Love you," meant "You are dead to me."

He had every reason to hate me. I had probably single-handedly destroyed Redondo Travel.
I had sold my clients out for a companion ticket
and a glimpse of something I could have seen any
night on the Discovery Channel. I had let senior
citizens be frisked, their shrunken orifices examined
for snake eggs and skinks and God-knows-what
else. I saw a message from the Giannis. Whatever
it said, I deserved.

"Cyd, we're just calling to thank you. You
won't believe where we are—Scotland Yard. Isn't
that exciting? I don't know how you did it from
there, but a man from the U.S. Embassy said you
cleared everything up. Can you book us another
flight? No hurry, we're having fun."

I almost threw up with relief. Clearly, these
"frail old people" weren't so frail. I guess after
the Depression and World War II and the whole
"duck and cover" thing, the past forty years had

probably been dull as dirt. But still, I wanted it to be adventure by choice, not by law enforcement. In six minutes I had them booked, upgraded, and discounted from Heathrow to JFK, with tickets delivered to their hotel, a limo courtesy of Redondo Travel to and from the airport, and a bouquet of prosciutto to be delivered to their house.

I had to call my lieutenant brousin, Frank. I woke him up, but he wasn't too mad once I told him about the whole Bunty/Bobby situation.

"He had frogs there? Were they African frogs?"

"How would I know? It's not like they had frog passports. I'm not sure it was Bobby, though. He seems really upset about his mom. Supposedly they're all working for a Chinese businessman, Mr. Chu. Can you check him out?"

For now, I didn't mention Jimmy. I needed to at least hear his side of the story before I turned him in. And I couldn't do it on the phone: I had to see his face. Plus I had to prepare Uncle Ray, soften the blow somehow.

"Bunty imports from South America too," I said. "Does this get me off the hook?"

"Not for running away to Africa."

I hung up on him and headed into Cassandra's bathroom. I wanted to wash my face, but I also wanted to check out the competition. What did "natural" girls have in their medicine cabinets? Let's just say it wasn't quite as "natural" as you might think: no Tom's of Maine toothpaste or rock deodorant here. Clearly, she knew that stuff didn't work and had supplied herself with Crest White Strips, Garnier hair dye, and Degree "Fusion." There was an interesting collection of "natural" hued makeups, not to mention the highly chemical packet of birth control pills. It was a brand I had used in my twenties, but it gave me a rash. Did Roger know she had hemorrhoids? I noticed a velour bag hanging in the closet, the kind hotels use to put hair dryers in, and figured I'd see whether she got those perfect waves with a diffuser.

Inside was a curved, sharply pointed object that looked just like…well, like the rhino horns I'd seen on the Internet—the ones that were incredibly rare and valuable and horribly illegal and were responsible for there only being two hundred rhinos left in the world. I couldn't believe it. Was everyone on this friggin' continent smuggling animals and their by-products? This was exactly the kind of the evidence Roger needed. I took the horn out and replaced it with a rabbit vibrator I found in her drawer, hoping she wouldn't notice for a few hours.

I had to get back to Dar es Salaam, where there were cell phone towers and taxis. Happily, I had a special relationship with FedEx and American Express. With my deal, if I lost my card, they guaranteed a replacement delivered within twenty-four hours, anywhere in the world. I lied and reported my card stolen, then called my contact at FedEx. She promised that the driver would deliver the card before ten the next morning and give me a ride back to the city.

I heard footsteps and shut down the computer, hiding the rhino horn in my bag. Cassandra stuck her head in. I gave her the codes for her new upgrades and thanked her. As a goodwill gesture for the other guests, I sprayed both touring vehicles with the last of my Obsession on the way back to the tent. At least someone would see lions.

When I checked the bathroom sink, Barry wasn't there. I completely panicked. Had he gotten out? I would never find him in the jungle, but some vulture might.

"Barry? Barry? Here, boy." Sometimes I forgot he wasn't a dog.

I went through the tent inch by inch, starting by the flaps and working my way to the middle, looking for anything that might be moving. I couldn't blame him for bolting. He had been stuck in my purse like a used tissue for days. I felt like crying. How could I be so irresponsible? Poor Barry, who hadn't asked for any of this. I decided to make one more circuit, but before I started, I needed a drink. I couldn't remember if there were still any airline bottles in my bag. And as I walked toward it, I saw a twitch and there was Barry, making his halting way across the zipper.

Then, I did cry, for the second time in three days. I cried for Barry and Roger and the end of my travel consultant career. I cried for the barbecued goat. I cried because I was homesick and because I was finally on my own. I set the alarm clock on my newly charged phone and finally fell asleep, tangled in mosquito netting and jungle sounds.

• ● ● ● •

I was packed and ready when I heard careening tires and spotted my ride. There was nothing like the blocky whiteness of a FedEx truck to ruin the illusion of the exotic. My friend Sara from college said it was like coming across a McDonald's in Iceland. Part of you was disoriented and a little disappointed, but part of you was relieved as hell.

The driver almost rolled the truck over pulling in. He was barely taller than I was, with a dirty blond John Denver haircut, a wide neck, bow legs, and an ill-fitting uniform: his FedEx shorts were so long they looked like gaucho pants. He ran up to Faraji, who shook his head no. They argued, then almost as an afterthought, he tossed my replacement Amex card at my host and started the vehicle. I grabbed the package, jumped on the running board, and started pounding on the truck. It jerked to a stop. The driver leaned out.

"What?" He had a peculiar smell: part monkey cage, part emergency room.

"Cyd Redondo, Redondo Travel," I said.

"Yeah, so?"

"You're supposed to take me with you. Your dispatcher made special arrangements for you to take me back to Dar."

"Nobody rides in the truck."

After I threatened to get the Worldwide office on the phone, he finally caved.

"I have more deliveries," he said. "I'm not going back right away."

"That's fine." I climbed into the passenger side, setting my carry-on at my feet, and holding my bag with Barry and the rhino horn tight in my lap. I had put Barry back in his aerated Tupperware, so he wouldn't get gored. There was a weird antiseptic smell coming from the box of light green Handi Wipes on the dashboard. I had only seen white ones and wondered whether the whole "green is for hope" marketing idea was taking Africa over as well.

The driver veered around potholes, sweat popping out on his forehead. This guy seemed too nervous to be in charge of vital deliveries. It was like putting a meth head in charge of our nuclear arsenal. I heard a banging in the back.

"What was that? Shouldn't you check?" I said.

"Check on what? What do you mean?"

"Check on the packages. Should they slide around like that?"

He ignored me for a mile or so, then stopped the truck. "Delivery," he grunted.

I looked around. Delivery to where? A tree? When I turned around, the driver smashed a thick wet stack of Handi Wipes over my face. I managed to loop my purse twice around my wrist before I passed out.

# Chapter Thirty-seven

I came to in the back of the FedEx truck, feeling like I'd swallowed one of those oily green Glade air fresheners or a soylent green milkshake. Since when did they make Handi Wipes with chloroform? For overwrought mothers? This kind of behavior was not up to FedEx standard. Besides, being abducted twice in one vacation did nothing for my self-esteem. I had three days left in Africa and I was not ready to spend them tied and gagged in a boxy vehicle.

I was trussed up beside what I assumed was the real FedEx driver, a tall, chiseled man the color of Irish Breakfast tea, in a t-shirt and boxers, lying on his side with an ugly lump on his cheek and a bleeding forehead. Mostly he looked embarrassed. I wriggled behind him and tried to untie his hands with my teeth, but every time we hit a pothole, which was every five seconds, I lost my grip and jarred every tooth in my head. Then I remembered I had something sharp. I ass-walked over to my bag.

It took forever to get the zipper undone. I kept reaching into the bag with both hands until I finally jabbed myself with the rhino horn. That sucker was sharp. Now, if I could just get a grip on it before we hit another fricking pothole. I'd never appreciated the Metropolitan Department of Public Works so much in all my life. Once I grabbed the horn, I tried cutting my gag, but all I did was jab myself in the cheek. My fellow hostage got the idea and did a handoff with the horn, working my gag off.

"Cyd Redondo, Redondo Travel." I hooked the horn into the side of the gag and pulled.

"Hugh Dakar, FedEx. That guy came out of nowhere. I was doing a pickup, and next thing I knew I was in my underwear and tied up back here. So I am fired. So I am fucked."

"No you're not. We're going to get your truck back, okay?" I had untied myself and had the rhino horn in my hand.

He stared at it. "That psycho said he believed in putting animals down humanely." He pointed at the rhino horn. "You are a psycho too?"

"No. It's not mine." I said. "Long story." But I didn't want to think about that. I wanted to think about how I was going to get the two of us out of here and find a way to Dar es Salaam.

The truck stopped, slamming us against each other. If we started screaming too soon, we could endanger some innocent person who just wanted his *Sports Illustrated* or insulin. I couldn't hear anything clearly. Eventually, because I had a gun and because Hugh looked scared, and mostly because I couldn't stand not knowing what was going on, I cracked the back door and peeked out.

I instantly wished I hadn't. I knew where I was—Bunty's compound. The place where creatures were tortured and then, apparently, FedExed to psychopaths overnight. I hesitated. If we stayed in the truck, we might have a chance. Staying in here was the smart move, no question. I turned to Hugh.

"Try to get behind those boxes if you can."

He backed up, the snaps on his shorts scraping against the ridged, metal floor. A monkey was going nuts outside. I decided to look out just one more time. After all, Roger had said Bunty and the thugs were away. I stepped down out of the truck, purse anchored across my chest, .38 in my hand, and stuck as little of my face as possible around the side.

As I did, Bunty's Range Rover pulled up to the house. I edged out a little further and spotted Roger kneeling by the crocodile pen, taking pictures. Oblivious. Bunty, Henrik, and Jock got out and started walking in his direction.

Then, everything happened very fast, probably

because I stepped out and fired my gun over the house.

Before I could pull back, Bunty, Henrik, and Jock pointed automatics at me. The faux FedEx driver dove behind a tree near the house.

"It's that wee bitch," Jock yelled.

"I am not wee," I yelled back, jumping behind the truck. How could I get their focus off Roger? I decided shaming/infuriating was my best option and used my outside voice.

"Hey, Bunty. Did you really think you could kill me? Sister Sandra Ignatius would be appalled." I heard feet move toward me. More running. Where were they? "You're a disgrace to the neighborhood, you crippled, pencil-dick matricidal motherfucker." Someone cocked a rifle. "And by the way, your mother left the apartment to me." Bunty and Henrik came around the truck, guns trained on me. I could probably only get one of them before I died.

There was a huge crash, followed by a rush of wings and yowls and breaking crockery. The bad guys ran toward the cages. Three seconds later, I was knocked to the ground.

"Get under the truck," Roger said, crouching behind me.

"You first," I said, not eager to crawl in front of him. I hadn't been to the gym in a week. We scrambled on our stomachs. Great—another outfit ruined. I did manage to hold onto my Balenciaga this time, at least.

"What the hell just happened?" It was chaos. Someone had knocked over the clay pots and opened the pens. The animals that were able to move were escaping, including gobs of snakes, heading this way.

"That should slow them down. They're too greedy to shoot their own merchandise," Roger said as I moved behind, using him as a snake shield.

"You did this? Good thinking, Rog," I said as a bullet hit about four inches from my leg. I saw two monkeys run in front of Bunty and head for the trees.

"If you hadn't shown up to ruin yet another operation, everything would have been fine."

The shooting finally stopped. There was more shouting.

"Really?" I said. "One of the guards was about to shoot you. And, I was kidnapped." The bullets started again.

"Kidnapped? Come on? How many times are you going to trot out that old chestnut?"

"Fine, I'm out of here. Deal with this yourself." I turned to crawl sideways, then froze.

Our old friend the leopard had joined us under the truck and this time, he was not in a good mood. He gave a lightning fast swipe, mortally wounding my bracelets.

"Hey! Bad cat!"

"No Obsession today?" Roger said, trying to swap places with me. It's not like we could move that fast on our stomachs. Then something else moved to my right.

"Shit," Roger said, gripping my shoulder.

"Shit? Shit is not what I want to hear. Shit is not helpful." I turned my head and saw a huge lizard—maybe six feet long—with skin like mildewed chain mail. It was dripping drool in a particularly disgusting way, not that drool is ever attractive. "What is that?"

"A Komodo dragon. God knows how they got it. I wonder if…?"

"Roger. Focus."

He lowered his voice. "Be quiet and don't move."

The two animals had noticed each other and were about to go at it right over us. I was not interested in being part of a fang/saliva sandwich. Out of the corner of my eye, I saw three black snakes and a chubby porcupine go by.

"I say we risk the lizard. Its teeth don't look that bad," I said.

"It's not the teeth, it's the drool," Roger

whispered. "It's toxic enough to drop a water buffalo. Basically it dissolves anything it touches."

"That is disgusting. What do we do?"

"There's not much to do, Cyd," he said. "Just be still and hope they go away."

"Yeah, right, just long enough for Bunty to shoot us." I watched a tiny river of drool work its way toward my Balenciaga. That bag had been through enough. I pulled it closer and inched it open.

"Stop moving. I'm not kidding." Roger said.

"I haven't spent ten years putting half my salary in a 401K to be dissolved by saliva," I whispered, sliding out the rhino horn.

"Where the hell did you get that?"

"Your eco-girlfriend, Cassandra. She was hiding it in her room," I said, handing it to him and pulling another weapon out. The leopard growled. The lizard eyed the bottom of my shoes.

"Occupy the leopard. I'll take care of the lizard," I shifted slightly to get in range.

Roger paled. "Cyd? Don't. Please don't, it's…"

"It's what?" I said, pointing my weapon straight at the lizard's eyes and spraying.

"Endangered." The leopard swiped at Roger. I turned and sent a shot his way as well. The cat backed off, yowling. "What the hell was that?" Roger said.

"Giorgio," I said. "I'm saving my bullets for the bad guys."

A shot almost dinged my ring finger. The truck vibrated to life and we barely avoided tread marks as it rolled over us toward the road. Without it, we were as exposed as Jayne Mansfield's nipple. Henrik and Jock yelled, alerting Bunty. Bullets spattered behind us. We sprinted for the back of the truck—the door was still open. A truck driven by a lunatic was better than an amputee with an AK-47.

Roger stopped, staring at the carnage. A shot whizzed past his head and blasted a tree limb to our left. "Jesus," he said, "what have I done?" There were disoriented animals everywhere. It was terrifying. But so was Bunty with Roger in his sights.

Shit, I thought, for about the fifteenth time that day.

The smuggler was peg-legging toward us, right between the leopard and the Komodo, who'd resumed their death match. I probably should have shot him, all things considered, but out of respect for Mrs. Barsky, I didn't. Instead, I sacrificed my last stiletto, nailing Bunty right in the forehead while shouting, "Call your sister."

He pitched forward. As I grabbed Roger, I heard a hiss, then a scream. I didn't look back.

We caught up to the truck as it slowed for a

pothole. Once we catapulted ourselves into the back, I checked on Barry while Roger shut the doors. Hugh was on his side, motionless. Roger pointed to the bullet holes peppering the walls of the truck. "Looks like a flesh wound. He's in shock."

I dug through my bag for something to staunch the wound. I decided it was no time for modesty and grabbed a handful of panti-liners, tanga-style, of course. They were individually wrapped, so they were probably sanitary. I slapped some Neosporin on them for good measure and pressed them onto the wounds. Roger kissed me on the head.

"What?" I said.

"Resourceful is the new sexy."

"Stop it and help me."

Roger held down the makeshift bandage while I cleaned the nasty bruise on Hugh's cheek. He moaned and shifted.

"It's going to be okay, Hugh. We're going to get you out of here. We are, right Roger?" I asked as we hit a crater-sized pothole. The jolt knocked a massive FedEx box over.

It flew open, spilling dozens of stuffed animals. How cute, I thought, until I noticed the hunks of red cottony flesh beneath the pink fluff, the gouged out eyes and missing limbs. God, had the Chief's goat guts been right? Roger picked up a pink-and-white dolphin sporting a rubber knife through its fin. "Did that guy, the driver, have a birthmark?"

"Gee, I guess was too busy being chloroformed to notice."

"It's just that it might be Grey Hazelnut."

"He's a nut, all right." I put down the panti-liners. "Wait. You know him?"

"He's an extreme animal activist. Calls himself the UnaVet. These look like they're from his Planet Reality toy line. He was probably there to save the animals." I picked up a fluffy green monkey with an amputation scar. Roger shrugged. "He thinks children should know the truth."

"And you think that makes him what? A good guy?"

"He's blown up a few research facilities. I guess it's all relative." With that kind of non-answer, I finally believed Roger worked for the government.

The truck swerved left and slammed to a stop, throwing us all against the cab wall. Then the door smashed open and the cavalry arrived. To arrest me.

# Chapter Thirty-eight

Red dust flooded the truck, so it took a second to notice the barrel of a Glock 9mm pistol pointed straight at us. Roger put his hands up, so I figured I should too. My bag was too far away to hook over my raised arms. I could see a silhouette in the door. It coughed.

Roger leaned forward. "Gant?"

It was the guy I'd met in Atlantic City, wearing the same Eurotrash suit. It looked damp. He lowered his gun. "Claymore? Seriously? You let Hazelnut get the drop on you again?"

"Screw you. What about Bunty?" Roger said.

"No sign. I left the forensic team there."

"Hey! Could we get some help here?" I pointed at Hugh. "He's been shot. He needs a doctor."

Gant stared into the truck, then turned to an agent who looked about twelve. "Flesh wound. Nigel? Medivac. And work the truck."

The kid ran to a black Range Rover, setting off

a chorus of crazed birds. He made a call, snapped on white rubber gloves and booties, then ran back toward us and jumped in. Gant gestured me down. I looked back wistfully at my bag, then followed Roger onto the narrow, pockmarked road. There was screaming, somewhere behind the shrubs.

I turned to Gant and held out my hand. "Cyd Redondo, Redondo Travel. We met in Atlantic City."

"Agent Gant. Interpol." He kissed my hand, then snapped a handcuff around it.

"Whoa! Roger? What is happening?"

"Gant, hold on a minute," Roger said, as I pulled my other hand away.

At that moment, two more cheap-suited Interpol henchmen climbed out of the brush carrying Grey Hazelnut, his bare, bowlegs flailing. He saw me and kicked harder.

"You! Do you have any idea what you've done you, you miniature bimbo? The global implications of your little performance? The millions of dead animals on your head." He lunged for me before one of the agents handcuffed him to the door handle of the Rover.

"Come on, Gant," Hazelnut said. "Show some mercy. I've had a bloody week. I got photos of Mr. Chu's poachers mutilating a male rhino. Cassandra

Phoenix almost got her knees broken going under-cover to buy the horn."

Roger shot me a look. I felt nauseous, glad my purse was still in the truck.

"We had all the documentation, a perfect chain of evidence, and—bam—last night some fucker steals it. Can you believe it? And today I had the boxes, I had the waybills, I had Bunty, until this breadhead fucked me. She's up to her neck in it. Take her in, not me."

"That's exactly what I'm trying to do, if you'd contain yourself, Doctor Doolittle."

"Roger! What is he talking about?"

"Miss Redondo, there's no need to be coy. We know about your family. We know all about your smuggling ring."

"My family? We're travel agents! And I'm the last person on earth who'd smuggle anything, ever." Roger was staring at something behind me. He went pale.

"Boss?" It was Nigel. "These were in her purse." He held out the rhino horn, the ivory neck-lace, Barry's Tupperware, and the gun. He had my bag hooked over his shoulder.

Gant grabbed my free hand and snapped on the other cuff, while Hazelnut jerked on his cuffs while he threatened various parts of my anatomy and unborn children.

"Gant? What actual jurisdiction do we have here?" Roger said. Finally.

"As much as we pay the Tanzanian police for."

I knew from experience that was true.

"She's here because she's decided to cooperate," Roger said, moving between us. "That's all evidence she's turning over."

"Really? I didn't get the paperwork."

"I've been a little busy."

"Cooperate with what?" I said. Roger squeezed my shoulder. "Ow."

"Graham, just ignore her. She's been hysterical all day." I kicked him as hard as I could with my bare foot. "Look, forget her. I've got photo evidence on Bunty's whole operation. We just need a warrant for the FedEx waybills and we have him."

"Is this because you banged her?"

"I beg your pardon?" I said, my eyebrows levitating above my head.

"Apparently, you have a great coccygeal vertebra," Gant said. All the agents laughed.

# Chapter Thirty-nine

I don't remember much about the next couple of hours. An airlift came for Hugh, at least. Nigel and a fat agent who smelled like mothballs and cumin drove me back to Dar es Salaam. They put me in room 555 at our old hotel, with Nigel posted outside my door. The room looked empty without Barry. Or my purse. This was the first time since I was eleven that I'd been outside the house without a handbag. I felt completely helpless. My clients couldn't contact me, I couldn't check my makeup or take my birth control pills or mop up spills. And then I remembered my father's compass. For a minute, I couldn't breathe. I'd let my dad down too.

But I couldn't think about that while I was still covered in monkey blood, dragon spit, and mud. I needed a shower. They'd taken out the phone, so I couldn't call Housekeeping for extra body lotion— why do hotels only give you enough for one leg? I convinced Nigel to walk me down to the front desk for supplies. The desk clerk took one look at the state of me and handed them right over, *gratis*.

"Thank you, Hadhi," I said, checking her name tag. It's important during an emergency or complete emotional breakdown not to lose your manners, especially with someone who might at some point help you escape.

After my shower, I put on the hotel robe and looked at my ruined clothes. Had the Andersons ever gotten monkey blood out of anything? I wasn't ready to give up that skirt. After all, I was already going to have to switch from FedEx to DHL.

Nigel brought me some food, but I couldn't eat. Or sleep. I decided to try cable. I flipped past CNN International, as I was afraid I might be on it, and kept flicking until the power went out. I automatically went for the flashlight in my purse. My Balenciaga was like an amputee's phantom limb. My fingers closed over nothing and I was left alone in the dark, distractionless.

I know the whole point of "if onlys" is that it's too damn late. Still, they were a great way to occupy yourself when you were deprived of cable. If only I hadn't gone looking for Bobby, if only I hadn't called FedEx, I wouldn't have been chloroformed or exposed to toxic saliva. And if only I had kept my bag attached to me at all times, I'd still have two more vacation days.

Of course I was avoiding the real issue: if only I had listened to Uncle Ray and stayed in Bay Ridge, I wouldn't be humiliated, heartbroken, and the target of an international criminal investigation. I couldn't stand that he'd been right and I'd been so wrong. Was I destined to live in the attic, paying penance, for the rest of my life?

At about five in the morning, there was a knock on the door. I pulled my robe tighter and looked through the peephole. It was Roger.

"Go away."

"I have your clothes."

"Leave them with Nigel."

"We need to talk."

"I don't want to talk to you, ever."

"It's about your uncle. Do you want me to broadcast it in the hall?"

I unhooked the chain, opened the door, and slapped him as hard as I could.

"Ouch," Nigel grinned.

"You're next," I said, and let Roger in. He was holding a plastic bag with a few of my things and rubbing his cheek. He had a black eye and his knuckles were bruised.

"Here." He handed me the bag. "I could only find one malaria pill."

"That's because I gave all mine to you."

"I'll get you some more. I'm sorry."

"About which part? The sex part, the lying part, or the surveillance part?"

"All the parts. Well, actually not the sex part."

"Ah yes, the recorded sex, thanks for that."

"I had nothing to do with that, I swear. Besides, that's more humiliating for me that they were listening in, than it is for you. You don't work with those guys."

"Apparently, thanks to you, I do now. Just tell me about my uncle."

He took the armchair. I stayed where I was, trying to keep a height advantage. He handed me a document. "Your 'confidential informant' paperwork. Please sign it and do what I tell you, so they'll let you go."

"Absolutely under no circumstances am I doing anything you tell me to. Was the thing about my uncle just another trick to get in here, or what?"

"No. Interpol thinks Bunty's been working for your uncle, that he's the U.S. distributor. They've been interested in you and your family for months. That's why your hotel room in Atlantic City was bugged."

"Bullshit."

"It doesn't look like bullshit to them. Everything points to Redondo Travel as the perfect cover. You hooked up with Adventure Limited—a shell company, by the way. You arranged the trips, it's your clients who have the animals in their luggage, and you got us dodgy shots and visas. You've probably done at least twenty illegal things just since we met. Jesus, Cyd, you stole that diplomatic bag, not to mention all the evidence they found in your purse."

"But you can explain all that."

"Yeah, well, I tried. But they figure I'm compromised because of...well, our relationship."

"We didn't have a relationship. We had an accident," I pulled my robe tighter. "I certainly hope you enjoyed yourself, you opportunistic son of a bitch."

"When I slept with you, it wasn't on the job. I was just on assignment at the Reptile Expo. I didn't know you might be involved until later. That night, I swear, it was just me." Part of me wanted to believe him, but it still didn't add up.

"The first night, maybe, but what about since then?"

"We haven't had sex since then. I didn't feel like I should."

He was right. In the midst of all this craziness, he had technically been chaste. This was too confusing to think about because, right now, I wanted to stay as mad as possible.

That was easy after he had the nerve to tell me that it was really my fault. When I introduced myself to Gant in Atlantic City, the agent recognized my name. Once he knew Roger had an "in" into the family, they ordered him to come on the trip with me. He said he had hated lying to me, but figured at least he might be able to protect me if I were innocent.

"If? Great job with that, Rog. Thanks a lot. You're just trying to rationalize completely despicable and unforgivable behavior."

"I know it's unforgivable, but Cyd, come on—I was just doing my job. You more than anyone should understand that. And my job is important. Surely you see how many bad people are involved and what's happening to these animals." I kept my eyes on the stained carpet. "I know you're furious at me. I get it. But don't try to take that out on Gant. That man has no sense of humor, believe me. He's a Swede. And the thing is, Gant doesn't really want you. He wants your uncle."

"Godammit, if you insult my uncle one more time…" I said, coming at him. He caught my wrists before I could make contact and held me in front of him. My robe had come loose. He took a quick look, then averted his eyes.

"Cyd, this is exactly why I'm telling you this. Gant's bound to say worse. And an assault charge is the last thing you need."

"I assaulted you. You're a federal agent of fish or something, right? Aren't you going to arrest me?"

"Self-defense." He let go of my hands.

We were standing too close. That mole was still beside his mouth. I backed up. "I swear on my life my uncle doesn't have anything to do with this, and neither do I."

"I know you're not involved. You care too much about your clients to put them in danger on purpose. Someone used you. Maybe that's why your uncle didn't want you going on this trip, to protect you. Did you ever think of that?"

"He didn't want me to come because he believes the world is a dangerous place. And he is fucking right," I said. "Are there any donuts in this godforsaken country?"

"Here," Roger handed me a granola bar out of his pocket. "Sign the papers, please." He opened the door. "And don't kick Gant in the balls."

"I wouldn't be able to find them. Get my purse back and check on Barry."

"It wasn't an accident, Cyd, you and me. Fate, maybe. Take that malaria pill."

The agents were coming for me in an hour. I used the room iron on my rust-colored pencil skirt and my white tie-front blouse. I put on my last pair of shoes, the Soffts three-inch. I felt nauseous every time I remembered that I had been a suspect, not a girlfriend, for the whole trip. I guess it was fitting I'd met Roger at a reptile convention.

But the worst part was that everything I'd done, from getting us shots to stealing the rhino horn, had put my uncle in danger. I knew there was no way Uncle Ray, who had bought my confirmation dress and taught me how to figure out compound interest, could do any of the horrible things Roger thought he had. Then I remembered the dead parrot, the computer break-in, and the idea Uncle Ray didn't like me coming to the docks, and for a tiny instant, I was worried.

At seven, Nigel knocked. I opened the door. Standing in front of him was Akida, dressed in full room-service attire. Thank God I played Five Card Stud on alternate Thursdays.

"Come in," I said. Nigel held the door open as Akida entered. He nodded at me and started to lay out the breakfast. On the tray was a note that said *What can I do, Cyd Redondo?* When Akida handed me the check, I wrote *Get me an outside line, thanx*, and gave him a huge tip on the room, as Interpol was paying. After he left, I figured at least I had one friend. Or did I? Maybe this was another setup. I had a piece of toast and three cups of coffee. Ten minutes later, Nigel took me downstairs.

The Serengeti Ballroom was their interrogation suite. I guess the Tanzanian jail was too awful even for Interpol, or at least for Gant, whose razor-sharp polyester creases hadn't budged in twenty-four hours. His grooming suggested the primal cruelty often inherent in frat boys and certain Catholic nuns. He had a fat lip, though. Had he and Roger actually come to blows? I handed him my paperwork.

"Smart girl." Gant looked at my breasts. "Smarter than you look."

"Believe me, with that tie, you don't have a chance," I said.

"Come on. If Claymore was in, you can't be that picky."

"She's not that picky." A woman in a pinstriped suit came through the door. It was the Eileen Fisher woman from Bay Ridge and Atlantic City.

"Miss Redondo, Agent Fisher."

"You. I knew it," I said. "I knew there was something dodgy about you. You never pulled off that Eileen Fisher, by the way." I turned to Gant. "Your undercover operatives suck."

"Well, you would know," he said. "Coffee?"

I declined for fear I might throw it in his face. I sat down at the conference table, and watched Agent Fisher lay out dozens of photos. They were all of me: me paying off Lieutenant Panza, me at gunpoint at the airport, me buying the ivory necklace. Me, me, me.

"Perhaps you'd like to call the embassy before we talk?" Gant asked. The photo of me with the diplomatic bag was on top. I shook my head. "Good. Let's get started. Tell me when your Uncle, Raymond James Redondo, first became involved with Robert Barsky?"

God, Roger was right. They were after Uncle Ray.

"They went to high school together, forty-five years ago. That's hardly involved."

"Well, then why has Mr. Redondo been paying the mortgage on the Pet World property for the last six years?"

"What?" How did I not know about this? I tried to come up with an explanation. Any explanation. "No. Uncle Ray was just helping Mrs. Barsky out after her husband died. He said she was going to lose the store."

"Yes, and he was going to lose his laundering operation."

"I swear on my life that my uncle has nothing to do with this smuggling operation. It's not possible. If he were laundering money, I would know."

Gant and Agent Fisher looked at each other. I jabbed my middle fingernail into my palm to keep from screaming.

Gant pointed to the photos. "Let me remind you that in addition to the contraband items in your bag, we have you on film committing various other criminal acts. You've had four clients arrested for contraband in one week and apparently you are currently wanted by the NYPD for questioning in a homicide investigation. You have two choices. You give us all the details of the smuggling operation and agree to testify against Mr. Redondo, or we nullify the confidential informant agreement and prosecute you for those offenses and any more we can come up with."

I couldn't testify against my uncle. What did it matter if I wound up in a Tanzanian jail? My career and love life were over anyway. And even if I agreed, I didn't know anything. I just kept my eyes on the photos and thought about how fat I looked. Finally, I took my best shot.

"Mr. Gant. Ms. Fisher. I'm more than willing to cooperate. Honestly, if I knew of any evidence in this matter, I would absolutely give it to you. But I don't have any. Truly, I am willing to do whatever you ask to convince you of my uncle's innocence. Anything. But if that's not enough, you're just going to have to arrest me."

Gant and Fisher frowned, then left the room. I waited at the window, looking down on the traffic and wondering how I could save Jimmy, and whether I should. They came back with a proposition. It was bad.

# Chapter Forty

Agent Fisher explained that there was a way to prove Uncle Ray's innocence—but only if I were willing to work undercover on "Operation Slither." The name really inspired my faith in our government. If I participated successfully, all charges against me would be dropped.

"By doing what?" I asked.

"You'll be smuggling animals yourself," Gant said.

"You mean the ones they've probably put in my 'lost' luggage? And this is going to help my uncle how?"

"If you're able to turn the contraband over to us at JFK, you'll go a long way toward proving your family has no involvement. If, of course, the animals disappear at any point, that will certainly verify our suspicions. It goes without saying, per your contract, that you will not contact your uncle prior to or during your trip."

"And if I get caught with the animals?"

"Then we've never heard of you and you'll get what you deserve," Agent Fisher said, holding up the rhino horn. There was something about this setup that bothered me, but I was too tired and too unmoisturized to think it through.

"And if I deliver the animals safely, my uncle's in the clear and you won't come after me or any of my clients?"

"All the assurances we're offering are in the paperwork."

I bit my lip and signed. Roger came into the room, just as they took me to the door.

"What about Barry? What's going to happen to Barry?" I asked Roger.

"He's recuperating. The agents were a little rough on your purse before they knew he was in there." Roger glared at Gant.

"Barry who?" Gant asked.

"The Madagascan chameleon, sir."

"He's named after my ex-husband," I said. "They have similar tongues."

Later that night, Roger came by my room again. This time, I was too disheartened for violence. I left the door open and sat on the bed.

"You named our chameleon after another man?"

"Our chameleon? Yes, I did. My ex—ex being

the operative word, as in someone I am no longer with."

"You never told me you were married."

"You never asked. At least I was single when we met. Unlike you. Or was Alicia made up too?"

"No, she's real. I did live with her for a long time. Too long. Mostly, I told you the truth." Roger sat down beside me. "Cyd? Are you sure you want to do this? It's not too late to change your mind. You haven't actually smuggled anything yet."

"Yeah, but then Gant's still after my uncle and my clients. I have to do it."

"What if you get caught?"

"I'm not going to get caught," I said, remembering the percentages I'd read online and hoping I could be in the majority for once.

He asked for my pill bottle. "I managed to get a few, thought you might need them." He threw a handful in.

"What about Barry?"

"You'll see him tomorrow."

"And he's okay?"

"He's okay."

After Roger was gone, the first order of business was to order dinner, i.e., Akida. Forty-five minutes later, there was a knock on the door and there he was.

"Where's Nigel?" I asked.

"I gave him an offer he could not refuse, like in *The Godmother*," Akida said, putting down the food. There was a throwaway cell phone on top of my burger bun.

"It is untraceable, as you wanted. But, Cyd Redondo, I have made a reservation for you under another name, if you desire to return home tonight. I have a passport for you, as well." He shrugged. "As in your country, certain rules may be bent."

"I want to, Akida, but somebody's got to face the music. But thanks. Thanks for everything."

"Cyd Redondo, before I followed instructions without thinking. I am not following instructions anymore."

"I know. And this phone makes up for everything. Thank you. Please give my love to Bopo and Shawana."

Akida grasped my arm in the Tanzania way— by the elbow. I shook it for a long time, then kissed him, which embarrassed him completely.

"Come to Brooklyn someday, Akida."

"It is my dream. Godspeed, Cyd Redondo." He hurried out the door.

I turned on the shower so no one could hear me talking through the door and checked my watch. It was lunch time in Brooklyn. Where would Uncle Ray be? I took a chance on Peppino's. Mario and I were partners in Cotillion a million years ago. I worked on my story as I dialed.

"Cyd. You're the talk of the town." Mario said. Great, I thought.

"Any chance my uncle's there for lunch?"

"No, haven't seen him. Seen any lions?"

"No, just a leopard," I said. "Look Mario, I need to get a message to Uncle Ray." I made Mario write everything down, hoping my uncle would understand my "code" and, if Jimmy did have anything to do with this, he'd take precautions.

"Come in for some sausage when you get home," Mario said.

●  ●  ●  ●  ●

The next morning Nigel knocked right on time. I grabbed my pills and extra toiletries, put on my sunglasses, and walked out with as much dignity as was possible without makeup.

"Claymore's not such a bad guy," Nigel said, as I stepped out of the elevator.

"Perhaps you haven't slept with him." I took a deep breath and walked into the ballroom. Gant, Roger, and Agent Fisher stood by the conference table. I saw my Balenciaga bag. It was all I could do not to run over and hug it.

It looked like there was a new stain on the side. I hoped Bay Ridge Leather had a multi-stain discount. The bag felt suspiciously light. I checked the side: no compass. I distracted myself with what looked like a coffee cake and a few pastry containers at the end of the table. I was starving. As I got nearer, my starvation turned to dread. I had seen those containers before.

# Chapter Forty-one

"Why are those here?" I asked.

"Well, we think the smuggling ring has placed animals in your waiting luggage, but we can't count on it. You'll have to carry some on board just in case." Gant picked up my open carry-on and pointed out the ground rhino horn powder in my compact and two ivory necklaces in a tampon holder. Not my brand, by the way, if anyone were asking.

"Great," I said. "I think I can handle that."

"Well, I certainly hope so," Gant said. "We don't want the live animals to be hurt or suffocated."

Live animals?

Agent Fisher held up one of my La Perla bras, which now had four slits cut into it.

"Stop. That's a La Perla. Do you have any idea how much that costs?"

"Yes," she said. She lifted two tiny bright green snakes and stuffed them into the slits. "We've drugged them, so chances are they'll sleep the whole trip." She took out a tiny needle and thread and sewed up the holes.

"Chances are? I can't spend twenty-three hours in a confined space with snakes in my bra. You've got to be kidding."

"You can distract yourself with these." She held up a money belt full of eggs. "You'll have a few turtles taped to your legs and some other items. I'll dress you when you're ready." Now I understood why Roger had brought my palazzo pants and tie-front shirt. "Come on, you really can't expect me to get through Customs with all of these."

"That's exactly what we expect you to do. That's the agreement you signed."

There were still four or five containers to go. I didn't want to show weakness. Would vomit be weak?

"Of course, as your 'plus one,' Agent Claymore, will be carrying as well."

"Well, that's romantic," I said, trying not to look at my wriggling bra. "Look guys, honestly, I don't think I can do this. I'm going to freak out before I even get on the plane."

"You know the alternative," Gant said.

"Gant? Could we have a minute?" Roger said.

Gant pointed to the security cameras, and left with Agent Fisher.

"Why don't you let me hypnotize you?" Roger

said. "I can make you unaware of the animals. I can keep you from acting guilty and keep your heart rate down, which will keep them calmer too. What do you think?

"I don't want to be hypnotized, especially by a federal agent. I told you that already."

"I know, but it might be the only way you can get through this."

"How do you know it will work? It doesn't work on everybody, right?"

"You're suggestible," he said.

"You're an asshole."

"I meant clinically. Will you let me try?"

"Am I going to be a zombie or something? I mean how will I feel?"

"Like yourself, but calm."

"What do you mean? I'm always calm."

He patted me. "Of course you are. You'll just be more calm. You'll be completely awake and aware. You'll know about the animals, so that you don't injure them, but you won't feel them moving or be bothered by them."

I caught the squirming plastic tubs out of the corner of my eye.

"Can't you just make me unconscious instead?"

"You're going to have to take off those sunglasses."

"Turn around, then," I said. My emergency

mascara was in the side of my bag along with a rust-colored lipstick. I went for my compact and almost spilled the rhino dust. I guessed I'd have to do without powder.

"Okay," Roger said. "Just listen to my voice and look at this." He reached into his pocket and pulled out my father's compass. I gasped. "I grabbed it at Hazelnut's. I didn't trust them, either. Don't worry. I'll be there the whole time, and so will your dad. Now just sit back and keep your eyes on this," he said as he began to swing the braided chain back and forth.

Once I was officially "under," Roger gave me back the compass and, to my delight, a pink Tupperware with holes. Barry twitched. I swear he recognized me. Roger said not to mention the chameleon and to keep him in my purse, not my carry-on.

Then Agent Fisher returned and escorted me into the ladies' room. She was drenched in Estée Lauder Pleasures. Between that and the reptiles, it was hard not to gag. Once she finished rigging me, I had four baby snakes in my bra, ten endangered reptiles in my fanny pack, and six tiny turtles in bubblewrap taped to my calves, like space-age leg warmers. Amazingly, I was still conscious and breathing. I guess hypnosis worked. I wondered if it were covered on my health plan? Fisher told me I had to be careful when I sat down.

"No kidding."

"I'm serious. You're wearing about seventy-five thousand dollars' worth of endangered reptiles purchased by the U.S. Government. This isn't a joke."

"If you don't trust me, then why don't you do it?"

"It's below my rank." So much for the sisterhood. She pointed to the door.

By the time the agents got us to the airport, our flight had been delayed. Was there an expiration date for hypnosis? I reminded myself to ask Roger about this once we were through security. When we finally checked in, I explained that our luggage had been lost on arrival and asked to file a claim, per Gant's instructions. The clerk disappeared, then came out beaming.

"Miss Redondo, Mr. Claymore. I'm delighted to say that we have located your luggage and it has been placed on the plane already for your return. Since it has not officially entered the country, there is no need to recheck." This was so wrong, but then I thought about how Uncle Ray taught me how to ride a bike, took the luggage receipts, and kept my mouth shut.

"I can't believe they expect people to fall for

that," I said. Roger patted me on the shoulder. "No patting. I'm fine."

Roger reached down to adjust his "package," which was larger than I remembered. What was down there—a monkey? If so, I hoped it had claws. He had saved my dad's compass, but had he done it out of kindness or manipulation? And what the hell had he told my subconscious when he was futzing around in there? I might be walking through the airport naked, for all I knew. At the very least I looked bloated and bowlegged.

We reached the first security point. The guard asked me to take off my shoes. Detached, I wondered whether any turtles had wriggled downward, but my feet were reptile-free. The agent, dripping blobs of sweat onto his checklist, said something too fast in Swahili to a man on the other side. The man answered and they pulled our carry-on bags out of the line. I was cool as a cucumber. Roger, not so much.

"You are with the Redondo Travel tour, correct?" the agent asked, then put a special tag on both of our carry-on bags and we were off for the second security screening. This was the trickiest part; I took deep breaths like Roger told me to. I zipped my purse so nothing (i.e., Barry) would fall out, laid my quart bag of hotel toiletries on the conveyer belt and walked through the metal detector, hoping my reptilian underwire wouldn't set it off. They seemed to be pulling about every third person for a pat-down. The guard gestured me over. Roger paled.

I raised my arms, preparing for arrest. A woman the shape of a hunk of fresh mozzarella moved up my arms, her thick fingers squeezing every few inches. She was just getting to my shoulders when one of the guards called to her and she stopped. The second guard gestured me through. I waited to see if they would frisk Roger. After all, he seemed to be wearing three shirts and a safari vest with multiple pockets. Even I would have frisked him. But he, the bastard, walked right through. We went into the jammed waiting area, and I heard a familiar voice that sent my heart right past the turtles and to the floor.

"Cyd! Cyd Redondo! It's us!"

I turned to see my favorite clients, the Minettis, in matching magenta shirts, sunburned and beaming and heading, arms wide, right toward us.

# Chapter Forty-two

I knew Marie would come in for one of her intense, bony hugs: the kind that could result in species extinction. I had to head her off. I gripped her outstretched hands, keeping my arms stiff, and kissed her on both cheeks,

"Very European," Marie said. "This is so swell. We're on the same flight. Don't you look great? And you've finally put on a little weight. That's what happens when you're happy."

How much reptile water weight I was carrying? Herb stepped up and offered his hand.

"You must be Roger. Herb Minetti and my better half, Maria."

"Delighted to meet you." Roger shook their hands.

"You know Cyd is too good for just anyone, mister," Herb said.

"Don't I know it." Roger put his arm around me, lightly. "Here, let me help you with those bags."

He picked up the two Rick Steves rolling duffels I'd selected for their trip.

"We love these carry-ons, Cyd. You know they lost our regular luggage, so these were a godsend."

"Lost your luggage?" I was suddenly nauseous. "Why didn't you call me?"

"We knew you'd worry. We carried on all the important stuff, just like you said, so we were fine."

I looked at Roger. There were animals in the Minettis' luggage. I knew it. I kept reminding myself that Google said over ninety-five percent of smugglers got through, but should we really trust Google when it's important?

They called our flight. Roger winced and pointed discreetly at my chest.

"Bra," he said. "There's something showing."

I looked down to see a tiny snake tongue flicking through my cleavage. Clearly hypnotized, I pressed it back in, buttoned up and headed up the stairs to the plane.

I stopped at the top and took a minute to say good-bye to Africa. I would never forget the smell of ginger plants and monkey droppings, the taste of *ugali*, or the leopard that had licked my face. Then I thought about Mom and Uncle Ray and the Minettis and wondered if it had been worth it, after all.

Once we were on the plane, I grabbed some

electrical tape out of my bag—one of the few things Gant's men didn't steal—and ducked into the lavatory to close up the snake escape hatch. I hoped it would hold, especially since I didn't seem to notice when they were moving. I got back to the seat and gave Roger a thumbs-up, then reached for the goodie bag. This time Roger had already gotten us extras. I put them in my purse, which now seemed terrifyingly empty.

"Those guys took my blush, Roger. That's a felony in Brooklyn."

"I know. They're assholes," he said, eyeing me a little too long. He had what looked like an enormous erection pushing up his seat belt. I looked down. He caught me.

"Sorry." He made an adjustment. "It's the horn."

"I certainly hope so."

The Minettis were across from us. They held hands during takeoff. I wondered how different this flight might have been if Roger had been a real "plus one." Travel was supposed to make or break a couple—it was a crash course in what someone was really like—what they ate, how they slept, how they tipped, how they handled stress. I apparently handled it with a series of jailable offenses.

I made sure no turtles were trapped between my calves and the leg rest, twisted around to the front, and fell asleep with my head against the tiny chilled window. I woke up as we were making our descent into Heathrow. Damn. I'd slept through the warm chocolate chip cookies. If any of us were caught in Customs, I might never be allowed to fly again.

I saw something crawl across Roger's chest. And back the other way. I shook him awake, gestured him to the bathroom and followed him. Of course, there was a line. Could monkeys undo buttons? Finally, he got inside. I introduced myself and handed out Redondo travel cards, to cover the high-pitched squeaks. Finally, Roger came back to his seat. Where was the monkey? As the plane headed downwards, he grabbed my hand and we taxied to the gate.

Roger and I kept behind Herb and Maria, checking each other for leaking species as we walked what seemed like five miles between the plane and Arrivals. I figured the Minettis would be okay here, as they didn't have animals on their person like Roger and I did. The four of us arrived at Border Control, where the agent asked if I were carrying any fruits or vegetables into the country. As he didn't ask about snakes, turtles, or rhino dust, I gave a resounding and convincing "No." Now I just needed to get to the Minettis' bags before they did.

"Roger, can you take Maria and Herb downstairs? I'll get our luggage."

"You're going to let that tiny girl get the luggage, Roger? Cyd can come with us."

"Yes, Cyd, I'll get it," Roger said.

"No! I mean, thank you, but because the luggage was lost, there may be some paperwork and I'll be able to handle that a lot quicker. Don't worry, Herb, they have carts. Really, you three just relax." I bolted down the stairs like I was running for the R Train.

It was hard to push through a throng of irritated travelers without smushing my cargo, but I did my best. Thank goodness I'd picked out the Minettis' luggage for them—black and white polka dotted hard shells—as Herb was colorblind. As the two cases tumbled down the chute, I lunged for them, possibly losing a couple of turtles. It was a case of priorities. Herb and Maria I'd known all my life, the reptiles I'd just met.

I wheeled the two cases into the jammed women's room and waited for a stall. For the millionth time, how could it possibly take some women so long? Once it was my turn, there was barely room to get the two cases through the door, much less open them. I had to lay them on top of the seat. I'm always irritated when a toilet flushes itself, but this time I was on the verge of screaming.

Per my instructions, both the cases were locked. Good thing I had a TSA lock opener on my keychain, lifted from a TSA guy I'd dated two years ago. I checked Herb's case first. I could hear angry women trying my door about every twenty seconds, but the bag was clean. I opened Maria's to find three cute stuffed toy tigers tucked under a floral muumuu. Then one of them blinked. And yawned.

It couldn't have been more than a couple of weeks old. It was obviously drugged, so I moved it gently aside to check for anything else in the bag. I had to think fast. I moved the drowsy little cub to my Balenciaga—the first time I was glad it was empty—wiped the toilet spray off the luggage, and opened the door to the furious stares of a plane load of tourists, swearing at me in Italian.

I had asked Roger once what happened to the animals they confiscated at Customs. He had told me, the cuter they were, the more likely someone would make the effort to save it. This little guy was off the cuteness scale. I moved to the pull-down diaper changing station. I had checked for security cameras, but kept my back to the door just in case. I wrapped the sleeping tiger cub in the airline blanket I'd lifted from the flight and laid him down on the changing table. I made sure he couldn't fall, then ducked out with the bags and looked for Roger. He was standing by the carousel with the Minettis.

"I need a pay phone," I said.

"You can use my cell," Roger offered.

"Pay phone," I said again, trying to make my predicament clear. Herb spotted one on the far wall and I went to make a quick anonymous call to Security to report the tiger, while Roger grabbed the purple case and his duffel.

As I was dialing, I heard a squeal. A woman with a bare-assed baby came running out of the bathroom and ran to a guard. I hung up, relieved. Gant hadn't said anything about other people's animals, right?

I rejoined Roger and the Minettis in the next line and waited with trepidation as they put Maria's case through the X-ray machine, cleared it, then let all of us go. At least my clients were safe from international prosecution. As we walked out the doors into the terminal, two Animal Control officers ran into the toilets.

I stopped by the BA counter and changed the Minettis' reservations, insisting they should stay in London for a few more days. That would also prevent their seeing me arrested at JFK.

As I tried to figure out how not to hug them good-bye, my name came over the loudspeaker.

# Chapter Forty-three

Was I on camera hiding the tiger cub? I gave them quick European kisses, gave Roger a worried look, and headed for the Information Booth. As I turned, the Minettis yelled "We love you, Cyd." Suddenly, I had the feeling things were crawling around on my chest and legs. I thought for a minute I was going to be sick, then it passed. I arrived at the booth and gave my name.

"Are you feeling all right, madam?" the Pakistani clerk said. I could feel a cold drop of sweat moving down between my breasts.

"I'm fine." I smiled and took the phone. "Cyd Redondo, Redondo Travel."

"Cyd." It was Uncle Ray. "Are you all right? You got to London okay?"

"We're fine. You got my message?"

"Loud and clear," he said. "Don't worry about JFK, everything will be fine. Hang in there. Love you."

"Love you too. Bye," I said, relieved. Again, I felt a crawling sensation, but it stopped.

I was almost frisked a final time at the gate, but saved by a woman with five Duty Free bags. Before I knew it, we were back in the bulkhead. I wanted to put my feet up on the wall just for a minute, but was afraid my pants would drift down, revealing reptiles. Roger asked if I had anything to do with Animal Control showing up.

"Let's just enjoy the flight," I said.

We had our warm nuts and champagne, then Roger drifted off, leaning against my shoulder. I tried to watch a travel show, but it was filled with too much irresponsible information. I finally settled on reruns of *Bones*. At this point, Roger had slipped down and was practically nuzzling my neck. He was sleeping so peacefully, I let him stay. He readjusted again right next to my ear.

"I love you, Cyd." His voice was almost too quiet to hear.

Even before the words got to my brain, I could feel something moving in my shirt. Something squirmy and slimy and maybe poisonous. All at once, I felt snakes and lizards and turtles squiggling all over me. I could swear a snake was headed down my arm and flicking my nipple. I barely stifled a scream and shook Roger's arm as hard as I could.

Two of the flight attendants noticed my distress.

"Are you all right, Miss Redondo?" the attendant with the heavy gold jewelry asked.

"Nut allergy," I said, on reflex. Both of us looked at the almost empty warm nut ramekin. "I forgot," I said, unconvincingly. Could she see the waves of reptiles moving under my shirt? Or was I going to be detained as a terrorist rather than a smuggler? I shook Roger's arm harder. Finally, he woke up.

"I need my EpiPen," I said.

"What? What are you talking about?"

"I'm having an allergic reaction," I said slowly, gesturing to the attendant, then looking down at my cleavage. "I feel like I'm breaking out in hives and having trouble breathing. Almost like snakes are all over me. Please help me."

He finally got it, and came with me to the lavatory.

"Roger you have to get these out now. Really. I am fricking freaking out."

"Hang on just one second. They're in zip-locks, it's okay."

"The ones in my bra are not in zip-locks, and anyway, a zip-lock is not Tupperware. They have fangs. Do something," I said. I started scratching at the zip-locks taped to my thighs, trying to get them off me. He grabbed me by the shoulders.

"Stop. Just look at me. Look me square in the eye and don't blink."

As I looked into those Raisinet eyes, I swear I felt a lizard headed for my thong.

"Okay, blink when I get to three." He had me blink in an irregular pattern and count down from ten and suddenly I was breathing. The flight attendant knocked on the door, asking if everything was okay.

"Fine," Roger said, "just give us a second." I put everything back in place and straightened my hair. Roger helped me back to my seat.

"I thought you said I would stay hypnotized."

"It's supposed to last until you hear the trigger."

"What's the trigger?"

"I can't tell you. If I say it, you'll wake up again."

But I thought I knew. Was "I love you" an ironic trigger, or a real one? They announced our descent into JFK.

"So," I said. "I just have to get through Customs and that's it, right?"

"Right. It's almost over."

"And what happens then? Do you take the animals? They're not going to die, are they?"

"Not if I can help it." He picked up my hand and kissed it gently. "You've done great. I'm so glad you decided to look after yourself for once. It was the right decision."

"What are you talking about?"

"You decided to let your uncle take the fall, like he should."

"Roger, what are you talking about? Fisher said if I got through without getting caught that would vindicate Uncle Ray. That they wouldn't go after him."

Roger swore. "Gant is such a shit. That's why they wanted me out of the room. This is the thing: you were supposed to be the test."

"I know, I'm testing their Customs controls."

"No, the test was for your uncle's network. Gant loaded you up with so many things, there's no way someone wouldn't pull you. So, the idea was, if you got through, then your Uncle had connections every step of the way. If the animals get out of JFK without being confiscated, then he's guilty. They've got him."

"Kind of like if you drown, you weren't a witch."

"Kind of like that."

I couldn't believe how stupid I'd been. Something had seemed fishy, but how could I have missed this? I knew I could be naïve sometimes, but I didn't really think I was a completely fricking moron. Dammit.

The wheels snapped down and two minutes later, we were on the ground. I figured there was still time between landing and the Customs Hall to get a message to Uncle Ray. I reached for my phone.

"Don't," Roger said. "All his lines are tapped. The office too."

I put the phone back and grabbed my bottle of pills, figuring the Valium Roger had given me was the only thing that would get me through Customs. Roger tried to stop me, but I sucked four down before he could tell me they were malaria pills.

I felt light-headed when I stood up, but I figured it was just stress. I was tempted to leave my carry-on, but, of course, Roger got it down for me. We chatted with the flight attendants about the weather and then the door opened onto the jetway and I got a blast of the diesel fuel and salt air that meant home.

Once we were inside the terminal, we followed the signs for Arrivals. We had apparently come in just behind a crowded flight from Nicaragua and there were probably a hundred people ahead of us in Passport Control. Roger kept glancing at me.

"I'm still hypnotized, don't worry."

"You're sweating," he said. "A lot."

"Yeah, well, I've been hiking with these bags." Actually, I did feel a little clammy.

"Let me carry that, then." He took the carry-on. I kept a tight hold on the Balenciaga and Barry.

Finally, we were next in line. I tried to be as

normal as possible while they checked our passports. I figured I should at least get back into the
country, where I had rights and knew attorneys
like my Uncle Tony, before I did anything stupid.
Roger kept a tight hold on my arm as we waited
for our luggage. As the carousel went around and
around with nothing on it, I got dizzier and dizzier. At one point, I saw my purple polka-dot bag
and lunged for it.

Roger caught me before I wound up face-first
on the carousel. "What are you doing?"

"There's my bag. Beside the goat," I said.

He pulled me away from the carousel and
turned me toward him. "What's going on?"

"Nothing," I said. "Will you please get my
bag?" He turned me back around. The carousel
was empty.

"How many of those malaria pills did you
take?" he asked.

"Four?" I said.

"Christ. Okay, just hold onto me and I'll get
you through this. Whatever you see, ignore it. It's
probably a hallucination." Easy for him to say.

"Even her?" I asked as Agent Fisher breezed by
with a diplomatic bag and jumped the line. Right
now, she had the head of a Gorgon and the legs of
a female wrestler.

"Ahhhh!" I said as she appeared to bite off the head of a tiny Asian Customs Agent.

"Shhh. There are our bags. Please stay here." He put down my carry-on and started chasing the rubber merry-go-round.

I felt dizzy again and leaned against the railing, being careful of the reptiles. A well-coiffed, too-tanned couple in suede ran over my foot with their luggage cart. I yelped. They just stared at me and turned into lizards until I remembered what I had to do. I picked up my carry-on and headed for the final Customs checkpoint.

"Cyd!" Roger cried, but I kept going.

Finally I arrived at the counter behind two people who had nothing to declare.

I smiled and said "I do."

"You do what?" The Customs agent looked down at me. He had a veiny nose and smelled like stale beer and air freshener.

"I have something to declare. I have a declaration."

He rolled his eyes. "Yes, miss, what is it you want to declare? Your independence?"

"No. I have five snakes in my bra." And then, I guess, I fainted.

# Chapter Forty-four

I came-to with no fanny pack, no turtle warmers, and no bra. At least I'd lost the La Perla saving my uncle. My purse, carry-on, and suitcase sat in the corner of the pale green, stuffy room, but before I could get to them, a thin, elderly man in a lab coat and granny glasses appeared.

"Miss Redondo. How are you feeling?"

"Where am I? What happened?"

"JFK. You fainted in the Customs Hall."

"Am I under arrest?"

"Of course not. We think it was just a reaction to your malaria pills."

"What about the animals, the ones I was wearing?"

"Yes, Bud told me you were hallucinating. That's very common. Don't worry, it's temporary. Just take those pills one at a time from now on."

"No, really, I had animals all over me."

"Of course you did."

"Where's Roger? My plus one?"

"As far as I'm aware, you were traveling alone. I'm sure it will all make sense once you get some sleep. Come on, I'll get you a taxi." He went out of the room and I tried to figure out what the hell had possibly happened. Were the animals still in my luggage? I was dying to check, but contained myself.

The doctor came back, gathered my things, took me out into the freezing New York night, and helped me get everything into a cab. He leaned in through the window and patted my arm.

"Tell your Uncle Ray that Doctor Bronson said hello," he said, then waved. The cabbie asked where I was going.

"Bay Ridge. Redondo Travel."

I pulled Dad's compass from the side of my bag and held on tight until I saw the Verrazano Bridge, brake lights scattered across it like Red Hots, and we turned onto Third Avenue.

The office was dark. I overtipped the cabbie, took a minute to figure out how to maneuver all my luggage and still hold my flashlight and Mace, then stood at the back door, listening. My head hurt from whatever it hit when I fainted, and I wondered if I were still hypnotized. I guessed not, as I hardly felt calm. Where was Roger? Where was Gant? Oh, God, where was Barry?

I unlocked the back door and hit the lights. Everything looked normal. I made my way down the hall and collapsed into my beloved ergonomic chair. I put my Balenciaga on the desk and opened my carry-on: no tampon ivory, no rhino compact. I unlocked my hardshell case and moaned: there were all the clothes I'd chosen so carefully for my safari and could have used for bartering, but no animals or animal parts. Who had gotten them all out? Uncle Ray? Or the FBI? And how long had I been unconscious? And where was Roger?

Finally, I opened my purse, then sighed in relief. The pink Tupperware with the holes was still there. After everything I'd been through, losing Barry was the one thing I couldn't handle. I unburped the top carefully and looked in. He was there, but not moving. Then, one of his eyes twitched. Maybe he was just traumatized. I knew exactly how he felt. I got him some water and a piece of wilted celery from the fridge and took him out to recuperate on my mouse pad. Looking at Barry made me think about Roger and I didn't want to think about Roger.

Instead, I booted up the computer while I filed my first (and possibly last) boarding passes in case the airline didn't give me the miles. I heard a noise in the back and whipped around. It was strange not to have a gun. I grabbed a strappy sandal from the suitcase and ducked down under the desk.

"Cyd? Cyd, are you here?" Uncle Ray stood in the doorway, his gray overcoat damp with mist and his jowls particularly jowly. His color was bad and he seemed shorter. I stood up. "Hey, kiddo. I didn't mean to scare you. Your mom got worried. I thought you might be here."

There he was, the one I'd run to with every skinned knee and failed test and fender bender of my life. It seemed like the most natural thing in the world to run to him with this. Instead, I threw the shoe at his head.

He ducked and it missed him by a foot. Damn. My aim was off.

"Still throwing like a girl." He smiled. "You did good, Squid."

"At what? Getting you arrested? Decimating the world's rhino population? Getting my heart broken? What?"

"Surviving," he said. "You got thrown right in the soup and here you are, in one piece. I underestimated you. You should have been in on this from the beginning. You did good."

It would have been nice to have heard that about getting a B+ in Algebra in seventh grade or when I was learning to parallel park. The unqualified praise made me wobbly for a minute. But it didn't change anything.

"Who the hell is Doctor Bronson?"

"An old friend."

"An old friend? Really? Like a Bobby Barsky kind of old friend?"

He gave me one of his looks. "We all went to school together."

"What school was that? The school of international assholes?"

"Cyd, language." It was just like him to try to make me feel like I was six.

"And since when does JFK have an attending physician who makes animals disappear?"

He sighed. "Since I got your message."

I honestly thought I might throw up. "So Interpol was right."

"I don't think Interpol is ever actually right. They're too disorganized."

"They weren't too disorganized to play me. I led them right to you."

"It's all fine." Uncle Ray saw my face and sighed. "Come on, we'll talk." He gestured toward his office.

"We don't have time to talk. They're probably on their way to the house right now."

"We have all the time in the world." He unlocked his door and moved behind the desk where it all started. I didn't want to sit down. I could still see that parrot. I knew now it could have been Barry.

Uncle Ray got out a bottle of Jack Daniels and two glasses, then pulled out my chair. "They can't just catch you with the merchandise. Animals come into the country all the time. They have to prove you had prior knowledge that a shipment was illegal."

"But you did have prior knowledge."

"It doesn't matter. They have to prove it. And they can't. That's why it's such a great model. Anybody carrying heroin can't really plead ignorance, but if a dealer tells you an animal's clean, you can."

"Well, if that's true, where are they? The animals I was carrying. Why didn't I just breeze through Customs?"

"Because you got us a warning. Those animals were planted by Interpol. They didn't have our paperwork. Thanks for fainting, by the way, that was really smart."

I really was going to throw up. "Why? Why on earth are you involved in this?"

He poured us each a shot of Jack. "We needed to diversify."

I pushed mine away. "Diversify? That's what you call it?"

"The business is in trouble. Real trouble. Has

been for years. On its own, I give Redondo Travel six months."

"No way. I do the books, we're still in the black."

He gave me a pitying look. I shot the bourbon.

"You think it's easy to support you and your mother?" he said. "Aunt Helen's cancer surgery? Private school for the twins? Jimmy's never going to be able to hold down a real job. Where do you think all that money comes from? Commission on a few cruises and senior golf trips?"

I thought about our commission situation. I probably had been kidding myself. Not for the first time today, I felt like a complete, worthless moron.

"I was looking for a new opportunity when Bobby got in touch and said he needed a warehouse in Brooklyn."

"Did he say for what?"

"Not at first. But after 9/11 things got tougher in Customs and he knew I had some connections, so he offered me a, well, a bigger role."

This had been going on since before 9/11? No wonder Interpol assumed I was in on it. Christ on a bike. How much had I been involved without knowing it? Was Redondo Travel just a laundering facility for animal trafficking?

"And what does that involve, exactly? I mean when I'm not the mule? How does it work?"

"We have people in Customs. Jakarta, Africa,

the United Arab Emirates, all over. Bobby was doing this in Indonesia before, so he has the connections. He handles Dar es Salaam and Cape Town and I set up the UAE."

"How do you have connections in the UAE?"

"You booked me that tour of the best Dubai hotels. Remember?"

God. I did remember. So I had been part of it. A big part. I nodded, zombielike.

"I'd heard they were happy to turn a blind eye for a price. In this case, a couple of first-class flights. Bobby gets the packages to the Dubai Airport and there, my Customs guy redoes the waybills."

"Redoes them how?"

"He marks the animals 'captive bred'—they're only illegal if they're caught in the wild—then they come into JFK legally." Mrs. Barksy's FedEx package and the embassy papers and had both said 'Captive Bred.' Of course. "And even if we get caught, the penalties are a joke. It's like a fifteen-hundred-dollar fine and no jail time."

"So, if it's so easy, then why stuff reptiles into the Andersons' luggage?"

"That came from Bunty's boss, Mr. Chu. The Customs guy in Dubai got greedy and top brass was looking for a way to cut out the middle man. Bunty told them about us and they had him set up Adventures Limited. He figured no one would suspect someone with a walker and as long as we put a special sticker on the luggage and had people in Baggage at both ends, it was still safe."

"Not for the Giannis, it wasn't."

He threw out his hands. "They're not in jail, are they?"

"No, but they would be if it weren't for Roger." God, this really was all my fault. I had participated at every stage. It didn't matter if I didn't know it, that just made me stupid.

"They're fine. It put a little excitement in their lives." He saw my face. "Cyd, I told you, we're in trouble. There's a five hundred to a thousand per-cent markup on this stuff, even with the occasional losses. High profit, low risk. Good business."

I could still smell the toxic paint on the birds, see the parrots with their eyes stitched. I saw the Minettis in their Sketchers, trusting me to give them a safe, happy vacation.

"Endangering our clients? Parrot sausages? Smothering baby tigers? That's good business to you?"

"It's mostly reptiles. Those animals are gone, anyway, Cyd, the rare ones, whether we're in it or not. There are too many wackos who'll pay top dollar to get them. Besides, family's more important than a few snakes, right?"

"I'm having a really hard time telling the

difference at the moment. What about all those lessons you taught me? About being honest and paying your taxes and taking things on the chin— what about that? Was that just bullshit? God, I can't even look at you right now." I got up.

So did he. "You're right. That's why I'm turning myself in. I already called the Precinct. I'm on my way now. I just came to say good-bye. Anyway, what kind of example would I be for you and the boys if I didn't stand up like a man and take responsibility for my actions?"

What was he talking about, turning himself in? What did he mean by good-bye? I couldn't breathe. I grabbed the back of the chair and lowered myself into it, then poured myself another shot to keep from crying. I choked down the tears, but couldn't stop my hand from shaking. Finally, I stared up at him. "Mrs. Barsky. Did you kill her?"

"Of course not. How could you think that?"

"Well, who did?"

"None of our people. No way. Bobby adored that woman. Leave it to the police, Cyd." He started for the door. Right that minute, I wanted him dead, but I couldn't bear to think of him in jail.

"But what about Mom? What about Louis and David?" And what about me?

He came around the desk. "They have you," he said. "That's not nothing." He kissed me hard on the head, then put his coat back on and straightened his tie. "Someday when you have kids, you'll understand."

"Should I call Uncle Tony?" He was my youngest uncle and the lawyer in the family.

"He's meeting me there. Don't worry about Redondo Travel. I've made sure it's clean. Go home and see your mother."

And then he was gone.

I closed the office door and sat down behind Uncle Ray's desk. Despite his "confession," could I trust anything he had ever told me? And was the business really safe, or would it be seized by the FBI in the morning? And what about Mrs. Barsky? And Pet World? Maybe Jimmy had killed her and Uncle Ray just couldn't face it. I couldn't think about all of it then; I was jet-lagged and heartbroken and a little drunk. I put my head down and drifted off.

# Chapter Forty-five

I woke up to voices, the smell of Estée Lauder Pleasures, and what sounded like my ergonomic chair hitting the wall, rhythmically. What the hell? I rose, my tongue thick and stale from the Jack Daniels, and looked for a weapon. As it seemed my kitten heel aim was off, I opted for one of Uncle Ray's golf clubs and cracked the door. I could hear my brousin Jimmy's distinctive wheezing—he'd always been asthmatic. As I crept down the hall, the familiar perfume got stronger, so I should have been prepared when I saw Jimmy on top of Agent Fisher, but it was still a shock.

"On my chair? Really?" I threw on all the lights. Jimmy's Hugo Boss pants were on the floor, surrounded by animals flopping in zip-locks and coleslaw containers, the tiny thuds like nail files through my heart. They gave Fisher's cloying perfume a base note of reptile house.

"You asshole!" I knocked Jimmy as hard as I

could with the seven iron. He fell straight to the floor, out cold. Agent Fisher slid up her skin-tight leather pants and smiled, pulling a gun out of her jacket. Too bad Interpol had kept mine. I dropped the golf club, provoking a spider monkey chirp.

"Thanks for the help," she said, looking down at Jimmy. "He is an asshole. Not bad in bed, but basically useless otherwise. He couldn't even stab a parrot."

"You're the one who killed that poor parrot?"

She smiled, then had the nerve to rub it in with "jazz hands." I looked around at all the animals who'd managed to survive the intercontinental journey suffocated in my luggage and down Roger's pants. Granted, being down Roger's pants might be okay for me, but for a monkey, not so much. Then I wondered whether Interpol was really tapping our phones, and if not, how long someone could leave a message on my cell. I wasn't going to be shot in my own office without taking Agent "can't wear Eileen" Fisher down with me. I sank onto my desk, shielding the phone from view.

"The parrot was your fault. You hadn't filled the trip and your uncle needed a little nudge. Besides, the bird had mange—no one was going to pay what it was worth. I hate waste." She started packing up boxes with one hand, keeping the gun pointed in my direction with the other. When she approached the tiny monkeys, they went berserk, howling and squealing, and I saw my chance. I leaned my hand back toward the phone. While she grabbed for them and swore, I hit the mute button on the phone, hit speed dial for my personal phone, mouthed "Cyd Redondo, Redondo Travel" to myself, then took the mute off and hit "speaker."

She finally wrangled the errant monkey and turned the gun back on me.

"Great, Agent Fisher. So you work for Bunty?"

"You can't be serious. He works for me, when he's lucky."

"Does Gant know? Does Roger?"

"Men see what you want them to see. I mean, did Claymore see a pathetic divorcée who lives with her mother? Of course not. He just saw legs. Of course they're short legs, but there's no accounting for taste."

"Taste? Really? You have the nerve to bring up taste after that hideous tunic thing?"

"I was undercover."

"I completely knew something was off with you."

"Please. Who's been one step ahead the whole time?"

Fisher was right. They'd all played me completely.

She turned toward me, took out her cell phone, and dialed. "Yes, this is Agent Fisher. Just letting you know that we have apprehended most of the Brooklyn contingent. Mr. Redondo is currently in custody and I am on the trail of the missing animals." She looked at me and winked. "I appreciate it, sir, but no thanks necessary. Just doing my job."

There was a sad, drugged squawk. Clearly the parrot tranquilizers were wearing off. I looked at my hangdog brousin, still out cold on the floor, and at our tiny, beloved office, now defiled by leather pants. I would never be able to erase the image of Agent Fisher shoving endangered species into crates like yard sale items. The Jack Daniels started repeating on me and I just wanted to lie down, but I had to keep the FBI super bitch talking.

"But why? Why us?"

"We needed a small-time travel company on the downswing."

"We are not on the downswing."

She rolled her eyes. "Your cousin was already helping us at Pet World. We needed more couriers to up our odds in Africa. Seniors were perfect, they always look harmless. And Jimmy told me how desperate you were to get away, so we offered you the trip, figuring you wouldn't look too closely. And you didn't."

She was right. I had trusted Uncle Ray's word it was okay.

"Your uncle's been very helpful. We needed

someone smart on this end who had a lot of connections." I was never going to be able to smell Pleasures again without gagging. I wasn't sure I could ever even go back into a mall.

"Who's we? You and Bunty?"

"The Buntys of the world are a dime a dozen. He just happened to have no scruples and a mother with a pet store. My partners are legitimate businessmen powerful enough to pay off any official who needs to be paid off and offer something in return. You understand the barter system, right?"

Sadly, I did. "And you really think you're going to get away with this? What are you going to do, kill me and Jimmy?"

Fisher pulled on some doctor's gloves and regarded a particularly wiggly takeout container. "I don't have to. Your uncle's confessing. Touching, isn't it? If you finger me, the FBI will think you're just trying to save him. And who would believe it, anyway? I'm a decorated agent, I've broken open three smuggling rings in three years." She reached into the carton and pulled out two wriggling baby snakes. I hoped they could bite through rubber. "Of course, I managed to cut myself into them, but the FBI doesn't know that and my partners aren't going to tell them. I'm too valuable. And Gant's the one who brought me on. He's not going to do anything that makes him look bad." She started putting the animals into two pieces of rolling luggage. I started to move. She turned the gun back on me and lifted a takeout container with two golden frogs inside. They were smaller than mini malt balls.

"Actually, better safe than sorry." Fisher opened the top and one of the frogs jumped out, a few feet from Jimmy. "These are from Madagascar. They're twice as potent as the South American ones."

"You killed Mrs. Barsky."

"The frogs killed her. I was just the delivery system."

"But why?"

"She was snooping around, asking questions. She didn't want to carry the reptiles anymore. And besides, she was old."

That did it. I pondered my odds. A gun usually beat a golf club, but I figured it was worth at least bruising her before I died. I reached for the seven iron. But instead of shooting, she moved to my desk and reached for the mouse pad. I had forgotten about Barry.

"Haven't you killed enough species already?" I asked, my heart in my throat.

"Go ahead, save one." She threw the long-suffering chameleon as hard as she could.

# Chapter Forty-six

I dropped the golf club and dove for an airborne Barry. Fisher grabbed Jimmy's keys and hit me on the head with the butt of her gun. Just the thing when you're hungover.

With Barry safe, I pretended to be knocked out and watched her roll the animals out. Finally, I heard the back door slam. Had the frog already touched the still unconscious Jimmy, or was it repelled too? Did all this really have to happen when I had jetlag?

Thank God Barry was okay. I put him back in his Tupperware and in a drawer for safety, picked up my bag and the golf club, and dragged Jimmy out into the parking lot just as the Lincoln Town car was pulling out. I managed to smash the right rear brake lights before Fisher headed down the alley. She waved, probably assuming I was car-less and not knowing Jimmy kept an extra set of keys in his wheel well. I ran for his Trans-Am and gunned the engine, spitting stones as I hit Third Avenue.

I kept my eye on the broken taillight and called Frank. He said he'd send an ambulance for Jimmy and he kept me on the line while I tried to figure out where Fisher was going. I looked back once as the bridge disappeared, said a quick prayer, and followed the car toward the Fort Hamilton Expressway.

After about a quarter mile, I saw someone tailing me. In a Prius. Fisher's Lincoln took a left to the docks. I turned left too. So did the Prius. I made a couple of quick turns and lost the tail, then circled back and spotted the Lincoln pulling into the Cruise Terminal. I slowed down and pulled over. The element of surprise was all I had.

Frank confirmed my location and said officers were on the way. Then I saw a light in my old friend Lou's parking/seafood shack office. He wasn't usually there so late, but it was worth a call.

"Yeah, this is Lou."

"Lou, it's Cyd. What are you still doing there?"

"I forgot Beth's birthday. I'm afraid to go home."

"Look, I'm in the parking lot. It's a long story, but I need to create a distraction. Do you have anything handy? Klieg lights, big vehicles, loud noises?"

"Is this for real?"

"Yeah, I'm trying to stall some animal smugglers until the cops get here."

"Have you been drinking?"

"No," I lied. "Seriously. I'll fix things with Beth." I heard him take a sip of something.

"I have some searchlights."

I saw three figures on the inky dock, in front of the Cruise Terminal concession stand. I reached into my purse. My hand closed around the two-cup Tupperware bowl I had managed to get past Customs.

"Give me ninety seconds, then shine it halfway between the dock and the Cruise Terminal," I said. I bolted from the car and ran. Ninety seconds is not very long. Two men were pulling the luggage out of the Lincoln and putting it into a mouse-gray van.

I put my camera phone on "record" and "zoom" as I made for my intended spot, making sure I got all their faces and hoping I still had some battery left. I used the cover of the open trunk to open the Tupperware and toss the contents around, then ducked behind some barrels and waited.

The searchlights finally smashed on, lighting up the entire dock and parking lot. Fisher and her cohorts froze, then, as I had hoped, ran toward the nearest cover, the overhanging awning by concessions—until they stopped. Stuck. Totally stuck.

I was definitely going to nab the North American distribution rights for bird lime. That stuff fricking worked. The three of them jerked around, trying to get their feet off the ground. I knew it wouldn't take long for them to take off their shoes, but at least Fisher had pull-on Ralph Lauren boots under her leather pants, so that gave me a few seconds—just enough time for me to throw one of the faux fishing nets from the Terminal restaurant over them.

"You can't pull off leather either, you bureaucratic slut!"

Fisher sprayed bullets at me through the net. I guess I hadn't really thought the whole net/bullet thing through.

Something stung my side. I ducked back behind the barrels. When I peeked back, they had their shoes off and were pulling off the net. With no cover between me and the Trans Am, I could only hope Frank's guys were on the way. I was starting to feel faint.

The burly guys got free and started grabbing animals from the Lincoln's trunk while Agent Fisher ran right at me, gun out. I prepared myself for the fate I probably deserved: death by Eileen Fisher.

Then someone dove from the side and she disappeared. Flashing lights appeared and half the Precinct rushed for the guys at the dock.

I stood up to see Agent Fisher on the ground,

a figure standing over her. It was Roger. He handed Fisher off to the cops and walked toward me.

"Were you tailing me?" I asked. He nodded. "You suck at it." I tried to stand up.

He reached over and took my Balenciaga off my shoulder. A neat bullet hole had pierced the strap.

"Dammit," My knees buckled. I gripped Roger's shoulder.

He saw the blood dripping from my side, pulled out a handkerchief, and pressed it into the wound.

"God, Cyd, I'm so sorry. I'm so sorry."

"Don't worry. I know a guy."

# Chapter Forty-seven

Dr. Kevekian came down to the Federal Building and patched me up. The bullet wound was just a graze. With any luck it would take a half inch off my waist. To be honest, it was my purse I was really worried about. It was really hard to match "Marilyn" red.

I had to give a full statement and verify my status as a "confidential informant." It helped that the Interpol wiretap and my speaker phone message had recorded Agent Fisher's confession and I had video of the animal exchange on the dock.

According to the FBI, Roger really was a fifteen-year veteran of the Fish and Wildlife Service (which was a real thing). He was a star, apparently—one of only six Special Operations Agents in the country, which didn't seem like nearly enough, given the general slaughter going on. I had hoped he'd be the one to spring me, but he was busy with interviews and paperwork, so Agent Gant offered to drive me home. He wasn't my favorite person at the moment, but he was free. He didn't say much until we pulled up at the curb.

"Your uncle is sticking to his confession. He confirmed both you and your cousin were unaware of any criminal activity. Interpol owes you an apology. I owe you an apology."

"And what? You're just going to keep your job? After harboring that psychopath? After sending all those animals to the bad guys?"

"Actually, I've been promoted. For breaking up the ring." I guess governments were the same everywhere.

Gant got out to open the door for me at least. I swallowed a yelp as I grabbed the dashboard. Holy God. Apparently, getting up from a sitting position used more of your waist than I remembered, but no way I was showing weakness in front of him. I'd scream later.

Every light in the house was on. This homecoming was going to be worse than getting shot. My mother opened the door, ran down the stairs, and grabbed me for all she was worth, right on top of my bullet wound.

"Ow!"

But she wouldn't let go and for once, she didn't even sigh.

The next morning at 8:05, I had a chat with Mrs. Barsky at the Greenwood Cemetery, plot 1783. I brought flowers and some watery decaf. I told her about most of my trip and how Bobby had called her a saint. I left the other parts out. I figured, if the dead were all-seeing, she already knew; if not, who was I to spoil her eternal rest?

A week later, things were almost back to normal. My wound was healing. Jimmy might have dodged an indictment, but my mousy mother had acted against type and had thrown him out of the house, so Eddie packed him off to work construction for some distant cousins in Fresno, which was the Brooklyn equivalent of prison. It didn't really change anything for me, as he was just absent as usual.

I went back to booking trips. Uncle Ray had done all the paperwork before he turned himself in: Redondo Travel was mine, impending bankruptcy and all. I was determined to turn it around, legally. The Andersons, the Minettis, and the Giannis were our new marketing strategy: they couldn't say enough about Redondo Travel's personal service. And after the article about me in the *Brooklyn Daily Eagle,* even Peggy Newsome's clients were stopping by to see my gunshot wound. I'd already filled a golf/seniors Zumba package to Palm Beach and a Seniors Walking Tour to Zurich. I still needed a big idea, and fast, but my old boyfriend Sam at Bay Ridge Savings had promised me a bridge loan, so I'd bought myself a couple of months.

We never found the frogs Agent Fisher let loose, but the Precinct's expert said they were only poisonous for a few days after they lost their native food source, so I decided they were welcome to hang around.

It was a tough decision, but I took Barry to the Brooklyn Zoo. Gant had arranged for an "importation certificate" so I wouldn't be arrested, and the reptile keeper said I could visit the chameleon anytime. He had a pretty cushy glass enclosure with a plaque that read "Sponsored by Redondo Travel." Nothing like free advertising.

I was at the zoo visiting Barry when Roger found me. We hadn't seen each other alone since the night on the pier. He was dressed in a leather jacket and jeans, with those same eyes and, worse, same sandals. Who wore a leather jacket and sandals? I pointed through the glass. Inside, were four tiny Barrys, zapping lettuce with tongues about a quarter inch long.

"Barry was a girl?" Roger said.

"The curator told me even that David Attenborough guy can't tell a boy from a girl when it comes to chameleons." I smiled, happy that at least in this case, I'd helped populate a species rather than end one.

Roger and I sat on a bench by the orangutans and he told me the burly guys had rolled over like kittens. It turned out when Agent Fisher had caught the infamous Mr. Chu, she had taken over his name and network. Her compatriots were pretty sure she'd killed him. Aside from being fired and charged with international conspiracy and animal trafficking, the confession I recorded in the office meant Agent Fisher had taken my place as prime suspect in Mrs. Barsky's homicide by frog poison. Roger said Grey Hazelnut had paid off the Tanzanian Police and was in the wind. Neither Bunty nor his body had been found. Now that I knew he hadn't murdered his mother, part of me hoped toxic saliva might have been a wake-up call. Besides, I didn't get my new apartment until he came home or the court appointed another executor.

Roger asked about my family. I wasn't ready to talk about my uncle yet. It was too raw. And too confusing.

"I've done what I could," Roger said.

"Thanks. For that, and for saving my life."

"I didn't save your life. Your purse did. As usual."

"It's a bag, not a purse." We watched Barry's daughters take out a spider.

"I have a big favor to ask. Could you drive me to the airport? I'm on my way to Indonesia."

"Another undercover case?"

"Interpol requested me again."

As we drove, I looked over at his dimple. It was just as cute from the side. The list of his betrayals was pretty much burned in my brain, and saving me from Agent Fisher couldn't wipe all of it out, even if I wanted it to. We rode along for awhile in silence. When we got to the turn-off for Departures, he asked me to veer left, down a service road.

"Why? Where are we going?"

"It's something the Customs guys told me about. I thought it might help if you got homesick for Africa."

We stopped in a big stand of trees near the fence that marked off the cargo runways. I could hear the growl of a 777 taking off and smell diesel fuel, but there was something else in the air. It smelled, like, well, monkey dung. Other noises started to filter in: vervet monkey calls and loud squawks. Three bright blue Macaws shot across the clearing.

"What the hell?" I said.

"When the animal cages go across the tarmac, sometimes the crafty ones escape. There are supposedly hundreds of species here; the airport staff call it the 'Suburban Serengeti.' Come on."

He led me down a path to a large, white *Out of*

*Africa* tent. Leaning on the side was the collapsible snake handler. Roger twirled it, for old time's sake.

"Don't you have a plane to catch?" I said.

"In the morning. I thought I'd spend the night trying to convince you to be on it with me."

I have to say, he made a compelling case. His first kiss was tentative and tasted of tarmac and Altoids, but his second was like rocket fuel. I tried to be cool, but I totally failed as I felt his long fingers on my back, and then tight around my waist. When I pulled back and saw the pleading look in those Raisinet eyes, I completely folded, mashing my lips against his and gasping as he lifted me over his shoulder and through the "tent threshold," then threw me down onto the camp bed he'd made for us. It collapsed on contact, but by then Roger was on top of me and grinning and by some miracle I hadn't thrown my back out, so, there in the jungles of Greater Manhattan, I gave into the best—and maybe worst—of my animal instincts, untied my consignment wrap dress, kicked off my Charles Davids, wrapped my legs around Roger, and held on for dear life.

The first time was frantic, a "we survived the leopard trap, komodo drool, and FBI bastardry" kind of sex, complete with canvas burn and a few insect bites where nobody wants them. It was a blur of my hands flat on Roger's "four pack," his dark, silky hair on my breast, monkeys bouncing on the roof of the tent, and macaws squawking. Or was it pigeons? When Roger pressed my wrists above my head, who cared?

The second time, after a lantern-lit picnic of airline nuts, olives, and tiny bottles of Jack Daniels, was different—just as intense, but in slow motion. Roger lingered over every part of me until I felt memorized. His fingers were dry and warm and insistent and the mole by the side of his mouth added a grace note to each kiss, from the back of my neck to the tip of my coccygeal vertebrae. The damp ground, the distant sirens, the vibration of A380s, none of it mattered if he was touching me. After he'd fallen asleep, I listened to the birds and smelled the night trees and traced his dimples with my finger. I'd never wanted someone as much as I wanted Roger, but I still wasn't sure what had been him and what had been the job. One night wasn't long enough to figure that out.

The planes and the monkeys woke us up. In the light, we were suddenly shy. Roger kissed me once, then we got dressed and broke camp. Neither of us spoke. I guess he didn't want me to say no and I didn't want to have to say it. Finally, he pulled a ticket out of his pocket and held it out.

"Here. You've never been to Indonesia, right?"

"Not yet," I said. Part of me wanted to just let

him whisk me away. But if my time in Tanzania had taught me anything, it was that I had to do my own whisking. I turned and grabbed his hand. "Someday. But right now, I need to stay here." We just looked at each other. "You can still get a partial refund if you turn it in before the flight."

He grinned and closed my hand around it. "Nope, this is yours, either way."

When we were packed, he said he'd pick up the tent and the snake handler next time he was in town. We sat on the endless hood of the Galaxie and watched the planes take off until it was time for his flight.

We drove to the Terminal, I parked illegally, and we stood on the curb as luggage crashed around us. He kissed me one more time, hard enough to almost make me change my mind. I wasn't ready to say good-bye and I wished it were the old days and I could have seen him off at the gate. Instead, I watched him walk through Security and disappear.

I drove back on the JFK until I saw the bridge. Fifteen minutes later I was in my new ergonomic chair—the other one had been retired for sanitary reasons—when the phone rang.

"Cyd Redondo, Redondo Travel."